TALES OF CAPE NOIRE

AIRSHIP 27 PRODUCTIONS

TM

An Airship 27 Production
airship27.com
airship27hangar.com

Cover illustration © 2020
Interior illustrations © 2020 Rob Davis

Editor: Ron Fortier
Associate Editor: Gordon Dymowski
Production and design by Rob Davis
Promotion and Marketing Manager: Michael Vance

ISBN: 978-1-946183-85-9

Printed in the United States of America

10 9 8 7 6 5 4 3 2 1

TALES OF CAPE NOIRE

TABLE OF CONTENTS

THE BATTLE OF BUGOSI MANSION

by Fred Adams, Jr.

Albert Carrington the Third stepped from his Cadillac and into a puddle of oily water. His fifty-cent shoeshine was his last concern, however. He was playing the biggest gamble of his life at that moment, and it would leave him either rich or dead. It was a dangerous game, and it was one he didn't ask for. His only choice was to roll the dice.

The lanky mouthpiece had to choose between two of Cape Noire's most powerful crime bosses, the slick Ace Bricker, his firm's former client (although Ace didn't know it yet), or the monstrous Harry Beest. Whoever got left out of the picture would be furious. Carrington had thought long and hard before he made up his mind, banking on the one he would choose to protect him from the one he didn't.

The warehouse door was shrouded in shadow. No one was in sight, but Carrington knew eyes were watching his every move over the sight of a gun. He pulled his briefcase from the passenger seat and closed the door. He straightened his tie, pulled the brim of his fedora down and headed for the entrance.

He was ready to knock at the steel door when a gruff voice said from behind him. "Hold it right there, bub." Carrington felt the cold muzzle of a revolver under his right ear. "Whaddaya do'in' here?"

"My name is—"

"We know who you are, shyster," a second voice said with a sneer. "The man asked you why you're here."

"I'm here to see your boss."

"He expecting you?"

"No, but he'll want to hear what I have to say."

"Uh-huh, and what's that?"

"I'm sure he'll tell you if he wants you to know."

That remark earned Carrington a whack on the side of the head from the pistol that rocked him on his ankles. He felt a trickle of blood run down his cheek and into his collar but knew better than to flinch or to

5

protest. Show fear, he thought and these animals will eat me alive.

"Don't crack wise, or I'll hit you harder next time."

"Keep him here, Rippy," the second man said. "I'll go upstairs and check with the Boss. A dark figure opened the door and slipped inside, closing it behind him. The gunman held his pose, revolver to Carrington's ear while with his free hand he shook out a cigarette and lit it with his lighter. A puff of smoke wafted over the lawyer's shoulder. A minute passed then two. The door swung inward, and he was told. "C'mon in."

In the dim light, he saw aisles of crates stretching for half a city block, most if not all of it stolen or smuggled goods. The hoods pushed Carrington against the wall and patted him down, disappointed that he wasn't carrying anything more dangerous than a fountain pen. Rippy opened his briefcase and pawed through it. "Nothing but papers, Mose."

All right." Then to Carrington, "You follow me. Rippy follows you. Behave yourself."

Carrington didn't need to ask "or what." The men led him across the warehouse to a set of oil-stained stairs that climbed to the second floor. At the end of a short hallway, Mose rapped at a door then turned the knob. The three stepped into a room that could have been a parlor in the Grand Bay Hotel. Carrington's shoes sunk into the carpet like it was a bed of moss. The floor length curtains were green velvet, and the leather armchairs looked as if they cost a grand apiece. Paintings that belonged in a museum hung from the walls.

But Albert Carrington didn't notice any of these things. His stare was fixed on a six hundred pound gorilla immaculately dressed in a pinstriped suit, starched white shirt, and red silk necktie, Harry Beest.

The mobster eyed him up and down, weighing, measuring, appraising him. His nose twitched. From five feet away, he could smell the lawyer's subtle aftershave and a trace of cigarette smoke, but no fear. "You're bleeding, Counselor," Harry said with a voice like gravel in a cement mixer. No response. Beest looked to Mose, who shook his head, then he turned to Rippy, whose eyes darted back and forth. "He got bright with us, Boss. I had to set him straight."

Beest turned his gaze back to Carrington. "What do you have to say about that, Counselor?"

"Nothing." Carrington smiled, and he pivoted left and nailed Rippy in the jaw with a right cross that would ring Dempsey's chimes. The hood went over backward and landed tits up on the carpet. His partner reached into his coat, and Harry snarled. "Leave it there, Mose. You two searched him. You know he ain't armed." He smiled then, showing a set of square yellow teeth that could bite off a man's hand.

"Where'd you learn that move, Counselor?"

"I boxed at Harvard."

Harry nodded. "Okay, so you got balls. Now tell me what you want." Carrington looked pointedly at Mose. "Go ahead," Harry told him. "He'd know five minutes after you left anyway, unless of course he left with you, if you know what I mean."

The lawyer nodded. "My partner recently died."

"Yeah," Beest said. "Huey Blankenship. He'd steal the cane from a blind man. What about him?"

Don't take the bait, Carrington thought. Have to stay on track. "I took over his case load, including the liquidation of several estates." He paused for dramatic effect. This is it, he thought. Roll the dice. "One of them the late Professor Bugosi." The next ten seconds would determine whether Carrington lived or died.

Beest's hairy paws gripped the desktop, and Carrington could hear the wood cracking. Harry's nostrils flared, his eyes widened, and a deep rumble vibrated in his chest. Bugosi—the crazy scientist who put Harry's human brain in a gorilla's body. The lawyer's eye flicked nervously to a six-foot crate standing in the corner of the room. As quickly as Harry's spasm of rage began, it faded away. He took a deep shuddering breath and said through his teeth, "Carrington, you'd better have a very good reason to say that name in front of me, a very *very* good reason."

"In my briefcase is the deed to his mansion. It's stood as he left it the day he was killed, furnishings, library, papers," he paused, "and his laboratory." Carrington let this piece of news sink in. "As executor, I have a free hand to dispose of the property. I realized that there are two parties who might be interested, you and Ace Bricker. I came to you first."

"Why not Ace? I thought you were his lawyer."

"Was his lawyer. I thought it over and figured I'd get a better deal with you."

Harry nodded and leaned forward in his chair. "The lab, what shape is it in?"

"It has suffered some damage, but nothing that can't be replaced or repaired."

Harry's brain spun like a whirligig. The lab where he was turned into a monster could be used to turn him back into a human again.

"I have the papers in my briefcase." Carrington nodded to his bag. "If you're interested, we can sign the sale agreement right now."

Harry's huge head nodded slowly. "Sure. I'll sign."

"Don't you want to know the price?"

"It doesn't matter."

Carrington smiled inwardly. He was right; desperation made Harry easy to play. "I do need to ask one thing of you."

"What's that?"

"As in court, somebody always loses, and somebody's always sore. Today, you win, and Bricker loses, and he will be sore. I need to know you'll protect me from him."

Harry laughed. "From the way you handled Rippy, you look as if you don't need protection. Get out the papers."

As Carrington reached into his briefcase, Rippy woke up, scrambled to his feet and started for the lawyer.

"Hey!" roared Harry, freezing everyone in the room. He pointed a thick, gnarled finger at Rippy. "You touch him, I'll pull your goddamned arms off." Rippy stepped back, speechless, looking as if he'd just been slapped.

Carrington laid the papers out in a neat row across Harry's desk. "If you'll just sign here, and here, and here..." Harry held Carrington's fountain pen in his paw and scrawled his name across the dotted lines.

Carrington signed on the lines below, and as he did, the plan was already taking shape behind Harry's sloping forehead.

"Do you like bananas, Carrington?"

The lawyer blinked, surprised at the question and wondering where it was leading. "Uh, yeah, sure I do. Everybody does."

"My birthday was yesterday, and somebody with a real funny bone sent me a present. Other guys get a case of whiskey or maybe champagne. I got this." He rose from his desk and yanked the lid from the crate in the corner. In it was a full bunch of bananas. "I didn't laugh when I saw it, and I promise you when I find out who the jerk is that sent it to me, he won't be laughing either."

But Harry was already laughing inside at how Fate had turned her wheel, and how the pieces of a plan were falling into place. "Counselor," he said. "I'd like to put you on retainer. Name your price."

The lamp bounced off the wall and then the floor before rolling to a stop. If it hadn't been brass, it would have exploded into shards, but instead, it left a lamp shaped dent in the plaster.

"That shyster bastard," Ace Bricker screamed. "I'll eat his eyes for breakfast—one at a time so he can watch me chew on the first one." The barrel-chested hoodlum paced back and forth behind his desk. As he did, he puffed at a cigar that dribbled ashes down his red silk vest. He stopped pacing and stared into Benny Capriotti's face. "Do you believe it?" he shouted. "He went to that animal instead of me."

Benny shrugged. "What's to believe? Some people got no loyalty, some people got no sense, and some people got neither. Question is, Ace, what do we do about it?"

Bricker was furious that Carrington sold the Bugosi mansion to Harry Beest. When Bugosi was killed, he was working in secret to develop synthetic opium that could be made for next to nothing and converted into heroin at an enormous profit in partnership with Ace. Since Bugosi's death, his house, his laboratory, and his library full of his notes were all out of reach. Just this week, the courts released Bugosi's estate, and Bricker learned about it less than a day before he learned that Carrington, whose late partner Huey Blankenship had been Bricker's lawyer, had sold him out in favor of Harry Beest.

It was bad enough that Bricker's considerable investment in the synthetic narcotic was down the chute; what made it worse was that the gorilla man might take the project over and run Ace out of business by undercutting his prices, a dime on a dollar for the same thrills.

"So, do we hit Carrington?" Benny said. His squinty eyes and pointy head were a giveaway that his mother was sucking on a gin bottle while he was still in the womb. Benny wasn't stupid, though, in fact he was smarter than the average hood, and a lifetime of ridicule and abuse had honed his mean streak to a lethal edge. "Word is he's been holed up in Bugosi's mansion for at more than a week and Beest's trigger men are standing guard."

Bricker thought it over for a minute. A bomb in the place would satisfy his lust for simple revenge, but it would destroy all of Bugosi's work, including his notes and formulas for the artificial hop. "No, it's too late to do Carrington. We have to kill Harry Beest. Take away Carrington's protection, and he'll come crawling back."

Benny let out a low whistle. "That's a tall order, Boss." Plenty of people had tried to kill Harry, and most of them ended up dead instead. Those who didn't never tried again.

"Put word on the street. Top dollar for the gorilla man's head. There's always somebody who'll take the shot."

"But once Beest hears you've put out a hit on him, he'll be after you."

"That's when we pull them out and see whose is bigger."

"You're talking a war."

Bricker nodded. "I'm talking a war."

"You know, Ace," Benny said, "Cape Noire's general population of murderers, gun thugs and button men will all go after Harry at once and end up killing each other over who gets the bounty instead of killing the ape man. Also, as word gets around, it'll reach Harry pretty fast, and he'll gun up and surround himself with protection. Better to sic one pro on him, let him take his time to set up the hit, and spring it on Beest without any warning."

Bricker didn't say anything for a whole two minutes, his gears turning. Finally, he said, "Benny, you're absolutely right."

"That's why you keep me on the payroll, Ace."

"Get on it. Get me the best."

Benny nodded and left the room. When he closed the door, Bricker was pacing again, and muttering under his breath about what he wanted to do to Carrington and to Beest. Benny had seen Bricker's unbridled rage many times before, but this time, Ace had two toes over the edge of madness.

He left Bricker's office and in the hallway, he passed Grimes and Hanchin, two of Ace's torpedoes. "Well?" said Hanchin, "what's the word?"

Benny paused for a second then said, "The word is: load the guns."

Albert Carrington poured a snifter of vintage cognac and settled back into a red leather armchair, one of two facing the desk in the late Professor Bugosi's study. The desk, swept clear when he'd arrived at the mansion, was now piled with leather-bound journals, stacks of files and loose papers, and Albert's own notes in his meticulous hand. Seventeen days had passed, and he hadn't set foot out of Bugosi House. Of course, he didn't want to leave at the moment. He was sure there was a hefty bounty on him, dead or alive from Bricker, but he had factored that into the equation when he thought the deal through.

Most of Huey Blankenship's work for Bricker involved bail and defense for the mobster's thugs when one of them got pinched by the law, but when Bricker made him a liaison between himself and the Professor, Huey had gotten to know Bugosi pretty well in the last year of the scientist's life. Bugosi liked to talk, especially after a few snifters of brandy, and soon Huey was privy to the crazy's doctor's experiments, especially the cheap, synthetic narcotics. Then Huey caught the Flu, which segued into pneumonia, and he shared the information with Carrington on his death bed.

But of course, that wasn't why Harry wanted Bugosi House. The ape-man knew nothing about the synthetic drugs. Bugosi's transplantation of Harry's brain into a gorilla's body was legendary. The ape man would have killed the Professor, but he knew that only he had the know-how to return Harry's brain to a human body. At one point, Harry went wild when he found out that Bugosi was secretly experimenting with brain transplants again, this time to put a human brain into a synthetic man, but he stopped short of killing the Professor. Instead, Harry wrecked Bugosi's laboratory and destroyed his experiments, but the Professor lived to continue his bizarre research.

Harry would give or do anything to be restored to human form, and now that Bugosi was dead, his only hope was to find another scientist who could untangle the Professor's cat's cradle of secrets and make them work in the laboratory.

Carrington's job: put the wheels in motion; restore the lab and find a doctor as brilliant and as crazy as Bugosi had been who would reverse the incredible experiment. As he combed through Bugosi's heaps of journals and piles of calculations, he was ostensibly searching for the notes on brain relocation. What Harry didn't know was that Carrington had his sights on the synthetic opium formula, the real prize. Harry would rip Carrington's heart out of his chest if he even suspected the real motive for helping him, but if things worked out, Harry would regrettably die on the operating table, and Carrington would waltz away with a formula worth millions and millions of dollars.

In the meantime, Harry held up his end of the bargain. For his safety, the lawyer was confined to Bugosi House, guarded every minute by no less than three of Harry Beest's gun thugs to keep Ace Bricker from having him whacked. It was a prison, sure, thought Carrington; a cage, but a gilded one. He had spent the first week taking inventory and making lists of what was needed to restore Bugosi's laboratory. What Harry's men couldn't steal, Harry would buy, and soon, the lab would be operating again.

Carrington was especially happy today because after a long separation, Rita Mayfield, his fiancée would be coming from San Francisco for an extended stay. She had balked at coming to the gloomy mansion at first, maybe a little spooked by its history, but she finally agreed that being with him in that place was safer than being without him elsewhere.

Mose came in without knocking. That was one thing Carrington had to be wary of. Beest's men were protecting him, but at the same time, he understood that they were protecting Harry by watching his investment closely. "Here're those catalogs you wanted."

"Set them on the desk."

Mose pushed a pair of books out of the way and set the catalogs on the corner of the ink-stained blotter. Medical equipment suppliers. Carrington was being circumspect, trying to not order too much from the same place and attract attention as he restored Bugosi's laboratory. "A crate full of stuff came an hour ago."

He handed a slip of paper to Carrington, a bill of lading for a fluoroscope, the same gadget that let a shoe salesman show you how your toes fit in a new pair of brogans. Unlike a standard X-ray machine, you didn't have to use film and saw the image instantly. Bugosi's had been destroyed in what Carrington liked to think of as "the night of the Beest," a phrase he didn't dare say out loud.

"Okay, Mose, I'll be down in a little while to make sure everything's correct."

Mose looked around the room, eyeing the floor to ceiling bookshelves. "You gonna read all them books?"

"If that's what it takes, Mose, yeah, I'll read them all."

The door opened and Rippy came in. Under orders from Harry, Rippy was civil, but barely, nursing a grudge at Carrington for decking him in Harry's office. More than the bruised jaw, Rippy hated being shown up in front of his boss, and having to take orders from the mouthpiece was about as much as Rippy could tolerate. "Boss called," he said, ignoring Carrington. "He's coming over now." He turned to the lawyer and gave him a hard stare.

Carrington noticed something he hadn't before: Rippy's eyelids were straight lines rather than curves over and under his eyes, as if the eyes behind them were flat as a sidewalk. The lawyer responded by raising his snifter in a mock salute and taking a drink, staring back over the rim of the glass. The corner of Rippy's mouth twitched.

Mose saw the tell and hustled him out of the room before the situation boiled over. He needed to speak to Carrington, tell him to not needle Rippy, but before he did that, like all things, he'd have to clear it with the Boss.

Alone again, Carrington rose from his chair and drained his drink. He gazed at the bookshelves and said aloud to himself, "Not all of them, only as many as I have to."

Twenty minutes later, Harry's special order Buick limo wheeled through the guarded gate and up the mansion's curving driveway. The sight of the place and all the memories it conjured made Harry grind his teeth. I've got to get past that, he thought, look forward instead of back. Harry opened the door for himself and climbed the steps to the entrance. The door swung open ahead of him, and Harry stepped inside.

In spite of his self-admonition, the scents that lingered around the place made his sensitive nostrils twitch. Chemicals. Ether. Ozone. The smells of science. Mose took Harry's hat and vicuna overcoat. No matter how many times Mose saw his boss, he always marveled at Harry's sartorial splendor.

Mose shouldn't have been surprised. He knew that when Harry was transformed, he had the legendary tailors from A. Sulka and Company of Fifth Avenue in New York, clothiers of the Quasimodo of Crime, Pretty Louie Amberg, flown to Cape Noire to measure and fit him for a classy wardrobe. "If they're busy admiring my outfit," Harry said, "maybe they won't notice my hairy mug." Harry's three-piece herringbone suit fit him perfectly, complementing his simian shape rather than exaggerating it.

As Harry's eyes adjusted to the dim light, he could see that cleaning the place was a low priority. "Joint looks like a dump," he said. "Where's Albert?" Harry had taken to calling Carrington by his first name, as he did all of the members of his gang.

"Right here, Harry." Carrington was coming down the grand staircase. He had put on his tie and jacket and looked like an executive on his way to a board meeting. He carried a ledger under one arm. "Let's go in the parlor."

Because the gorilla man couldn't fit in the armchairs in the study, he met with Carrington in the parlor, where he could settle his bulk on a divan, whose French Provincial legs creaked under his weight. "Whaddaya got?" he rumbled.

Carrington opened the ledger and set it on the coffee table for inspection. For the next ten minutes, he pointed out figures, transactions, and totals as Harry listened, fingers interlaced across his lap. His breath, in and out sounded like wind in a chimney flue and in spite of liberal doses of mouthwash, smelled like a wet dog.

"How soon?"

"We're still receiving equipment, but in two weeks, the lab should be fully operational, based on Bugosi's diagrams and notes. Do you want to see it?"

Harry hesitated but finally nodded his head. He'd have to do it sooner or later, so he might as well get it over with. "Yeah. Let's take a look." They left the study and started for the staircase. Mose fell in behind Harry.

The laboratory occupied a good chunk of the mansion's second floor. It seemed strange to Carrington that Bugosi would put his lab anywhere but in the basement of the house, that is, until he saw the basement. Low-ceilinged and dirt-floored, it was crisscrossed with load-bearing walls separating rooms, the enormous furnace (which doubled as a crematory kiln for some of Bugosi's less successful results) and a huge coal bin to accommodate it.

The second floor had walls knocked out and plenty of window casements to install ventilation ducts and blowers. The lab took up three quarters of the second story of the mansion as one continuous space.

Carrington led Harry up the staircase and to the locked steel doors down the hall. "Bugosi was able to partially restore the place before he died. You really made a wreck of it."

"I never do anything halfway, Albert."

The doors opened, and Harry hesitated on the threshold. He wasn't superstitious, but the memories of the room were powerful, the worst one waking to see his reflection, the sloping forehead, the hairy arms and face, the flat flaring nostrils, and the fanged row of teeth. The eyes were haunting, deep set under a shelf of dark forehead, the whites yellowed, around irises almost black they were so dark. Startled, Harry had seen that image and put his fist through it, then the horror dawned on him that he was punching his own reflection. That was his face he saw in the glass.

Carrington snapped the wall switches one by one and each corner of the lab lit with blazing electric light as bright as an operating room. "We've made a few improvements, but nothing that will change the functions Professor Bugosi described in his notes."

"The notes," Harry rumbled, closing his thick fingers around Albert's arm. "Did you find the notes about the transfer process?"

Albert winced at the pain of Harry's grip and hated to think how it would feel around his neck. "Not yet. The Professor left dozens of journals and mounds of papers. It's slow work going through them all."

"Hmmph." Harry grunted, a sound more like a bestial snort. He let go of Albert's arm.

The arm hurt like hell, but Carrington knew better than to acknowledge it."We've also cleaned the place up quite a bit."

"Yeah, I see that." Finally, Harry stepped in and turned from side to side, taking in the view.

Bugosi's laboratory now looked more like a hospital operating room, than a medieval torture chamber, which is how it had looked the last time Harry had seen it. The floors were scrubbed clean, the new equipment shone, and every square inch of brass and steel on the old hardware was polished to its highest possible gloss. The beakers, retorts, and test tubes gleamed in the bright light. Not a mote of dust hung in the air, and not a speck of rust tarnished one piece of metal. Shelves were stocked with bottles and tins of chemicals; tanks of oxygen and ether stood in a rank against a far wall.

"The old lab looked like something out of a Karloff movie," Harry said. "This looks a lot more modern."

"State of the art."

Harry walked among the lab tables, the work benches, picking up a piece of exotic glassware or an instrument, turning it over in his dark, leathery fingers. His eyes fell on the stainless steel gurney, the same one he'd lain upon the night he stopped being human.

Harry turned to Albert and tapped his forefinger against the attorney's breastbone. "Get it ready, find the notes, and find me another Professsor."

"We're working on it, Harry." Carrington shrugged. "Guys like Bugosi aren't exactly hanging around the bus stop, you know."

The gorilla man's head tilted back, and his eyelids closed to slits. He grabbed Carrington's arm again, less gently this time, and lifted his left foot clear of the floor while his right struggled on tiptoe. Harry put his face an inch from the lawyer's nose and said, "Don't get bright with me, Counselor, just get done what I'm payin' you to do."

Carrington nodded, a little more quickly than he might. "Sure thing, Harry, whatever you say."

Harry let go of the arm again, and Carrington's heels clattered on the shiny oak flooring. Harry nodded once, turned, and walked out of the room. Mose paused a moment, gave Albert a "you should know better" shrug, and left him alone in the brightly lit laboratory.

Carrington locked the door to the lab and was halfway down the staircase to the foyer where Mose was helping Harry into his topcoat when the doorbell rang. Mose opened it, and the three saw a pretty young blonde at the doorstep, holding a suitcase. Mose turned to look up the stairs to Carrington who said, "It's all right; she's my fiancée."

Mose stepped back and Rita Mayfield entered the foyer, smiling. "Hello, darling. Who are your friends?" Before Albert could reply, Harry turned to face her and her hand went to her mouth, eyes wide with terror.

"No need for that Miss, " Harry said. He gently took her hand from her face with a hairy paw and brought it to his dark pursed lips in a genteel greeting. "I'm Harry Beest, Albert's employer."

Carrington came down the stairs, and she broke away from Harry and ran to him. Carrington put protective hands on her shoulders and said, "This is Rita Mayfield, my fiancée." Then to her, "Harry has already introduced himself. This gentleman is Mose, a fellow employee."

"I'm so sorry," Rita stammered. "I was just—I mean I—"

"No apology necessary, my dear," Harry said with an open mouthed grin. "Happens all the time." He turned to Carrington. "Keep me posted about the talent search. And be sure to canvas the bus stops, huh?" He started out the door and turned. "A pleasure to meet you, Miss Mayfield. I hope the next time we meet, you won't be so surprised." Harry put his tan fedora on his head, adjusted the brim, and strode heavily down the steps to his shiny blue limo.

"Where to, Boss?" Ralph, his driver said to Harry's image in the rear-view mirror.

"The warehouse." As he rode away, Harry took a last look at Bugosi's mansion, and the corners of his mouth curved upward. Once he had the handsome attorney's body, he was going to take his cute little girlfriend too.

He could do it now; nothing could stop him, but Harry's few experiments with hookers had been less than satisfactory. A few had landed in the looney bin, and one ended up dead when he got a little too enthusiastic. What frustrated him most was the issue of his size. As a human, Harry was what polite society called "amply endowed," and now, like all his silverbacked cousins, he was hung like a little kid. No, he'd enjoy the dainty Miss Mayfield in the future; she'd be his first try with the new equipment.

As the limo rolled through the dingy backstreets of Cape Noire, Harry looked through the tinted windows at the decaying city. Maybe it was the fog; maybe it was the accumulation of decades of soot from the days when the factories were humming along; maybe it was just the corruption of a

HER HAND WENT TO HER MOUTH, EYES WIDE WITH TERROR.

dying animal pushing through its skin to the surface, but whatever it was, it was real. It was a metropolitan dung heap, but Harry was determined he would be on the top of it or die trying.

Ralph turned into the brick alley that led to the warehouse entrance. A delivery van was blocking the way. Ralph blew the horn and the driver, a little guy in coveralls and a leather cap came around the truck and stepped up to the window. He gestured with his hands and said something too low for Ralph to hear. Ralph rolled down the window enough to talk to him, and the little man threw something through the opening.

Harry's animal instinct went into overdrive. His long arm shot over the front seat and snagged the grenade in his catcher's-mitt paw. In the same sweep of his arm, he tossed the grenade back the way it came to roll under the feet of the fleeing driver where it exploded, spattering the alley with blood and red gobbets of flesh.

Men with guns ran out of the warehouse door. They were all Harry's. "Are you all right, Boss?"

"Yeah, I'm okay, but I don't think Ralph's doin' so good." He opened the driver door of the limo and Ralph's body sagged out. His left eye was missing because when the grenade exploded, fragments of the pineapple casing bounced off the Buick's bulletproof glass and its armor plated doors, but one found its way through the open window and Ralph's eye socket into his brain.

Sirens wailed in the distance. Harry told his men, "Get the limo out of here." He shambled away muttering, "Gonna need a new driver."

"He's so awful, Al, how can you stand even being around him, let alone working for him?" Rita shuddered. "And when he kissed my hand, God, I thought he was going to bite it off. Ucch."

"How was your meal?" Carrington gestured to the remains of her chicken *cordon bleu*.

"What?" Rita blinked at the *non sequitir*.

"How was your meal?" Carrington's meals were brought in from the kitchen of Mancini's Restaurant uptown.

"Uh, it was fine, really good food."

"And the champagne?"

She looked at her empty glass. "First rate, why?"

"And your rooms?" Rita's suite included a bedroom, private bath and sitting room.

"Like the Ritz if you ignore the barred windows, but—"

"Because that kind of living is what we're going to have from now on and it's all because I'm working for Harry Beest. You take the bad with the good, Rita."

"Well, I'm still afraid of him."

"It won't be forever, darling. In the meantime, we just have to tough it out." He leaned over to kiss her on the cheek, and the door opened. Mose came in. "If you don't mind, Mose, could you please knock."

Mose shrugged. "Sorry if I interrupted anything."

"You didn't—this time, but from now on, don't just walk in."

"Tell you what," the gunman said, "I won't barge in on the lady; I'll knock, so if you want privacy, enjoy it in her room. Fair enough?"

Carrington could tell from Mose's expression that that was the best concession he was going to get. "Fair enough. And if you don't mind tell Rippy."

Mose nodded. "Better me than you. Anyway, this came just now. Thought you'd want to see it." Mose handed him a Western Union envelope. It was addressed to Albert Carrington, but it had already been opened and read, probably over the phone to Harry when it arrived at the mansion. He unfolded the telegram and held it to the light.

The message was simple: CANDIDATE LOCATED PASADENA STOP ADVISE

There was no signature, but of course Carrington already knew who sent the telegram. He had put Willie Shenk, a private investigator on retainer with his firm on the search for the Professor's replacement.

"You wanna send one back?" Carrington realized Mose wasn't leaving until he composed a response.

"Yeah." Carrington found a scrap of paper and wrote the return message: SEND DETAILS IMMEDIATELY STOP. "Get it off as soon as you can."

Mose nodded and put the paper into his pocket. "Have a good night, Counselor, Miss." He left and closed the door behind him.

"I don't like him, either," Rita said, lighting a cigarette. "And that other one, Rippy? He gives me the creeps."

"Like it or not, those two and the rest of Harry's men you'll see around the place are all that's keeping Ace Bricker from filling me full of holes. Like I said, just sit tight. It'll be okay."

"I'm starting to feel sorry I ever let you talk me into coming here."

"You won't when I tell you why I'm here."

For the next few minutes, Carrington outlined his plan to Rita, as her eyes grew wider and wider. When he finished, he looked to the door. "What do you say we go to your room and talk it over, where we won't be interrupted."

For the first time since she'd arrived, Rita smiled. She stubbed out her cigarette and said, "Thought you'd never ask."

The steak was thick and juicy, and Ace Bricker was enjoying himself in a wrap around booth in Montenegro's, bookended between a pair of floozies who nibbled at his ears while he cut another bite of meat. The Ray Mountjoy Orchestra was playing an up tempo version of "Blue Skies," and the thought crossed Bricker's mind that the song was a message just for him. Maybe it was the steak, maybe it was the booze, maybe it was the company, but he was feeling the best he'd felt since that rat Carrington sold him out.

Ace was confident; he managed to land Bobby Toro, the Michaelangelo of Murder to do the hit on Beest. The deadly little man was proficient in the art of assassination, and for twenty-five large up front and twenty-five on delivery he would concoct a scheme that would not only kill Beest, but leave no evidence pointing to himself or his employer.

Ace looked up to see Benny standing in front of the booth, holding his hat by the rim in his fingers like he was hiding a hard-on. His expression didn't look like good news. "What?" Ace said over the music.

Benny leaned across the table and said in Ace's ear, "The hit went bad. Beest is alive and Toro's dead."

"God damn it!" Bricker grabbed the edge of the table and heaved it over, spilling food and drink, and startling the other patrons. Ray Mountjoy followed standard protocol when things went south: keep playing and play loud. Ace leapt to his feet, knocking his girlfriends aside, and started for the door.

The tuxedoed *maître d'* scurried over. "Mister Bricker, Mister Bricker, is something wrong?"

"Get outta my way." Ace planted his hand on the penguin's mug and shoved him backwards to stumble into a serving cart, tipping it over and scattering a hundred bucks worth of fancy French desserts across the dance floor. Bricker stormed out of Montenegro's and found his car waiting at the curb. As the dark Cadillac rolled through the city, Ace fumed. Beest was still alive, and worse, now he would be on his guard. He took a cigar from his breast pocket, bit off the tip, and shoved it between his teeth, not even bothering to wet it on his tongue before he lit it. He puffed at it for a good five minutes before he told Benny, "Go to Chicago. Bring back Dandy Jake." The legendary hit man charged ten grand just to talk to a client.

"I hear he's holed up in Canada," Benny said.

"I didn't ask you where he is," Bricker shouted. "I said bring him to me."

Benny nodded agreement, but Bricker didn't see it; he was already staring at nothing through the rain-streaked back window and chewing through the end of his cigar.

☠ ☠ ☠

Bobby Crandall parked his roadster under the bridge that spanned the estuary whose fingers poked into the marshes at the edge of town. Word of the assassination attempt on Harry Beest spread like ripples from a stone thrown in a pond. The radio reports said a gas main explosion had killed an unknown party, but Bobby found out in no time that the dead man was Bobby Toro. There was no doubt on the street who his target was.

A shadow crossed his windshield, and Bobby found himself staring into the stark white skull mask of Cape Noire's avenger. Bobby stepped out of his car. No matter how many times he saw Brother Bones in their ongoing association, the sight of the black eyes staring from the eye-holes unnerved him.

"What did you find out?" The sepulchral voice said. Bones stood draped in his dirty gray overcoat, his slouch hat hiding most of his mask.

"That the dead man was Bobby Toro."

"I thought as much. I knew he came to town, but I didn't know who he came to kill."

"Harry Beest."

"Yes, the location was a dead giveaway—pardon the pun. I hear Harry bought the Bugosi mansion a few weeks ago."

"The City has the deed recorded in his name. The tax stamps show he paid two hundred Gs for the place. Why do you think he bought it?"

"Certainly not nostalgia. I'm guessing he wants to restore the Professor's laboratory in the hope of becoming fully human again. I can understand the feeling."

"Wouldn't that make him an easier opponent—being human again, I mean."

"May be, but his own corpse was destroyed by Topper Wyld's men to make sure he'd never have his brain put back in his body. To do a transplant, Harry would need a new body—from an unwilling donor. Worse, unlike a plastic surgeon who can change only his face, this process could switch identities like changing a suit. He would be hard to see coming."

"You had a chance to kill Beest before. Why didn't you take it?"

"He wasn't my target, Bobby Crandall so I spared him."

The young card dealer was all too aware his grim companion was merely the agent of supernatural entities who directed him when there was a need for his lethal justice.

"So what now?" asked Bobby. "Are you going to get involved or not?"

"I don't know yet. I need more information such as who put the hit on Harry Beest."

Harry sat alone in his office, his hairy paw wrapped around a beer mug. He poured a triple header of scotch into it, drank it in one pull, then poured another round from the crystal decanter sitting beside his automatic with its oversized trigger guard. So the proverbial glove was down. There was no doubt that Ace Bricker was responsible. The attempted hit hadn't shaken Harry particularly. It was one try of many, and so far he'd survived them all. The cops were already on the pad, and a few extra bucks got them to report the explosion as an accident involving a gas line. What bothered Harry was losing Ralph as a wheel man. Ralph could shake the cops driving a garbage truck. He'd be hard to replace.

The one thing Harry couldn't afford to do was let the incident cloud his judgment. His first inclination was to hit back immediately and to hit back hard, but he knew if a war broke out, it would completely derail the main event, restoring Bugosi's lab and making him human again. Whoever won would be weakened, and the rest of Cape Noire's underworld would be eager to take down the victor. What he had to do this round was to keep moving forward and be watchful. The men around him were good, but Mose would have seen it coming and headed it off.

Then another thought swirled around his brain like the whiskey in his mug. Was somebody on the inside selling him out to Bricker? No doubt about it; he needed Mose close by to watch his back. Rippy could keep an eye on Albert for a few days. Harry reached for the phone. His fingers were too thick to fit the holes, so he used the blunt end of a fountain pen to dial the number for Bugosi House.

Rippy answered. "Yeah?"

"Guess who. Put Mose on."

Harry heard the clunk as Rippy set down the phone, and his sensitive gorilla ears caught every footstep as the gunman crossed the marble floor of the mansion's foyer. "Mose," he called. "Boss wants you on the phone."

More footsteps, then, "Yeah, Boss."

"You heard what happened a few hours ago, right?"

"Uh, yeah, Sammy called and filled us in. Glad you weren't hurt."

"I need you with me to piece this business out. Come in. Now."

"Both of us?"

"No, leave Rippy to babysit Carrington." Harry cursed. "Too many doors to watch at the same time."

"Okay, Boss. I'm on my way."

As Mose hung up the phone, Rippy said, "What's up?"

"Boss wants me at the warehouse. Said to leave you in charge here."

"Oh yeah?"

Mose didn't like the look of Rippy's smile; not one bit.

The next day, Doctor Anton Petrus climbed the zig-zag stairs to his cold water flat on the grimy tenement's fourth floor. What little light remained of the day barely shone through the soot-coated skylight overhead. The climb was no physical challenge for his slender physique; it scarcely disturbed his breathing. What hurt was the humiliation of the destination; he, Anton Petrus Ph.D., forced to live in the squalor of the filthy building surrounded by the lowest of human scum.

When he graduated from the Carnegie Institute of Technology just ten years before, the words his professors used to describe the young biochemist included, "brilliant," "promising," and "auspicious." When he joined the research faculty at Caltech, the words became "successful," "celebrated," and "remarkable." And a scant year later, the Board of Regents changed the words to "sadist," "fiend," and "monster."

His mistake was not using vivisection as a research tool, it was allowing weaker minds to share in the process, people who allowed their personal feelings to obstruct the greater goals. Petrus was on the verge of a major breakthrough in interspecies biology when his team turned on him and reported his activities to the police and the university.

Stripped of his position, his tenure, his salary, and his posh campus residence, Petrus was forced to take menial work in a pharmaceutical factory as a chemist for a pittance of a wage and to live in a flop house that bordered on the medieval; all because he wanted to further the advance of science. After all, what was life anyway but a bundle of chemical reactions, electrical impulses, and mechanical motions.

At the top of the stairs between the third and the fourth floor, one of the tenement's worst, a professional wino named Frome, the building bully, was sitting on the steps blocking the way. He was big, he was strong, and he was stupid. "My bottle's empty, four-eyes. What're you gonna do about it?"

Petrus had made the mistake once of giving him some money. Now, any time he was out of booze, Frome would lie in wait to ambush him for his pocket change or worse. "It's a bad day for panhandling, Frome, I have nothing to give you."

Frome stood, holding the wine bottle by the neck. "The hell you say." He snatched Petrus's rimless spectacles from his nose.

"Give them back," Petrus said.

"Or what?" Frome thrust his unshaven face close to Petrus and tapped the wine bottle against the side of the scientist's head. "Give me some money, asshole."

A shadow loomed behind Frome, and the look of surprise on his face was no less than that on Petrus's when a pair of rough hands seized the drunk by his collar and belt and heaved him over the banister to carom from railing to railing until he landed with a snapping of bones on the cracked tile of the foyer.

"Petrus?" said the shadow, whose face was a nearsighted blur. The scientist nodded.

"You're not the police," he blurted.

"Knew you were smart." The shadow chuckled. "Somebody wants to meet you."

"Meet me?" Petrus barely got the words out. The thug stooped and picked up the glasses Frome had dropped and put them on Petrus's nose. The face that came into focus was more menacing than Frome's; hard eyes under heavy brows, and its lopsided smile made it even more sinister.

"He's got a job for you."

Petrus peered over the banister and saw Frome's body, limbs twisted into unnatural poses. A second man as large as the one above him stood beside it. What need could men like these have for him?

The man on the stairs said. "Better get a move on before the cops get here and you get blamed for him." He pointed with his chin to the open stairwell.

Petrus nodded once again, and dazedly followed orders before he too was sent down the quick way. No doors opened for curious eyes to peer out as they zeed from floor to floor. The building residents kept their noses out of the hallway, like lesser predators do when tigers are prowling in the jungle. Poor Frome was just too drunk to read the signs.

At the ground floor, Petrus had to walk past the bully's body, lying in a twisted heap amid the emerald shards of his broken bottle. "Hope he wasn't a friend of yours," the killer said with a laugh that iced Petrus's guts.

On the street, a dark blue Hudson Terraplane sat idling at the curb, the driver a shadowy figure behind tinted glass. The Hudson's glistening chrome and pristine whitewalls looked jarringly out of place in the neighborhood. It hadn't been there when Petrus entered the building. These men, whoever they may be, were waiting for him, watching for him. They knew who he was and where he lived. What else did they know?

The man from the foyer, the one called Ray by his companion opened the back door. "Climb in, Doc." Like the tenement hallways, the street was empty. Eyes may have been watching from the shadows, but none dared show his face. Petrus climbed into the back seat of the Hudson, and Ray climbed in beside him, nudging him to the center. The left hand door opened, and Ray's companion climbed in from the other side, sandwiching Petrus in the seat.

"Where are you taking me?" Petrus found the courage to ask as the Terraplane rolled silently away from the curb.

"Okay to tell him, Mike?" Ray said.

"I suppose so. He won't be getting out anywhere along the way."

"We're going up the coast to a nice little seaside resort. You'll like it. Ever hear of Cape Noire?"

Rita finished drying herself with one of the big fluffy towels from the rack in her bathroom. She drew the curtain over the bathtub away a few inches to look outside. The window gave onto Professor Bugosi's garden, a tangle of ugly vines and twisted stalks, plants she couldn't identify in the gray light, plants that didn't seem to belong in this universe.

She slipped into her silk kimono and opened the bathroom door. She was just pulling her robe closed when she saw Rippy eyeing her through the bedroom doorway, a door she was sure she had closed when she went for her bath. The hoodlum was lounging in a chair in the sitting room, legs crossed and smoking a cigarette. She gasped and clutched the silk to her chest.

Before she could speak, Rippy said; "I'm lookin' for your boyfriend. Thought maybe you and he were playing rub-a-dub-dub in there. I didn't want to bust in and interrupt the festivities. Guess he ain't here huh?"

Rita held the kimono shut with a white-knuckled fist. "Get out of here," she hissed. "These rooms are off limits. Didn't your pal Mose tell you?"

"Must've slipped his mind."

"Get out," Rita shouted this time. She picked up a cut glass ashtray from the nightstand and threw it. The ashtraty missed Rippy's head by a foot and shattered on the wall behind him.

Rippy dropped his cigarette on the rug and crushed it out with his foot. "Sorry to bother you." He got out of the chair, gave her a salacious once over, and walked out, leaving the door to the hallway open. Rita darted across the room and slammed it shut, turning the key, her face red with outrage and embarrassment. The acrid smell of singed carpet stung her nostrils and her eyes teared up in spite of herself.

I've got to get out of here, she thought, whether Al comes with me or not. There's not enough champagne in the world to make me stay.

Carrington had been downstairs poring over one of Professor Bugosi's journals. He realized that if he found the notes on brain transfers, he had to keep it to himself until he found the formula and the notes for the artificial opium. He was sure that once Harry had the transfer procedures, he might not see Bugosi's study again for a long time, if ever. It was a temptation to bolt if he found the drug formulas first, but even if he could escape the mansion, Harry would hunt him down long before he could profit from the information. All he could do was plod on.

He looked up from the desk and saw Rippy standing in the doorway. Carrington hadn't even heard the door open. "What is it, Rippy?"

The thug stood staring with those flat-lidded eyes of his and said

"WHAT IS IT RIPPY?"

nothing. The corners of his mouth twisted upward in a cold smile, and he turned and walked away.

💀 💀 💀

The ride was a lot longer than Petrus expected it would be. When they stopped two hours into the trip on the side of a country road, he thought that it was the end, that Ray and Mike were going to shoot him and leave his corpse in some drainage ditch like a scene from a bad gangster movie. But instead, the men all lined up, including the driver, who Ray called Shenk, to piss out the coffee they'd drunk from a big brass thermos bottle fifty miles back.

Once they were back in the car, Petrus breathed easier. At least he was sure he would live to the end of the ride.

He relaxed enough that he nodded off into a fitful sleep for a while as the Hudson's radio played a live broadcast of Count Basie's Orchestra from the Roseland Ballroom in New York. He woke to a shake of his shoulder. "Wake up, Doc. We're here."

Petrus shook his head to clear it. The Hudson was pulling up to a wrought iron gate overgrown with vines. Shenk flashed the headlights. two long, three short, and a man with a pump shotgun over his shoulder stepped from the bushes with a ring of keys. The gate opened, and the car wound its way up a long tree lined driveway.

Petrus climbed from the back of the Terraplane to find himself standing at the entrance of a house, more than a house, a mansion, a grim pile of stone that thrust three stories into the night sky. The double doors opened, and Petrus was ushered inside.

He rubbed the back of his neck, stiff from the long ride. He looked at his wristwatch: two twenty-six. The foyer was large, befitting the size of the mansion, but it was ill cared for. Petrus noted a film of dust on the ornate mirrors, and webs spun at the corners where legs met the bodies of furniture. Gobs of dust, like grounded clouds lay in the corners.

"This way, Doc." Mike stood back and extended his arm like a hotel doorman inviting a guest inside. As Petrus passed shadowy doorways, he saw furniture, some of it shrouded with white sheets and some of it not, as if squatters had broken into the place and uncovered only what furniture was immediately needed.

Up a wide staircase and down a dim hallway to an open door. In the room Petrus found a dark-haired man in a vest and tie behind a desk and beside him, a thug in a cheap suit and a bad necktie slouched in an armchair.

"Good evening, Doctor Petrus," the man at the desk said. "My name is Albert Carrington. Please sit down."

Petrus took a seat in one of the armchairs and was very conscious that Mike stood directly behind him, the murderer's hands over the back of the chair on either side of his head. Carrington lifted a sheet of paper from his desk and studied it. "You have an impressive resume. It is a shame that a man of your stature and ability has been forced out of his position." No apologies for what amounted to abducting him and dragging him to this place, whatever it was.

"The men who brought me here said you have a job for me."

"Maybe. Think of this as an interview."

Carrington continued. "You are sitting in the study of the late Professor Ladislaw Bugosi." Petrus's eyes widened. "You know the name. I found some correspondence between the two of you in the Professor's file, so you have some knowledge of his experiments."

Petrus shuffled nervously in his chair. So, Bugosi was dead. That explained the lack of response to his letters the past several months.

"Professor Bugosi left a considerable amount of his work unfinished when he died, and my employer would like to see that work completed."

Petrus knew better than to ask who the employer might be, but instead said, "What work?," his curosity overcoming his trepidation.

"We'll get to that. First," Carrington lifted a sheaf of papers, "I have three problems for you to solve. They are from Professor Bugosi's journals. Think of them as an aptitude test."

The thug in the cheap suit chuckled. "More like your final exam for life."

"Shut up, Rippy," Carrington said without looking at him. The thug frowned but did as he was told. "Mike will take you to a room where you can work without interruption. Take as much time as you need. Solve the problems and then we'll discuss what we need done." Carrington stood and held out the papers to Petrus, who took them with a trembling hand, knowing that if he failed the test, his life was likely over. Mike took him to a room on the first floor that had nothing in it but a chair and a table with a goose necked lamp, a dozen sharpened pencils, and a quire of blank paper.

"I'll be right outside. Knock on the door when you're done," Mike said. "You want coffee?"

"No, thank you," Petrus said, sitting in the ladder backed chair. Mike closed the door, and Petrus heard the snick of the key in the lock. He spread the three sheets of paper Carrington had given him in the pool of the lamplight. The problems were neatly hand copied and represented approximately the first half of each, their solutions left to Petrus. The first was a complex mathematical formula involving differential equations. The second was a partial calculation whose symbols identified the problem as one of electrical engineering. The third was an incomplete formula involving organic chemistry. All were complex, but unless some factor was missing, he felt confident that he could solve them. It would take some time and thought, but he was certain he would succeed.

☠ ☠ ☠

Downstairs, the door to the study opened, and Harry shambled in with Mose behind him.

"You heard?" Carrington said.

"Yeah, I heard." Harry had been listening in on the conversation by way of a microphone hidden in the well of the desk. "You think he's the guy?" Harry's animal voice was hard to read, but Carrington detected a note of urgent hopefulness.

"He's a good prospect. We'll know soon enough. If he can complete those formulas from Bugosi's papers, he's got the ability. The question is, will he do it?"

"His record says he will," Mose said. "He got bounced off his job and almost did time for slicing up live animals in the lab. He's already halfway to yes."

"Sounds promising. So now we wait to see whether he's got the chops, huh?" Harry said.

"Yes," Carrington replied, "and while we're waiting, we need to discuss something else. Miss Mayfield. It seems that some people aren't respecting her privacy." Carrington went on to recount Rippy's visit to her rooms, and as he went on, Harry's head slowly turned from Carrington to the flustered gangster. "Mose agreed that her rooms are off limits to your men."

Still staring at Rippy, Harry said over his shoulder, "That true, Mose?."

"Yeah. That's what I agreed to. Made sense."

Harry crossed the room to Rippy, who sat upright in his chair and looked as if he might jump up and run away any second. Harry laced his fingers over Rippy's head and closed his palms on the gunsel's temples. Harry squeezed, just a little. Rippy's eyes bulged and the cigarette fell from his mouth to land in his lap. Harry put his nose an inch from Rippy's and whispered something Carrington couldn't hear. Then he relaxed his grip, but Rippy's eyes stayed wide in terror. "Behave yourself," Harry growled. "You been warned. Now get out of my sight."

Rippy almost fell over his own feet leaping out of the chair and running from the room. Harry turned to Carrington and said, "Please convey my apologies to Miss Mayfield. I'll apologize myself the next time I see her. I'm going downstairs now. There's nothing fit for me to sit on in this room."

Carrington smiled at Harry's back as he left. He was hopeful too. One of the incomplete problems Petrus was puzzling over was the formula for synthetic opium that Carrington had found just a few hours before Petrus arrived. Unlike the other two problems, it was incomplete in the notebook, but if Petrus could finish it, Carrington would become the richest man in the world.

☠ ☠ ☠

Outside the gate, Dandy Jake watched from a convenient clump of bushes. He had been in Cape Noire for only six hours, and already had his target in his pocket. Harry Beest's Buick limo was bulletproof, but Harry wasn't, and sooner or later, the ape man had to step out of it, and when he did, Jake would be ready. "Baby," his Thompson submachine gun was waiting in the back seat of his car. Tonight, or tomorrow, or the next day, he would get his shot at Harry. In the meantime, he had to be the mobster's shadow, a role he played all too well.

He looked down and saw a night crawler undulating over one of his pristine white spats. He delicately plucked it from the shiny leather and flicked it off into the bushes. He could have used a drink and a cigarette, but his code of discipline forbade either while he was on a job. Harry Beest would be his exclusive focus until Harry was dead.

Jake heard a furtive footstep behind him, and in one fluid move, he pulled a knife from his sleeve and whirled, holding it at the throat of a man he recognized as one of Ace Bricker's thugs. "What are you doing here?" Jake hissed.

"Boss said to check on you, see if everything was all right," the wide-eyed man stammered.

"You tell your boss when I'm on the job, I don't need minding. The next one of you sneaks up on me's a dead man." He prodded the thug's larynx with the tip of the knife. "No charge."

Bricker's man stumbled away, and Jake cursed under his breath, hoping nobody around the mansion heard him thrashing in the brush.

☠ ☠ ☠

In the mansion, Petrus set down his pencil, took off his spectacles, and rubbed his eyes. It had taken him a scant two hours to complete the calculations, and that only because he had to do the math longhand without logarithmic tables. He pushed back his chair and stood, gathering his work. He rapped at the door to be let out, and hoped that Mike didn't count the pencils.

Mike led Petrus to the study where Carrington was waiting behind the desk, but the gangster in the cheap suit was gone. "Finished?" Carrington said.

Petrus nodded and handed his calculations to the lawyer. Carrington opened his desk drawer and pulled out three sheets of paper, pages from Bugosi's notes. He compared each to Petrus's work. The first two had some variations in procedure, but arrived at the same answers. The third was the incomplete synthetic drug formula. It was all Carrington could do to contain himself. "Very good, Doctor Petrus. Perfect, in fact. You're obviously capable." He nodded to Mike, who opened the study door. Petrus turned and his eyes bulged at the sight of a gorilla in a pinstriped suit.

"Doctor Petrus, meet Harry Beest."

☠ ☠ ☠

An hour later, Petrus followed Mike to the third floor where he was to be locked in a room and "made comfortable." If he was going to be comfortable, why would they need to lock him in? He had been shown the laboratory, second only to his old lab at Caltech, shown the mounds of journals, and shown the trepanning scars in Harry Beest's grey scalp.

What Bugosi had done was monstrous, even to Petrus's thinking, and when Harry said, "Who knows, Doc, this works out, we could make a handy buck any time somebody's on the lam—fix him up with a new identity," Petrus realized he could have no part of the scheme. The question he didn't ask was: where will the new bodies come from? To change a killer's identity, Beest wouldn't have him put a brain in another criminal known to the law; he'd supply some innocent man or woman as the host, and if Petrus refused, he'd be dead. There was no doubt in the scientist's mind. He had to escape and now might be his only chance.

Mike led him down the hallway to a door. "Here you go, Doc."

Petrus jiggled the knob. "It's locked. You have the key."

Mike pulled a ring from his pocket and ran the keys around it until he found the one he wanted. He slipped the key into the lock and turned it. Behind him, Petrus pulled a sharpened pencil from either pocket of his jacket.

"Hey, this isn't—"

Petrus drove a pencil into either side of Mike's thick neck with surgical precision. One pierced his larynx, the other his carotid artery. The gangster tried to scream, but all that came out was a gurgling choke as bright blood sprayed the door. Mike sagged to the floor and groped for his pistol, but his weight fell on top of it. In a few seconds, he lay still.

Petrus grabbed the ring of keys where Mike had dropped them, and when he stood, he found himself staring into the face of a young blond woman standing in an open doorway across the hall.

"Are you escaping?" she whispered, unaffected by the dead gangster. She didn't wait for an answer. "Take me with you or I'll scream."

Ace Bricker was worried, not because Harry Beest declared war on him and his gang, but because he didn't. The gorilla man was known for his temper and reacting like a scalded dog when anyone scattered his marbles. It had been two days since Toro had failed in his try at Harry, and—nothing. Bricker was ready for any response, from a stick of dynamite in his tailpipe to an all-out assault on his headquarters in the old cannery on the docks. Neither had happened, and nothing in between. Waiting for the proverbial shoe to drop was fraying Bricker's nerves.

"It was probably a bad idea to send Spud to spy on Dandy Jake," Benny said. "The guy's a pro, the best, maybe. It might be a good idea to just be patient and leave him alone to do the job."

"I already lost twenty-five Gs on Toro. I want to be sure I get my money's worth this time."

Benny shrugged. Reasoning with Ace when he was in a mood like this was like talking a freight train into making a left turn. "If Jake's as good as his rep, it'll happen. In the meantime, we just have to sit tight."

"Well, it's driving me buggy. I need Beest out of the way so that I can get my hands on Carrington and Bugosi's formula."

"It's coming, Boss. we just have to be patient."

Bricker gave Benny a hard stare. "We been together a long time, Benny, but if you say that word to me one more time . . ."

Benny put up his hands as if Bricker had pulled a gun on him. "Whatever you say, Boss. Whatever you say."

� � �

Petrus and Rita stood in the darkened grounds near the carriage house where Carrington's Cadillac was parked with two or three other cars. The keys had gotten them out of the house through a delivery door off the pantry. "This one, Rita said."

"There are no car keys on this bunch," Petrus said, holding up the ring of keys he took from Mike's pocket.

"Al always keeps a set inside the left hand spare tire cover."

Petrus wrestled the spare from the fender well and when he separated the tire from its metal shell, a small ring of keys jingled on the gravel. He climbed behind the wheel and Rita in the passenger seat.

"Which of those keys on the ring fits the lock on the gate? Petrus asked.

"How would I know?"

"The doctor pulled a book of matches from his pocket and lit one. If it's on the ring, it has to be this one, this one, or this one," he said, pointing to each key in turn. The rest look alike, so they must be to rooms in the mansion. We'll just have to try each of the three." He put the Cadillac's key in the ignition then paused. he handed her the key ring. "Hold these. I'm going to let off the brake and push the car from behind to let it roll down the driveway without it making too much noise. You steer and stop it below at the gate."

Rita slid across the seat into the driver's position. Her foot barely reached the brake, and she hoped she could stop the car in time. Petrus pulled the handle, and the emergency brake ratcheted off. He went behind the Cadillac and put his shoulder to the fender. He strained and grunted, but the heavy car wouldn't budge. Rita stuck her head out the window. "What's wrong?"

"The car is too heavy. I can't push it by myself."

Rita climbed out of the driver's seat and came around the other side. She put her hands against the trunk and said. "Let's do this."

Between the two of them, they got the Cadillac moving, slowly at first, then a little faster as the car picked up momentum. Another twenty feet, and the front tires cleared the lip of the grade and the car started rolling on its own weight. Petrus ran along the driver's side while Rita ran along the other. Petrus would have left her there, but he foolishly had given her the ring of keys to examine. Rita jumped onto the running board and yanked the door open. The unsteered car was rolling at the edge of the gravel, and Rita scrambled into the seat a scant second before a big elm close to the driveway caught the edge and ripped the door off its hinges with a sound like a sardine can.

Petrus jumped in and grabbed the wheel. He turned on the lights, engaged the clutch and started the Cadillac in gear. "What are you doing? Rita said. "They'll hear you up at the house."

"There's a guard at the gate. If he sees us rolling down hill blind and quiet, he'll know something's wrong. The driver flashed his lights two slow and three quick when we came in. If we're lucky, he'll think we're part of the gang."

At the gate, Petrus flashed the signal with the headlights, and a man who looked like a mannequin from a Saville Street display window carrying a Tommy gun stepped from the shadows. He squinted into the headlights. "Who's that?"

"Mike," said Petrus, lowering his voice in imitation of his abductor.

The thug held his gun upward and took a set of keys from his pocket. He unlocked the gate just far enough to slip through. He walked up to Petrus's open window, then with a quick motion, lowered the machine gun to point into the car. "Good evening, folks. My name's Jake. Let's go for a ride."

Carrington tapped at Rita's door in the dim hallway and heard no answer. Surely she'd be asleep at this hour. He turned the knob and found the door unlocked. "Rita?" he called softly, then a little louder. "Rita?" As he went into the bedroom, he tripped over Mike's body. Carrington turned on the light and screamed in spite of himself.

A lot of things happened all at once.

Mose and Rippy came running up the stairs, guns out. "Rita's gone. Mike's in there dead." Mose ran across the hallway and kicked in the door to Petrus's room. Empty. They heard a car engine catch outside. Harry was waiting at the bottom of the staircase when they came down, Rippy shouting, "Petrus escaped. He took the dame with him."

Outside, Mose said, "I'll drive." The four of them piled into Harry's limo. Mose took the wheel and roared down the driveway. He slid to a halt in the gravel at the closed gate. "Get out there and open it," Harry growled at Rippy, who tried the gate and said, "It's locked. You got a key?"

"We don't need a key. Get in." Mose threw the armored Buick into reverse and backed halfway up the driveway and floored the gas pedal. The wrought iron gates were substantial, but the heavy limo twisted them aside like woven licorice. The car fishtailed on the asphalt, straightened out, and sped after yet unseen taillights.

☻ ☻ ☻

"Pull over here," Jake said, and Petrus did, putting one wheel over the curb. "Stay put." Jake got out of the back seat and stepped around to the passenger side with its missing door. "Now, both of you, out this way. No tricks. I ain't being paid to kill you two, but I will if you give me a problem." Jake pointed with the muzzle of his gun. "Over there, under that street light."

The shielded bulb threw a circle of light around its pole. Jake threw a pair of handcuffs to Petrus. "Cuff yourself to the dame. Your left to her right. Petrus clicked the cuffs on them, and Jake tossed a second pair to him. "Now cuff your right to her left."

"What are you going to do?" Rita said.

Jake smiled. "I'm going to wait." He pointed to a shadowy recess across the street between two buildings. "Right over there. But first—" He reached into his pocket and pulled out a wide roll of adhesive tape. "Can't have you yelling for help, now can we."

☻ ☻ ☻

Once Mose entered the city limits, he slowed the limo to a crawl, as all four of its occupants peered through the fog for Carrington's car and the fugitives. "There it is," Carrington said, pointing to his Cadillac parked half on the sidewalk.

"And there they are," Rippy added.

In the circle of the streetlamp, the four saw Petrus and Rita, arms around the lamp post as if they were dancing around it, but neither looked very festive. Mose pulled the car up near the post and he and Rippy got out the driver's side. Harry and Carrington got out the other. "What the hell's going on?" Harry rumbled. Petrus raised an arm and mumbled something behind the tape. Harry saw the handcuffs. He held the chain between his fingers and with a sharp snap, broke first one set of cuffs then the other. He grabbed Petrus by the arm and dragged him toward the car, the toes of his shoes barely touching the pavement. Petrus pulled the tape from his mouth. "Let me go."

Rita rushed into Carrington's arms and tugged at the tape over her mouth to shout a warning, but it was too late.

Harry snarled at Petrus, "You're staying right beside me until—"

A burst of machine gun fire ripped through the night, peppering the big sedan with bullets and drilling Mose and Rippy. Bullet-proof glass in the windows spidered as Harry threw Petrus to the bricks and shielded him with his bulk. Carrington pushed Rita to the sidewalk and put his body between her and the bullets.

"Why don't you shoot back?" Petrus said, his voice muffled by a mouthful of Harry's necktie.

"My automatic against that Tommy gun ain't gonna do much." Harry peered under the car and saw a pair of white spats leisurely crossing the street; Dandy Jake. Shooting under the car for his feet might work with a shotgun, but Harry's .45 wasn't accurate enough to even try. Besides that, it would give away that somebody survived the gunfire. His eyes darted around him and he saw his way out.

He rolled off Petrus and pried his fingers under a manhole cover. Harry pulled it loose and grabbed Petrus by the coat. He dragged him to the lip of the manhole. "Down there, he growled. Now. And don't get any ideas about taking off. Right now, I'm your only chance to stay alive."

Petrus put his feet into the manhole, feeling for the rungs. Harry took another look under the car and saw that he didn't have a second to spare. He put a paw on Petrus's shoulder and shoved him through the opening. A splash below told him the doctor had found the bottom.

Jake rounded the back of the sedan with the Thompson ready to fire. Like ducks on a pond, he thought, easy money.

With a roar, Harry sprang from a crouch holding the manhole cover in front of him like a shield. Jake panic fired the Thompson, and slugs ricocheted off the thick steel. A few slipped past the cover and caught Harry in the thigh. He grunted in pain and swung the steel plate sideways. The machine gun went sailing over the sidewalk and through a plate glass display window to land in the arms of a smiling mannequin in a ballroom gown.

Harry raised the manhole cover over his head. Jake reached into his coat for another gun. Harry brought the lid down two-handed to crush the thug's vertebrae, snap his collar bone, and push his head halfway into his rib cage. Dandy Jake's corpse fell to its knees, then pitched forward to the asphalt.

Harry looked down at his leg, where the blood was seeping through his trousers. "Damn," he said. "this was my best suit." He bent over the manhole. "Petrus." His voice rasped.

"Is it over?" the scientist's voice squeaked.

"For now, yeah. Gimme your hand." Harry reached his long arm into the manhole and Petrus seized him by the wrist. Harry pulled him up and out, dripping wet but still breathing. The scientist stared at Jake's grotesque corpse then turned away and retched. Rita saw the dead hoodlum and let out a shuddering moan.

"Shut her up," Harry snarled.

Petrus took a deep breath and said, "What do we do now?"

"First, we see whether this heap will start." Harry opened the driver's door. "The engine compartment's steel plated, but he still might have hit something vital with a lucky shot." He climbed in, and turned the key, and the engine rumbled into life. Harry reached out and grabbed Petrus by the arm yanking him off the sidewalk and into the car, dragging him across his lap and throwing him into the passenger seat. Carrington shoved Rita into the back and barely made it inside as Harry popped the clutch and the Buick roared away from the curb with a squeal of tires.

Sirens wailed in the distance. The Cape Noire cops were smart enough to announce their arrival way in advance to allow the people who might shoot at them to go elsewhere.

"Now you listen to me, you little weasel. I just lost two good men because of your tricks. You try something like that again, I won't be so damned charitable. Got me?"

"You won't kill me. You need me alive," Petrus said.

"Yeah, I need you alive, but if I pull off one your legs, you can still operate on crutches."

Petrus stared at the simian gangster and realized the threat was not an idle one. He shut his mouth and turned his eyes to the windshield.

Carrington stared at Rita, desperately wanting to ask her The Question, but he was smart enough to wait until Harry couldn't hear her answer.

☠ ☠ ☠

As Sergeant Dan Duffy barked orders to his men combing the shadows for evidence and undiscovered bodies, a dark figure watched from the roof of a haberdasher's shop. Brother Bones recognized the bullet-riddled bodies of Mose Alway at first sight, and Rippy Smith when the meat wagon crew rolled him face up onto the stretcher. Harry Beest's men. The third whose head was pushed grotesquely into his torso was a mystery until Bones saw the white spats over his shoes and his memory clicked. Dandy Jake Lonnigan, the dapper hit man who never worked for less than fifty grand.

First Bobby Toro, now Dandy Jake, thought Brother Bones; poetic justice. Two hitters who wanted to take over his job as the Mob's assassin when he was still Tommy Bonello. Since no dead gorillas lay on the sidewalk, it was obvious that Harry Beest won another round with Death. Harry buys Bugosi's mansion, and suddenly two of gangland's top button men try to kill him. Too bad Lonnigan failed, Bones thought. Cape Noire would be better off less one Beest. But if I play Harry as bait, he'll draw out whoever is trying to kill him.

An unmarked car pulled up, and Detective Dan Rains got out. He had a quick conference with Duffy that Bones couldn't hear then knelt by the bodies.

One of the cops called across the street from the abandoned Cadillac, "Sarge, Car's registered to Albert Carrington."

"He isn't one of these three," Rains responded.

Carrington; law partner of the late Huey Blankenship, Ace Bricker's lawyer. Cogs began to mesh, the focus narrowed, and Bricker jumped to the top of Brother Bones' list of suspects. Bricker was relatively new to Cape Noire's Rogue's Gallery, trying to push his way into narcotics and extortion, but Harry Beest wasn't involved in either and no competition. Bones was certain that the source of the conflict between the two lay in Bugosi House. His job was to find what it was, and if Fortune favored him, take down both of them in one swipe.

Harry drove the Buick through the gateway of Bugosi House and wished Mose hadn't been so quick with the gas pedal. Twisted iron sagged from the gate hinges. Those gates would never close again. There was no sign of Wally, who was guarding the entrance, and Harry figured he was just one more victim of Dandy Jake. "I've got to get inside to the phone and call the warehouse for reinforcements," he told Carrington over his shoulder." If Bricker came at him here and now, he'd have a tough time

DETECTIVE DAN RAINS HAD A QUICK CONFERENCE WITH DUFFY...

holding him off. What was the old saying? Third time's the charm, or maybe more like three strikes and you're out.

The four walked through the open front door of the mansion. Harry grabbed Petrus by the shoulder. "The keys, Doc. Mike's keys. Hand 'em over."

"I don't have them, she does." Petrus pointed at Rita.

"Counselor," Harry said, "Will you get them from her, or would you rather I do it?"

Carrington swallowed hard. "Rita, give me the keys. Now."

Rita hesitated but finally reached into her décolletage and pulled out the key ring. Instead of handing them to Carrington, she threw them to Harry.

"Okay, Doc. In you go."

Petrus went into his room and Harry locked the door behind him. "Now you," he said to Rita. "I have half a mind to leave Mike's body in there to keep you company." Rita's eyes widened. "But I'm not that cruel. Counselor, go drag the body out in the hall and then Miss Mayfield can go to sleep." When Carrington hesitated, Harry snarled, "Don't make me tell you again."

Al took Mike by the ankles and dragged him across the carpet. The thug was heavier than he looked, and by the time Al got him out of the room, he was sweating, though not all from the exertion. The thought of the scrawny little scientist having the balls to murder a professional killer like Mike and haul his body into Rita's room staggered the imagination, but it taught him that he would have to watch Petrus closely and never turn his back on him.

Rita turned to Carrington as she went into her bedroom. She opened her mouth to speak, but no words came out. She looked away and closed the door. Harry locked it. "Now, Counselor, you and me got to talk."

"What about—" Carrington looked toward Mike's corpse.

"Leave him." He ain't goin' anywhere. Come on. We got things to do."

Downstairs, Harry sank into the sofa. "Bring the phone over." Harry took the handset from the cradle. "Now, dial this number." Carrington dialed the warehouse, and he heard a gruff voice answer. "Yeah?"

Harry recognized Eddie Sacco's voice. "Who you got with you, Eddie?"

"Sam, Rico, Earl, and Grover. The other guys are down the coast working that warehouse heist in Fishtown."

"Bring everybody you got with you and come to the mansion. Gun up. Everything you've got handy."

"Boss, we got a truck coming in from—"

"I don't give a damn about the truck, Eddie. Get over here as fast as you can." He slammed down the phone, and Carrington was surprised the handset didn't break into two or three pieces, Harry threw the car keys onto the coffee table and pointed a finger at him. "You. Take the limo down to the gate and park it sideways so nobody can get in." He reached in his pocket and held out a snub-nosed revolver.

Carrington stared at the pistol but didn't take it. The revolver looked like a toy in Harry's paw. "Take it. Mike doesn't need it anymore." Carrington didn't move. "You're in this shit up to your knees, Counselor, and you're standing on your goddamned head. Take it. You might not think you want it now, but you'll sure as hell want it when the shooting starts. Ain't no negotiating with a bullet."

He took the gun from Harry as if it were a rattlesnake. "I've never used one of these."

Harry snorted "Didn't teach you that at Harvard, huh?" He gave Carrington a hard look. "Go block the gate 'til my boys get here."

As he walked out the front door of the mansion, all Carrington could think was, Not what I had in mind at all. What he wanted to do was take the limo through the gate and drive as far away and as fast as he could. He patted his breast pocket. The formula was there, and all he had to do was run away, but he loved Rita too much leave her to the tender mercies of Harry Beest.

If he could just get through this night, maybe everything would be okay. He would take Rita and the formula and get away somehow, and if he had to, he'd take advantage of Harry's shaky trust in him and put an end to the gangster. Carrington's hand tightened round the butt of the revolver. One shot was all it would take, maybe two, and he cursed himself for not having the resolve to do it when Harry handed him the gun.

Petrus stared at the locked door. It seemed that all the science in the world couldn't pull him out of the hole he'd fallen into. He had choices to make, and he had to keep his head. Logic must overrule emotion. If he refused Harry Beest, he would surely be killed, so he had to keep up the pretense of helping him. When the opportunity arose, when Beest was helpless on the operating table, he would see that the gangster's brain found a new home—in a vat of acid. In the meantime, he had access to the notes of one of the most brilliant minds of the century and must commit as much to memory as he possibly could.

Rita sat on the edge of her bed staring at the bloodstained carpet. Petrus was a murderer, Beest was a murderer, and now they were going to turn Al into a murderer too if she didn't stop them. Locked in this room, I can't do anything, she thought, but I won't be locked in here forever. I'll get out, and when I do, I'll find some way to kill Beest, and Petrus too if I have to. I've seen the way that ape man looks at me; I'll get him alone sooner or later, and when I do, he's dead.

Ace Bricker tucked a second revolver into the waistband of his trousers under his vest. Sometimes, whether you like it or not, you just have to handle things yourself, even if you're the boss. He decided that he would go after Harry Beest personally and put the freak in the ground with his own gun.

Benny came in carrying a Thompson machine gun under one arm and a bulletproof vest over the other. Benny wasn't as confident as Ace; he'd been in Bugosi's mansion before, many times, and he knew the pile of stone was as strong as a medieval fortress. What worried him was that Ace had seen the same things he had and probably more, yet he was determined to raid the place.

"How many we taking with us, Benny?" Bricker said around his cigar.

"Ten."

"That should be enough."

"By tomorrow I could recruit at least twice that many."

"And Beest could do the same or worse. No, we're going to hit him, and we're going to hit him right now before he can do anything to prepare for it." Bricker shouldered into the bullet proof vest, and realized he couldn't get at the pistols in his waistband. "Gimme my overcoat," he said, and Benny helped him pull it over the bulky vest. Bricker jammed the revolvers into his coat pockets. "Tonight's the night, Benny. Tonight's the night."

Benny wondered, was Ace reassuring me or reassuring himself?

Carrington sat in the limo watching and waiting. The more he thought about murdering Harry Beest, the better the idea seemed. Killing Beest would ingratiate him with Bricker again, especially if he had the formula to offer and Petrus to make it work. Maybe he could sell Bricker the idea that this was his plan all along. He wouldn't be as rich, but he'd be alive and Rita would be safe.

Headlights. A dark sedan pulled up to the gate and flashed the new signal. Carrington backed the limo away from the gate and the carload of hoods rolled through the twisted iron. Two of Beest's men got out, and their silhouettes included heavy ordnance. He heard Sacco say, "You two stay here at the gate. Shoot anybody who tries to come in." Eddie didn't wait. the car drove away before Carrington could even block the driveway again.

Carrington pulled Harry's car across the entrance, shut off the engine, and took the keys. The Buick's armor plating almost doubled the car's weight, and anyone who wanted to move it would need a bulldozer or a tank. As an afterthought, he opened the hood and pulled a handful of wires from the plugs and the distributor. No hot wiring the car to move it either.

Satisfied, Carrington started his walk up the long driveway then stopped, realizing that the sound of his shoes on the gravel would make a target of him even in the dark. A man with a Tommy gun doesn't need to be a good shot. He stepped off the gravel and continued his climb by walking on the grass.

☠ ☠ ☠

Across the road, a figure wrapped in shadows watched from the same clump of bushes where Dandy Jake had stood a few hours before. Brother Bones smiled grimly behind his mask at the thought that Harry Beest believed blocking the gate would keep enemies away. Brother Bones picked up the suitcase from the ground beside him. Harry was about to learn that security never lasted long.

☠ ☠ ☠

Ray let Eddie into the mansion along with Earl and Rico, who carried canvas bags full of guns and ammo. "Eddie, I want you down here with me. You two upstairs; one cover the back, one the front."

"Where are Rippy and Mose?" Eddie said.

"Dead, so it's up to us to last the night. I'd bet my left nut that Bricker's on his way now with all the guns he can carry. So let's get it set up." He threw Eddie the keys. "Go upstairs and bring down the Doc. Leave the dame where she is."

Harry opened the canvas duffel and pulled out a machine gun. He stared at the trigger guard, too small a loop to fit his finger. Harry took the guard between his thumb and forefinger and twisted it off the gun with a brittle snap. He took another from the bag and made the same modification. He set the Thompsons on the sofa and dug in the bag for spare clips for his automatic.

Eddie came back with Petrus in tow. Harry could smell his fear. "Okay, Doc. Here's the situation: the same people who tried to kill us all a little while ago are probably going to come here tonight to finish the job. You're a valuable asset, but lead don't discriminate. You want to live?"

Petrus nodded, "Of course I do."

"Then you're gonna pull your weight. We got a lab full of chemicals upstairs. Can you use them to booby-trap the place?"

He thought for a moment. "I'll have to go upstairs and see what's on hand."

At that moment, the doorbell rang—three short, one long.

"Who's that?" Eddie said.

"It ain't the Fuller brush man. Go let Carrington in."

Carrington came into the parlor, his trousers soaked almost to the knees from the dew-wet grass. His eyes widened at the array of guns on the coffee table. "Glad you're still with us, Counselor," Harry said. "The thought crossed my mind you might take off, but the skirt always brings 'em back, huh?"

"I need to see Rita. I know she's scared to death."

"When the party's over, assuming you live through it, you two can have a joyous reunion. First things first." Harry threw Carrington a pump shotgun. "They shoot skeet at Harvard?" No reply. "You watch the back door to the kitchen. Nobody in," he gave a meaningful glance at Petrus. "Nobody out. Got it?"

Carrington swallowed hard. "Yeah, I got it."

Petrus turned to Eddie. "You and Ray take the Doc upstairs and help him bring down what he needs. I'll be outside."

"Wait a minute, Boss," Ray said. "He killed Mike. We gonna let him get away with that?"

"Ask me that question later—if we all live through this. Now do what I tell you."

Upstairs, Petrus ran his hand along the shelves of chemicals. Given enough time, he could easily produce nitroglycerine, but the attackers would likely arrive far too soon. His eye fell on glass jars of various acids. "Take these," he said to Ray, "and be careful not to spill any." At the end of the long room, he saw the tanks of gases. "You'll have to help me, Eddie. We're going to take all of them downstairs." Twenty-four hours ago, Petrus thought his life was simply terrible; now, it was simply terrifying.

Outside in the bushes, Harry waited in the dark, all his senses alert. He'd learned from experience that his eyesight wasn't much better than humans', but his hearing and his sense of smell were far superior. So, he shut his eyes and drank in the night, the sounds of frogs in the pond down the hill, the sounds of crickets chirping, the distant rumble of a freight train miles away, and the moan of its whistle. Around him he could smell the dampness from the early evening rain, the sharp scent of the marigolds in the flower bed out front, and the decaying corpse of some unlucky animal in the brush nearby. Let them come, he thought. I'll know when they arrive.

It took all the stealth that Brother Bones possessed to climb over the wall and sneak up on Harry's guards. Sam and Grover took positions on either side of the gate. Because the stone wall was too tall for them to stand behind and still see to shoot, they hid in the bushes flanking the entrance.

Bones quietly slid under the Buick between the rear wheels and wedged a bundle of dynamite under the right tire. He retreated, carefully unspooling detonator wire as he went until he was thirty yards away. If his plan worked, the explosion would flip the car end over on its back, clearing the driveway. He settled behind the bole of a thick oak tree. Now, all he had to do was wait.

The wait was short.

In the basement, Petrus set the oxygen tank beside the ether. The furnace was cold; too early in the season for heat. He turned to Ray. "Put out your cigarette."

"Huh?"

"Put out your cigarette. Better yet, just head for the stairs and shut off the light." Petrus turned the valve on the oxygen tank and it hissed like a leaky radiator as it blew a cold blast across the basement. He then opened the ether valve only enough for it to leak out in a slight, but steady stream. At the top of the stairs, Petrus said, "Shut this door and lock it. Don't let anyone go down there." He smiled grimly. Let them come, he thought. They'll find more than an ape in a suit waiting for them. To Ray, he said, "Bring the bottles."

☻ ☻ ☻

Two cars came down the winding lane, lights off, and stopped around a bend, hidden from Sam and Grover's line of vision. Doors opened, and six men got out. Bricker told them, "The gate's got to be guarded. Moe, you go take a look and see what's what." And to the others, "You four skirt the fence so you can get into the mansion from the back of the property. Get inside if you can. We'll be ready to close on the place as soon as we can get through the gate."

Moe started down the road, almost tiptoeing, sticking to the soft earth at the edge. Others left the cars and followed the wall up the hill. From the shadows, Brother Bones watched and laughed.

In a few minutes, Moe returned. "The gate's torn up like somebody run a tank through it, but there's a big car parked across the road blocking the entrance."

Bricker ground his fist in his palm. "Damn it," he muttered, "I guess we'll have to—"

A roar erupted down the road, and the sky lit up with the bright orange of flames.

Bricker's mouth dropped open. What the hell was going on? "Come on," he shouted. climbing into the lead car. Whatever that was, it can't hurt us."

As they sped down the road to the gate, Bricker's mind raced. Was it a booby trap that went wrong? Was somebody else trying to rush the place? The cars rounded the bend, and as they reached the gate, Bricker saw two men lying face down on the ground and Harry's limo overturned on the edge of the driveway. The way was clear. "Go! Go! Get in there!" The cars rolled through the ruined gateway and onto the property. "Wait." Bricker said. "Stop." Benny slammed on the brakes and the car slid in the gravel. Behind them the second car came within an in inch of ramming them. They were fifty yards from the front door. "We'll go it from here on foot."

The roar of the dynamite made Harry's sensitive ears feel as if knives were thrust through them. They rang, and he shook his head to clear them. No dice. He could hear, but a loud whistling tone seemed to shoot from one ear to the other, making it difficult. He didn't have to tell Eddie and the others that Bricker had arrived. Behind him, all the lights in the mansion blinked out at once. Eddie had thrown the main switch. No light, no targets—for them. Harry closed his eyes and flared his nostrils, inhaling the aromas of the night. When they were close, he'd be ready.

Rita screamed, startled by the explosion. Then the room went pitch black. She sat on the bed and listened to her ragged breathing and the thump of her heart. How was she ever going to get out of this alive? Footsteps. "Rita?" Al's voice. Stand away from the door." He kicked the door as hard as he could, three, four times, but the solid oak panel held. "It won't give," Carrington said. "Go back in the bathroom and lie down in the tub. The cast iron will stop a bullet."

"Bullet? What's going on?"

"We're under siege. Go. Now. I'll be back for you. I promise."

"Oh Al—" Rita said, but he was already gone.

After circling to the rear of the mansion, two of Bricker's men found the coal chute on the west wall. With a little finagling, the lock popped open, and the pair slipped through the metal trap door into the basement. "What's that smell?" one of them whispered.

"Smells like the hospital," the other one replied. Light a match so we can find the light switch."

There was a scratch, a sulfurous flare, and an explosion as the tank of ether went up in a ball of blue flame, engulfing the screaming thugs.

Outside, Harry waited. His hearing was slowly recovering. He could hear the crickets again, they went silent in waves, starting up again in a minute, and he realized it wasn't a problem with his ears. A faint breeze ruffled the fur on the backs of his hands. He took a deep breath through his nostrils and smelled sweat, gun grease, and fear. The crickets went silent in front of him.

Harry roared, raised a Tommy gun in each hand, and pulled the triggers. He turned ninety degrees to his left then to his right as he emptied the drums, the flash from the barrels glinting off his eyes and teeth. Bricker's men, caught completely by surprise, fell like bowling pins. Bricker caught several in the chest, and was knocked off his feet. Only his lead-lined vest saved him from death.

Carrington came back downstairs to his post to find two of Bricker's men kicking at the kitchen door. He flattened against the wall, his shotgun aimed at the doorway and held his breath. Silence. Did they give up? Where did they go?

The blast of a hand grenade took the door from its hinges and slammed it into Carrington, knocking him flat and landing on him. The explosion caught the wall on fire. Through the smoke, he could make out a pair of shadowy figures crossing the threshold. "Come on, one of them said. We –"

Petrus stepped from a pantry alcove with a saucepan in either hand. He swung them, spraying the invaders with acid. The men dropped their guns and screamed, clawing at their smoking faces until Petrus picked up Carrington's shotgun and blew holes through them.

The little man heaved the door off Carrington and knelt beside him. "Can you move?"

Carrington coughed up a lungful of blood. "I can't even feel my legs."

"Lie still. I'll do what I can."

"Leave me. Get Rita out of here," the lawyer gasped.

Petrus scooped up the shotgun and ran for the back stairs.

Harry's burst of machine gun fire decimated Bricker's men, but sporadic gunfire still erupted in the woods around the mansion. Harry retreated into Bugosi's garden, his automatic clutched in his paw. The foul smelling stalks and creepers assailed his nostrils and masked the odor of his enemies. He'd heard two more explosions from inside the mansion, and he was sure that Bricker's men had closed from the front and the back. He had no way of knowing how many had come nor how many he'd killed, so he just had to continue shooting anything that moved. But at the moment, nothing was so much as twitching.

Petrus took the stairs three at a time and stumbled once, nearly breaking his shin. Outside Rita's door, he knocked and said, "Miss Mayfield?" Her reply sounded distant. Petrus fired the shotgun at the doorjamb near the lock. The buckshot tore a chunk of wood from the frame. He fired again. One kick and the heavy door swung open. As he ran into the room, Petrus wondered why Carrington hadn't done the same. Maybe he thought she was safer locked away.

"Miss Mayfield?"

"In here." Petrus strained his eyes and saw Rita emerge from the darkened bathroom. He took her by the wrist. "Come with me." Rita didn't argue.

Petrus led her down the back stairs one step at a time this trip. When they reached the kitchen, in the light of the fire, she saw Carrington. He had dragged himself to the pantry doorway and propped himself to lean against the jamb. Blood soaked the front of his suit, and his head sagged onto his chest.

"Al!" Rita ran to him and took his face in her hands. Petrus turned away to give the lovers privacy in their last moments.

Carrington groped in his pocket and pulled out a folded sheet of paper. He pressed it into her hand. "Take this. The formula. Worth millions. Petrus will know how to use it." He coughed up a mouthful of blood and went still.

Rita understood that this was no time for tears. She shoved the paper into her brassiere and said to Petrus. "Get me out of here." Petrus didn't argue.

Out in the trees, something moved. Eddie, perched in a second floor window, fired a burst from his machine gun. The flash was all the target Benny needed to fire three rounds into Eddie's chest. Eddie fell through the casement and rolled down the slate roof to land to the side of the portico.

Sirens wailed in the distance. "C'mon, Ace," Benny said. "We gotta move before the cops get here."

"I don't give one damn about the cops. I'm not leaving here 'til Beest is dead."

Benny suddenly realized that his boss had gone totally crazy. "Ace, this is nuts. I'm not hanging around." He got three steps before Bricker shot him in the back.

Now, Harry, Bricker thought. *You and me. Show your ugly face so I can put a hole through it.* He crept up on the stone fence at the edge of the garden, finger on the trigger of his shotgun, waiting for anything to move.

There hadn't been a shot fired for almost five minutes, but Brother Bones had no illusion that the gun battle was over. He slipped through the coal chute into the basement. In the light of his pocket torch, he saw the blackened ruin of the basement and the charred bodies of two men. He wedged a bundle of dynamite against the load bearing wall at the basement's center, cut stone blocks piled two feet thick, and spooled out the wires the way he had come.

Rita and Petrus ran from the kitchen door toward the gate in the back wall of the grounds. In the garden, Harry caught a whiff of Rita's perfume. The dame was out of her room and the house, and it was a good bet Petrus was with her. He rose from his crouch and started through the tangled vines.

A blast from a shotgun peppered his shoulder with double-aught buckshot, knocking him backward. Harry roared in pain and wheeled to see Bricker's dim form as he jacked another round into the chamber. "Got you now, you freak. This is gonna be the best day of my life." He raised the shotgun to his shoulder. "So long, ape-man."

A blast from the mansion shook the ground and knocked Bricker sideways. Harry, reflexes in high gear, sprung the eight feet between them and landed on him hard. He yanked the shotgun from the hoodlum's hands and sent it spinning into the trees. Harry clamped his paws over

Bricker's head and squeezed, and squeezed. Bricker's skull collapsed with a wet crunch as his eyeballs popped from their sockets with a spray of blood.

Harry rose to his feet and roared as he beat his chest with his fists, but his glory was short lived. Behind him, he heard a loud cracking noise and a deep rumble. He turned to see Bugosi House begin to collapse inward on itself like a house of cards, and with it, his hope of salvation.

"No! No!" he screamed. He stood dumbfounded as cop cars rolled through the gate below, lights and sirens going full tilt. Ray grabbed him by the arm. "Come on, Boss. We gotta get outta here."

Harry followed Ray across the garden where Harry sprung to the top of the wall in one bound and dropped to the other side. Ray took longer to clamber over the top, and a single gunshot sent him falling back into the grounds.

With no choice, Harry ran crashing through the trees and brush with no other thought but survival. A running jump landed him in the limbs of a massive oak. Animal instinct took over, and he swung and leapt from tree to tree, putting distance between himself and the cops.

In the crotch of a maple tree, Brother Bones watched. He had gotten one of Beest's henchman, but the mob boss had escaped. From the grounds, he heard the commotion of the police as they scattered around the property looking for the living and the dead. The Undead Avenger silently slipped away to a back road where Bobby Crandall awaited him in his roadster. As for Harry Beest; there will be other days.

Petrus and Rita were nearly a half mile from Bugosi House, their legs aching and their lungs burning, when they heard the biggest explosion. Looking over her shoulder, Rita saw flames shoot through the mansion's roof just seconds before the whole place fell in on itself.

"Good Lord," Petrus said. "I guess that's the end of this nightmare."

Rita put her hand over her bosom and felt the folded paper Al had given her as he lay dying. "But it's the beginning of a whole new dream for you and me."

Petrus heard an edge in her voice he'd not heard before.

"You're going to help me, and I'm going to make us both richer than you could ever imagine. I'm going to take over this town. Are you in?"

Petrus nodded slowly. "How could I refuse?"

In the dark, he didn't see Rita let down the hammer of Al's revolver and push it back into the waistband of her skirt. "And if Harry Beest survives this night, I'll have his head on my bedroom wall."

The resolve in her voice sent a chill through the scientist.

If politics make strange bedfellows, he thought, crime makes even stranger ones.

THE END

A PRETTY MONSTER

When Ron Fortier asked me to write a story for his Cape Noire anthology, I was delighted to take the assignment. I felt like the proverbial kid in a toy store with a ten dollar bill. Such a variety of characters and personalities to choose from; it was a tough choice. A few were already taken, but Harry Beest was still unclaimed, so I went with the ape man. While Harry isn't a super hero, being a gorilla gives him a few advantages strength-wise and agility-wise that makes him more than a formidable foe.

I modeled some of Harry's mannerisms and habits after the real life Brooklyn mobster Louie Amberg, a misshapen, dreadfully ugly murderer and crime boss who was nicknamed Pretty as a child, and who offset his looks with expensive tailor made suits that masked his deformity and lavish spending on women and booze. The two seemed brothers under the skin, even if one of the skins had fur on it.

This was a fun assignment, and I left the door open for a follow up if Ron decides to run the gang again. Hope you all enjoy it as much as I did writing it.

☠ ☠ ☠

FRED ADAMS, JR. is a retired Penn State University English Professor who spends his days writing pulp fiction and his nights working as a singer-songwriter. His Sam Dunne novel *Dead Man's Melody* was nominated as Pulp Novel of the Year in 2017's Pulp Factory Awards, and his Smith Brothers novel *The Eye of Quang-Chi* was nominated for the same award in 2018. His titles include *Hitwolf* 1 and 2, *Six Gun Terrors* vols. 1, 2, and 3, and *C.O. Jones: Mobsters and Monsters, Skinners,* and *The Damned and the Doomed.* His original Sherlock Holmes anthology *The Affair of the Chronic Argonaut* was recently published by Pro Se Press. Forthcoming titles from Airship 27 include *C.O. Jones: Home Front, Six Gun Terrors 4: The Town Killers,* a Sam Dunne Mystery, *Blood is the New Black,* and *Holster Full of Death,* a Dead Sheriff novel. He lives in Mount Pleasant, Pennsylvania in "perpetual terror of boredom."

Visit Fred's website at http://drphreddee.com/author

THE DEVIL YOU KNOW

By Andy Fix

The scream that tore through the air shattered his nerves like a fist through a plate glass window. Nothing Officer Brian McKluskey ever encountered in his seventeen years as a beat cop prepared him for such a sound, and a cold fear gripped his guts. The scream quickly lost all of its humanity and became a sound of primal terror and pain. It ended abruptly with a choking gasp, and McKluskey's training kicked him into action. He raced down the sidewalk as he drew his service revolver with a shaking hand. He glanced around to get his bearings, and he stopped abruptly. The sign on the corner proclaimed the two intersecting streets: Morneau and Edgewater. After a moment's hesitation, McKluskey steeled his nerves and crossed into the shanty town of Little Jamaica.

Even hardened officers of the Cape Noire Police Department avoided this neighborhood. McKluskey's patrol area ended where the hovels on the water's edge began, but somebody needed help. Both the cop's conscience and his duty drove him onward into the darkness.

Doors and windows slammed shut in the shacks and buildings around him. The denizens of Little Jamaica knew trouble when they heard it, and they wanted nothing to do with whatever was going on.

McKluskey slowed as he approached the alley that the scream emanated from. His skin prickled as the hairs on his arms and neck stood on end. A lone streetlamp flickered intermittently, offering only brief glimpses into the narrow space between two dilapidated buildings. With his gun held out in front of him, he stepped into the darkened alley.

The deficient bulb made another vain attempt at life, and in that brief flash of dim light McKluskey saw a dark figure crouched low over a mutilated body.

"Freeze, mister!"

The bulb flickered again as the figure glanced back at him. McKluskey's eyes widened as the alley was plunged into darkness once more. That face, shadowed by the brim of a hat, leered at him with an unmistakable skeletal grin. Only one man in Cape Noire wore such a mask.

Brother Bones.

☠ 55 ☠

Paula Wozcheski gagged from the kerchief covering her mouth and nose. It reeked of chloroform, undoubtedly enough to overcome any normal person. In moments, she fell limp in her assailant's arms.

"Quick, throw her in the back of the car," said a man's gruff voice. "With this dame's looks, she'll fetch us a fortune! What a looker, eh?" A coil of rope cut into her skin as it was knotted around her wrists.

While Paula appreciated the compliment, the men had sealed their doom when they grabbed her from behind. Chloroform has no effect on vampires, after all. Her feigned unconsciousness merely assisted in her search for their gang. They had snatched their last victim from the streets of Old Town. Once these kidnappers took her into their den, she would feast.

She rode in relative comfort, with the exception of the groping by the man in the back seat next to her. *This one*, she thought, *will die horribly.*

When they arrived at their destination, another man took her out of the car and slung her over his shoulder. He struggled as he carried her dead weight up a flight of creaking stairs.

"What the hell is taking you so long?" called out another from above. "We've got three more packages up here that we still need to ship out. Shake a leg!"

"Hey, back off," said the man that was providing her transit. "This broad weighs more than she looks."

Okay, change of plan, she fumed silently. *This will be the guy that dies the worst.*

She was dumped with little gentleness on a wood floor. The faint whimpering she heard must be coming from the other 'packages' the impatient man had mentioned. A door opened and then closed as the men left the room. Paula cracked open one of her eyes to take a peek. Her heightened vampire sight allowed her to see three other women on the floor in the dark near her. All was going according to plan.

With a slight flick of her wrist, Paula snapped the rope that bound her hands behind her back. She crawled over to the three prisoners. The darkness hid her face from them, but she saw them all clearly. *These are just girls*, Paula realized. *They're younger than me!*

"I'm going to get you out of here, ladies," she whispered. "Keep quiet and keep your heads down. I'll come back for you once I've taken care of those goons." All three girls, wide-eyed with fear, nodded their understanding.

Paula peered out the cobweb-covered window set opposite the door. The room overlooked an empty warehouse strewn with refuse. The light fixtures all hung dark, many of them housing broken bulbs or no bulbs at all. A thick layer of dust covered everything. This building hadn't been used for any legitimate business in quite a while. All the better.

A makeshift table surrounded by several overturned crates sat in a small circle of light almost directly below the window. Four men sat at the table, the flickering flame of a gas lantern in the center sending shadows dancing across their faces.

The tight dress and heels Paula was wearing certainly accentuated her statuesque physique and her long, shapely legs, but the outfit was not particularly suited for this kind of work. She would have much rather been wearing her normal gear for this kind of action. Unfortunately, her undercover role required her to look more like a street-walker than a masked vigilante.

Paula glanced back at the three young women huddled on the floor behind her, then she crashed through the window. She landed on her feet in a low crouch on the concrete floor some twenty feet below. The men at the table threw up their arms to cover their faces from the shards of glass raining down on them, unaware of the greater danger that was now in their midst.

Like a hunting tigress, she was upon them in a blur of speed. She grabbed the nearest man's head from behind and jerked it around with a loud crack. He wore a shocked look on his face as the life faded from his eyes. Paula flung his corpse at a second thug, then leaped into the air as a third fired his pistol at her. She landed on the table and sent him sprawling with a hard kick to his neck. The man clutched his crushed throat, making satisfying gurgling noises as he choked on his own blood.

Paula stood straight up on the table and peered over her shoulder at the fourth criminal. He sat on the floor beside his toppled stool, his eyes wide, his mouth gaping as he tried to collect his wits.

"W-what are you?" he managed to stammer.

"You," she said, pointing down at him, recognizing his voice. "You're the one who called me fat."

"Actually, I j-just said that you were heav- urk!"

Paula leapt down to the floor and sank her fangs deep into his jugular. He writhed and screamed in agony as she drank his life away, but her grip was too strong for him to do anything else. He died with a whimper, and she cast his lifeless body aside like so much garbage.

Several gunshots rang out as the last remaining kidnapper emptied an entire magazine of .45 caliber bullets into her back. She turned in slow, dramatic fashion to face him with a gore-smeared smile on her face. The effect this had was visible from the spreading wetness on the front of the man's trousers as he lost control of his bladder. Flames started by the overturned lantern burned between them.

"Run, fool," she hissed while leering at him. "Run to all those who prey on the innocent and tell them what happened here tonight. Tell them you've seen the devil herself rise from the flames of Hell to wreak vengeance upon your kind. Tell them you've seen the nightmare face of Sister Blood!"

And he ran as fast as he could, never once looking back on her horrible, laughing visage.

☠ ☠ ☠

Paula and the three girls made their escape as the flames consumed the warehouse and its grisly contents. No one would be identifying those bodies anytime soon. She spent an hour ushering them to St. Michael's church, and another hour there as she and Father O'Malley discussed what to do with the traumatized trio. None of them showed any inclination towards going to the police station. Father O'Malley promised that his deacon would see them to their homes in the morning. The girls would spend the few remaining hours of the night at the church.

All of this left precious little time for Paula to make it to the safety of her apartment before the sun rose. She closed the door of her blacked-out apartment just as the first signs of dawn were lightening the Eastern sky.

She awoke hours later as Nancy Hansen, her roommate and confidant, was fixing dinner.

"I'm telling you," said Nancy, "the cops put out a warrant for Brother Bones."

"That can't possibly be right," said Paula as she ran her hand through her raven black hair to work out the tangles. The last rays of the sun were fading from the night sky, and Paula's head was still a bit clouded from sleep. She must have misheard her roommate. "Did you say Brother Bones is wanted for murder?"

Nancy gulped down another bite of her sandwich before she answered. She never waited for Paula to wake up before she started eating dinner; the two friends had entirely different appetites.

"I just read it in the evening edition of the Tribune. A witness placed Brother Bones at the scene of the crime." Nancy flipped the paper open to the article. "Another murder in Little Jamaica."

"Another one?" Paula took the paper Nancy offered her. "That's the third one in, what, two weeks?"

"And just a grisly as the last two," replied the young blonde. "Body dismembered and burned all to Hell. Like they swallowed a hand grenade, or something." Nancy gave a shudder. "They haven't even been able to identify this new victim yet."

"But the first two victims, the prostitute and the vagrant, what did they do to deserve a visit from Brother Bones?" Paula shook her head. "Bones is a killer, for sure, but he's called 'The Undead Avenger' for a reason. What was he supposedly avenging?" Paula tossed the paper back to her friend after giving it a cursory glance. "No way Bones had anything to do with these murders."

"You may want to read the whole thing." Nancy pointed to the byline at the top of the article. "Sally Paige is the best crime reporter in the city. She backs her stories with solid facts."

"And what about her witness? They're probably spinning some outlandish yarn just to get their name in the paper."

"The witness wasn't some scared, superstitious nut-job, though," said Nancy. "It was a cop."

"That... that can't be right," Paula repeated. Frowning down at the newspaper, she continued, "I need to talk to Bobby about this and find out what's going on."

Paula weaved through the crowd at the Grey Owl Casino working her way towards the blackjack tables. Bobby Crandall's red hair stood out from everyone around him as he worked one of those tables. She easily picked him out even from the opposite side of the casino floor. But obstacles lined her path. Her cigarette girl uniform, by design, did little to hide her long legs and generous curves, and she drew the eyes of every man she passed. Of course, that was pretty much her job. So she flirted with every male customer between her and Bobby's table. After the better part of an hour and with a nearly empty cigarette tray, Paula got close enough to Bobby whisper into his ear.

"We need to talk."

The young dealer gave a startled yelp, but, being the professional that he was, he never broke his deal. Bobby coughed and continued on with his customers as if he hadn't heard her. But Paula noticed the reaction the gamblers missed. Her heightened senses picked up on all the cues: the hairs on the back of his neck rose, his heart beat faster, and the blood in his veins reddened his freckled cheeks.

When the last player busted out, Bobby gave her a quick glance over his shoulder. "I'm really hopping tonight. Can it wait for a bit?"

"Sure," Paula answered. "Meet me in the coat room at your first break. I'll keep an eye out for you."

Bobby gave an almost imperceptible nod as he started dealing the next hand, so Paula headed back for more cigarettes to sell. She refilled and sold out her tray two more times before she saw Bobby finally head off towards the coat room. She got there before he did, and she waited for him in the dark.

"Paula, you in here?" He closed the door behind him and moved through the rows of coats.

As he passed by her in the dark, the smell of him filled her nostrils and ignited her vampiric desires. Lust for his blood and for his body washed over her, and the tips of her canine teeth pricked her bottom lip as they grew longer and sharper. Memories of the recent passionate nights she shared with Bobby flashed through her mind. *I have to stop this*, she thought. *It's just not fair to him.*

She squeezed her eyes shut tightly, took a deep, calming breath, and managed to overcome her hungers. Instead of sinking her fangs into Bobby's neck, she reached out and brushed his cheek with her hand.

For the second time tonight, Bobby yelped in surprise. "Would you please stop doing that?"

"A bit jumpy, aren't we?" Paula moved around front, stroking her hand across his chest.

"I lead an uneventful, boring life outside of work." His voice dripped with sarcasm. "It makes me meek and timid."

"Indeed," said Paula. "I believe we need to talk about your extracurricular activities, my mild-mannered card dealer. Or, more accurately, the activities of your friend, Brother Bones."

"I don't know what goes on inside of Bones' head." Bobby's voice lowered. He looked around as if making sure not to be overheard, even though there was nobody else in the room with them. "I just drive him around and run his errands. We ain't exactly partners, you know."

"Have you made any trips to Little Jamaica recently? Like maybe last night?" Her finger ran down his back to the base of his spine. Bobby shuddered.

"If you're wondering about those murders, Bones had nothing to do with them." His voice had a slight quaver in it.

"Oh, I know he didn't kill those people." She breathed onto his neck. "It's not his MO. I just want to know what he's doing about it."

"Er... nothing."

"Wait, what?" All of her playful huskiness disappeared. "What do you mean? This is some seriously spooky shit going down. He should be all over that."

"Sorry, Paula. He hasn't shown any interest. I even asked him about it after I read the paper earlier tonight, and he just stared at me with his creepy, dead eyes. You know, like he does. Like I said, he doesn't share much with me."

"But this needs to be addressed. Innocent people are dying, and dying pretty horribly. Someone needs to do something."

Bobby moved closer and put his arms around her waist and pulled her to him.

"Can I see you later?"

"Bobby, not now, please! Someone has to stop this fiend. If not Bones, then who?"

"Well," he said with resignation in his voice, "I guess that someone is going to have to be you, then." He let her go and left the coatroom.

She stared at the closed door for a few moments after he left. "Then I guess it is up to me," she said to no one.

Paula spread her arms out to their utmost to catch more air under her leathery wings. She soared higher as she circled over the shanty town that made up the neighborhood of Little Jamaica. If any of the residents below happened to look up, they would have seen a giant bat glaring hungrily down at them. Fortunately for both Paula and the people below, anybody walking the streets at this time of night kept to their own business, so no one noticed her.

But she saw all of them. For the past five nights, Paula had crisscrossed the sky over the waterfront neighborhood hunting for a killer on the loose amongst them. She hunted, and she hungered. She couldn't feed while searching; that would only add to the fear that permeated the streets below. And a night off to hunt up a meal in her regular hunting grounds of Old Town meant the possibility of missing another attack here in Little

Jamaica. *But I do need to feed soon,* she thought. *Every person I see is starting to look like a very tasty morsel.*

A sudden flash from the streets below caught her eye, then a second one. A pair of thudding booms followed in quick succession, startling a flock of sleeping pigeons into the air.

Paula circled over to the source of the explosions. She tucked her arms in close, folding her bat wings to her side. She plummeted down towards a rubble-strewn lot before spreading her wings out once more and alighting on the ground.

With arms crossed over her chest and her wings wrapped around her, Paula rose to her feet. As she did so, the leathery skin of her wings became a black silk cloak engulfing a now human-shaped form. She opened her arms, revealing not a monstrous bat, but a stunning young woman. Paula's raven-colored bangs and shoulder-length hair perfectly framed her high cheekbones, while her dark eyes glittered from beneath a veil of black lace. The tips of two canine fangs peered out from between her scarlet lips. The neckline of the crimson silk blouse she wore plunged scandalously low, barely covering her bosom. Her black jodhpurs trousers hugged the curves of her thighs before fitting snugly into her knee-high leather boots.

Sister Blood had arrived.

"Now, just who de hell are you supposed to be?" The man's deep voice lilted with the singsong accent of a Caribbean islander, tinged with just a hint of mirth. Flickering flames from the burning debris limned the man's silhouette with a hellish glow, while the shadows cast his features in darkness.

Paula moved around him, putting the flames at her back so she could bring both figures into view. Just beyond the shadowed man was a young woman sprawled on the ground. A wide-eyed look of fear distorted her pretty brown face. Her torn clothing told which was the aggressor and which the victim here.

As the man turned towards Paula, the firelight revealed his fearsome countenance. He wore a threadbare tuxedo over his tall, spare frame. An upside-down cross was painted in white on his bare, dark-skinned torso. His pant legs ended in tatters, exposing bony calves and bare feet. Long dreadlocks spilled out from beneath a battered formal top hat, the ends of the braids sizzling and smoking like slow-burning fuzes. White paint covering the upper half of his face gave his features the appearance of a grinning skull. His pitch-black eyes reflected no light from the flames. *Now I see why this guy was mistaken for Brother Bones.*

"I am Sister Blood," she said, trying to keep the annoyance out of her voice. Her perfectly dramatic entrance hadn't sufficiently impressed him. "And these are my streets you are terrorizing."

"Oh ho, are dey now?" He held his arms out wide and laughed, gesturing grandly at the burning lot around them. "De streets you can have, my beauty, but de people here, dey belong to me."

Before Paula could reply, the man moved toward the cowering woman. In a blur of preternatural speed, the vampire caught him by the throat.

"Not her, she doesn't." Paula lifted the man by his neck so his feet dangled above the ground.

For an instant, the fiend's black eyes widened and turned a smoky gray color. But the clouded eyes quickly disappeared into pitch black again. A smile spread across his face as he grabbed her forearm. He clamped his legs around Paula's chest. With a powerful jerk, he arched backwards and flipped her onto the back of her head.

She lost hold of him when she hit the ground. As she rolled away from his grasping hands, she disrupted a section of the burning debris.

"No!" he screamed. "You fool, you've released her!"

Paula flung herself at the man, but he proved quicker than she expected. He cartwheeled sideways to avoid her, picking up a shovel that was lying in the dirt as he passed over it. She pivoted off of one foot and launched herself after him, only to find that she underestimated his speed once again. The head of his shovel smashed into her face.

Paula reeled backwards and tumbled to the ground. *That... hurt!*

She didn't have time to contemplate that impossibility any further, as her attacker was already lunging at her with his shovel held high for another strike. Before he could land that blow, Paula thrust both feet into his gut. Using his own momentum against him, she flung the man over her head. He landed with a thud several yards away.

A sudden movement caught Paula's eye. The woman who had been the intended victim bolted for the perimeter of the fire that ringed the lot. She passed through the opening Paula had created moments ago and fled up the darkened street.

The vampire shook her head to clear her vision. Her skull still rang from the blow she took from the shovel. When Paula opened her eyes, she gasped and jumped back. Her attacker was standing in front of her leaning on his shovel.

"Don't worry, beautiful lady. We won't be fighting no more tonight." He took a drag of the cigar hanging from his mouth. "She is gone now anyway.

And I don't like de odds. One sevite is a tough fight. But two of you?" He shook his head. "No, dat is too much for me. I'm kept on too tight a leash."

The man pulled a flask from inside his coat. He took a swig, swished the contents around his mouth, then spit a spray onto the cigar he held in his hand. The resulting fireball blinded Sister Blood, and she covered her face with her cloak against the intense heat. When she looked again, he was gone. Only a lingering smell of rum and sulphur remained.

It didn't take long for Paula to find the young woman. Even from the air, Paula could hear her desperate panting and the slaps of her bare feet on the pavement as she ran through the streets. She landed in an alley ahead of her and transformed back into her human form before stepping out in front of the near-hysterical woman.

The young lady jolted to a stop, eyes wide with fear and a scream threatening to escape her lips.

"Take it easy, honey," said Paula in the most soothing tone she could muster. "I'm not going to hurt you. I just saved you from that fiend, remember?"

Paula got her first good look at the woman. She was young, more of a girl, really. Full, black hair fell to her shoulders, and not a single flaw marred her rich, brown complexion. Her torn, dirty clothes looked as if they had been stylish and new until very recently, and they complimented her figure very - *Hey, wait a minute...*

"I know you! You're one of the girls I rescued from that warehouse last night."

The woman's eyes widened even more, but now from surprise. Her choked back scream came bubbling out as laughter, and her mouth split into a wide smile. The white-knuckled grip she held her beaded necklace with loosened and she tucked the charms back into her torn blouse.

"Oh, yes, yes! I do know you! It is a second time I am owing you my life, Sister Blood." Her accent hinted at a French origin, but with a strong Caribbean current flowing through.

"Call me Paula; Sister Blood is what the bad guys call me." Paula looped her arm through the woman's and guided her towards a better lit part of the neighborhood. "I'll walk you home. Tell me how you come to find so much trouble in such a short amount of time."

The woman cast her eyes down towards the pavement. "I... I have no

THE YOUNG LADY JOLTED TO A STOP, EYES WIDE WITH FEAR...

home. At least not anymore. The Baron knows of it now, so I can never go back there."

"Well, do you have a name, at least?"

"Yes, I'm sorry. We... that is, I am Giselle."

"Okay, Giselle. That's a start. Now tell me, who is this Baron? And how did you end up in this mess?"

"He is the Baron Samedi, a very bad spirit." Giselle's voice dropped to a whisper. "Oh, Bondye save me, he is after my soul!" She looked away from Paula and sobbed. After composing herself, she continued with a more even voice. "I came to Cape Noire from Haiti. My mother is Haitian, but my father is a Frenchman, a sailor who left when I was just a child. I have been searching for him for the past several months, and that search brought me to this city a few weeks ago."

"Back to this Baron Samedi guy. He's the one that attacked you earlier tonight, right?" Paula scanned every shadowed rooftop and every darkened alley they passed for any sign of Baron Samedi. Her head still hurt from that blow she took from his shovel, and she didn't want to be surprised like that again. "What does he want from you?"

"That I do not know. Tonight was the first I saw of him."

The streetlamps glowed at regular intervals, driving away some of the darkness and revealing buildings in better repair. Little Jamaica was behind them, and the more familiar Old Town now spread out before them.

"I'm taking you back to St. Michael's church again," Paula said. "Father O'Malley will find a place for you to stay."

"No, no! Please don't take me back there." Giselle's eyes grew round with fear again. "Please, it is only you who can protect me."

"Wait, what? Sorry, I'm not in the bodyguard business. I've got too much to do to follow you around while you look for your father."

"I do not need a bodyguard. Just a place to sleep. I can stay with you!" Her eyes went from fearful to hopeful. "Oh, please, it would mean the world to me."

"Now wait a minute, you can't... I mean, I don't... we..."

"Please, Sister...er..Paula," Giselle interrupted, "my life depends on it."

With a sigh, Paula held up her hands in concession. "Okay, okay, you can stay with me. But only until I take care of this Baron Samedi situation."

💀 💀 💀

Bobby Crandall whistled tunelessly as he walked through the darkened parking lot. He longed for his bed and for sleep after a long, busy shift at the Grey Owl Casino, but the ample tips he made tonight buoyed his spirits. His keys jangled in his hand as he approached his car.

A sudden chill shivered down his spine. He felt another presence, like someone was watching him, but he didn't see anyone else in the lot. What few cars remained at this hour were empty. His whistling died in his throat.

"We need to talk." Paula stepped out from behind Bobby's sedan.

The young card dealer jumped back, shrieking like a schoolgirl.

"Really, Paula? Really?" Bobby asked, the octave of his voice dropping back down to an acceptable level. "Why do you have to keep doing that, skulking around in the shadows and scaring the bejeezus outta me?" Grumbling, he bent over and picked up his dropped keys.

"I'm a vampire, that's what we do. Union rules."

"Hardy har har. What is it you wish from me now, oh Mistress of the Dark?"

"I need to talk to Brother Bones."

"It's not as easy as all that. I ain't his personal secretary, yah know." Despite his gruff answer, Bobby's eyes roamed over Paula's figure. He was so in love with her, despite her being a nightwalker. She had tried to break it off, but he was persistent. Vampire or not, he was devoted to her and so the relationship, awkward as it was, continued.

"Please, Bobby. It's important." She put a hand on his arm. "I need his help. A girl's life depends on it."

"Oh, all right." He opened up the passenger side door for her. "I don't make any promises, though. Bones does his own thing. You know that."

The drive didn't take long, as the roads were all but empty in these early, pre-dawn hours. Paula filled Bobby in on the events of the past two nights.

"You're right," Bobby said once Paula finished. "This is something that Bones should be into. But he hasn't moved from his room in days." Bobby glanced over at his immortal lover. "This is more than your typical thug or gangster, though, Paula. I hope you're not getting in over your head."

Paula rubbed a welt on her forehead. "Yeah, me too."

When they pulled up to the apartment, Bobby pointed up to a window with a faint light glowing from it.

"That would be Bones," said Bobby, pointing to the lit window. "He sits in there in front the window just staring out at the city. He doesn't sleep… ever. Just sits there. Sometimes I hear him talking to someone. He only comes out when he's ready for action."

Bobby opened the door and flipped the light switch, eliciting a gasp from both him and Paula. At the small kitchen table sat a lone figure clad in his ever-present skull mask and with his twin .45 pistols slung in their holsters beneath each arm. Brother Bones, the Undead Avenger, stared at the blank wall in front of him for a heartbeat, then he turned his dead eyes towards them.

"Paula Wozcheski," said Bones. His raspy voice sounded like tearing paper. "You have come to speak to me about the murders in Little Jamaica." It wasn't a question.

Bones' unblinking gaze bored right through them. Bobby and Paula shared a shocked look with each other before Paula walked over and sat across the table from Bones. Bobby noticed for the first time that a black coat and hat rested on one of the chairs at the table.

"Yes, I have," said Paula. "What do you know of them? Why aren't you doing anything about it?"

"I do not choose my own path," he said. "My vengeance is directed by a higher power."

"Dammit Bones, that's not good enough!" Paula slammed a hand on the tabletop. "I don't know the first thing about this guy, this Baron Samedi."

Brother Bones rose and grabbed his coat and hat.

"Samedi is not of this world. Tread carefully."

Paula turned to Bobby with a look that bordered between exasperation and pleading.

"Would you get a load of this guy? Some help!"

All Bobby could manage in response was a shrug.

"Bobby Crandall," rasped Bones as he pulled on his coat and donned his hat. "Pull your car around, I have work to do."

"Aw, c'mon, Bones. I just got off work," Bobby whined. "I'm exhausted and starving."

Bones adjusted the fit of his hat, pulling it down lower over the boney brow of his mask. "Vengeance waits for no man, Crandall." He stepped past the Bobby and through the still-open door.

"Wait just a minute here," said Paula as she rose from the table. "What about me?"

The Undead Avenger stopped and turned slowly back to stare at her.

"I cannot join you on this path, Sister Blood," he intoned in his deathlike monotone. "We all have a spirit to guide us. Seek yours elsewhere."

💀 💀 💀

"Seek yours elsewhere," said Paula, mimicking Brother Bone's monotone. "What the hell is that even supposed to mean." She sprawled on the lone couch in her apartment with her arm flung over her throbbing head. "And why isn't this aspirin taking care of my headache?"

"Maybe because you're an undead vampire?" replied Nancy. Her roommate was sitting at her sewing machine mending the Sister Blood costume. "I'm surprised that Samedi guy was able to hurt you at all. Aren't you supposed to be invulnerable?"

"I was thinking about that too. Bones did say that Samedi was 'not of this world'. Maybe that has something to do with it? I don't know."

"Well, you may want to keep that in mind the next time you face him." Nancy held up the red silk blouse to make sure she hadn't missed any rips or holes.

"If I ever find him again. I should be out there looking for him right now."

"Well, your Sister Blood outfit is all fixed up, so you won't have to go looking in just your brassiere and garters." Nancy folded the blouse up and stacked it up with the rest of the clothes on the arm of the couch. "Say, if you need spiritual help, why don't you go talk to Father O'Malley at St. Mike's?"

Paula sat up and looked at her roommate.

"That's perfect! Father O'Malley had his deacon help out with Giselle and the other girls the other night. He might be able to offer some insight on this situation. What was his name...?"

"Deacon Devareaux," said Nancy. "Tonight's Saturday, so he'll be helping out at the soup kitchen after evening mass. If you hurry, you can still catch him there."

"Nancy, you're a genius." Paula stood up and grabbed the clothes off the couch. She looked around the room and asked, "Say, where is Giselle, anyway?"

"She said she had some things to take care of." Nancy shrugged. "Not sure I'd be out running errands if an evil spirit was after my soul, but what do I know?"

💀 💀 💀

A slim, dark-skinned man exited the front door of the soup kitchen. His black frock coat with white stand collar marked him as the clergyman Paula was looking for. He donned his hat, pulled a cane out from under his arm, and stepped down onto the sidewalk. He waved his cane out in front of him, gently tapping it on the ground as he walked. His head tilted to and fro, but more as if he were listening to something rather than watching where he was going. Dark glasses hid his eyes, and he seemed to ignore the tipped hats of those who passed him by.

Paula wasn't sure what surprised her more, the fact that the deacon was a black man, or the fact that he was blind.

She mirrored him from across the street until there was no one else around, then she hurried ahead and crossed over to wait by a corner street lamp. He stiffened as he approached her, and he came to a stop when he reached where she stood.

"Is there something you need, Sister?" He didn't turn to look at her.

Paula started in surprise.

"How did you… I mean, I'm not…" *How did he know I was here, much less recognize me as Sister Blood?*

"Are we not all brothers and sisters in the eyes of God?" He turned her direction and held out his hand. "Deacon Antione Devareaux, at your service." His mouth curled up into a mischievous grin. "My apologies. I did not intend to startle you."

Letting out a breath she hadn't realized she was holding, Paula shook his hand.

"I'm the one who should apologize, Deacon. I should have announced myself. I… I didn't realize you were…"

"Blind? No worries, sister. I manage very well for myself, so most people don't realize." He doffed his hat and tucked it under his arm. "Now, what is it I can do for you, Sister…"

The expectant pause at the end of his question hung in the air for a moment.

"Oh, sorry. My name is Paula Wozcheski."

Devareaux stiffened again, but only for a moment. "You are the one who brought the women to St. Michael's church the other night?"

"Yes, that was me. Thank you so much for helping them out the next day."

"All in service to Our Lord," said the deacon with a slight bow of his head.

"Actually, I've come to speak to you about one of those women, Giselle."

Antione was silent a moment, tilting his head.

"Come, walk me back to St. Michael's. It is late, and I don't see so well in the dark." He flashed her another grin and offered his arm.

Paula took his arm, and they walked in the direction of the old church.

"Giselle is still in grave danger," she said. "She is from Haiti, and she claims she's being hunted by an evil spirit. Someone named Baron Samedi. I wouldn't have believed her tale, but I saw the man myself, and he's terrifying. Do you know who — or what — he is?"

Deacon Devareaux nodded. "I was born in Haiti myself, and even though I grew up here in Cape Noire, I have been back to the island many times doing missionary work. I am familiar with Vodou, their religion. Baron Samedi is the guardian of the gateway to the spirit world. It is he who takes the souls of the dead either to Heaven or to Hell. It is said that if the Baron is knocking on your door, Death is not far behind him."

"So he is evil, then?"

"Not necessarily. People only fear him because they fear Death. He is portrayed as crass, rude, and debauched, but not completely without merit."

"He certainly doesn't sound like a fun guy to have at a party."

The deacon chuckled. "Being the guardian of the gateway, Samedi decides who gets to enter the spirit world and who doesn't. He can decide to send a spirit back to its body, thus denying Death. So some desperate people pray to him not to take their souls."

"He can do that?"

Devareaux shrugged his shoulders. "I am a man of God, and I believe only God has power over life and death. But…" The deacon gestured at the city skyline with his free hand. "We live in a strange place and in strange times."

You don't even know the half of it, Deacon, thought Paula.

"Why would this evil spirit be after Giselle?" she asked.

"Only Giselle can answer that."

Except she can't answer that, thought Paula. *Or she won't.* She chewed on her lower lip as they continued to walk in silence.

"Is that all, sister? You still seem uneasy."

Paula shook her head. "I'm just worried about Giselle, Deacon. She wasn't home when I left earlier tonight, and I'm not sure where she got off to."

"Oh?" He stopped abruptly and turned toward Paula. "You know where she is staying? I mean, you know she is safe, yes?"

Though Paula couldn't see the deacon's eyes behind his glasses, she could feel those eyes looking directly into her own.

"Um, yeah. She's staying in my apartment with me and my roommate Nancy."

"Ah, yes, young Nancy. I see her at mass often. Very good, very good." Devareaux started walking again. "If Giselle is with you, then I believe she is exactly where she needs to be."

"I hope you're right, Deacon. I'm worried about her right now, though. It's not safe with this Baron Samedi still running around."

"And look, here we are at the church," Devareaux said without looking for himself.

Paula had been so wrapped up in their conversation that she hadn't been paying attention to where they were walking. But as soon as she looked up, she saw that they were indeed standing at the front steps of St. Michael's church.

"How did you…?"

The deacon pointed up to the church's bell tower.

"I can hear the pigeons," he said with a grin. "I will pray for our sister Giselle tonight, and I am certain she will return home unharmed. Good night, Paula. Thank you for your company."

"I will take care Giselle, I promise." She watched the deacon climb the stairs and enter front door. "And thank you for your…guidance," she said, more to herself than to the man disappearing into the church.

"Giselle, if you want me to protect you, you really shouldn't stay out after dark alone like that." Paula pushed the evening edition of the newspaper across the table so Giselle could see the headline. "Baron Samedi struck again last night." She pointed to the gruesome photograph that accompanied the article. "This could have been you."

Giselle passed a hand over her wide eyes as she made the sign of the cross with a charm on her necklace.

"Bondye preserve us, how horrible!" Tearing her eyes away from the photo, she clasped Paula's hands in her own. "Please forgive me, Paula. I was following a lead on my father, and I lost track of time. I returned back here as soon as I realized the late hour."

"Everything is fine; just be more careful." Paula stood up and stretched her limbs, arching her back like a cat. "I've got the night off from work, and I'm famished. I think I'm going to go out and grab a bite to eat."

Paula walked into the living room to grab her Sister Blood garb from where Nancy had left them next to her sewing machine.

"When will Nancy be back?" asked Giselle from the kitchen.

"She'll be back soon," Paula called back over her shoulder. "Don't worry, though. Samedi has no idea where to find you. You'll be perfectly safe."

The darkness outside the apartment window disappeared in a blinding flash. A clap of thunder pounded her skull as a wave of hellish heat rolled over her. Paula slammed into the living room wall, and shards of glass and masonry shredded her clothing. Were she not a vampire, her body would have been pulped by the blast and the shrapnel.

The room reeled around her as Paula struggled to focus. Through the dust and smoke, she could make out a blurry figure stepping through the gaping hole that used to be her window and wall. The pungent smell of sulphur burned her nostrils. Sulphur and another odor she recognized.

Rum. *Oh, shit!*

Sister Blood raised her arm just in time to deflect the head of the shovel that was whistling down at her face. The sharp pain of the impact instantly pierced the fog of shock that clouded her thoughts. She lashed out with a foot and connected with the dust-shrouded form above her. Already off balance from his attack, her kick sent him careening over the coffee table.

Sister Blood rolled into a crouch and tensed for action. Across the darkened room from her rose a nightmare. The skull painted on his face and the cross that stretched from neck to naval reflected the pale moonlight. The ends of his smoldering dreadlocks glowed red in the darkness.

"I wish we had time to play, my pretty, but dis isn't your fight. Step aside."

"Giselle is under my protection, monster," she spat back at him. "You'll need to go through me."

"Monster?" he said with mocking innocence. "You wound me."

With speed that rivaled her own, Samedi lunged forward and raised his shovel to strike again. Sister Blood countered, but she realized too late that his attack had been a feint. He channeled his momentum into a spin, and his foot smashed into the side of her jaw, nearly removing her head from her her shoulders. She somehow maintained her footing, but she was forced to parry two more quick kicks with her elbows.

He uses his feet like most people use their fists, Sister Blood noted. She responded with a quick kick of her own and buried her foot into his gut. *Two can play at that game.*

Samedi shifted his shovel into a defensive grip as he gasped for air. After he regained his breath, his death's-head visage split into a wide grin.

"Let's dance den, Sistah Blood."

He jumped at her and made a quick jab with his shovel, but his attempted feint was only half-hearted. Sister Blood didn't take the bait this time. Instead, she sidestepped to put herself between Samedi and the doorway to the kitchen. She hadn't heard a noise from Giselle since the initial explosion, but she had to still be in there. The only way out of the apartment was through the front door, and Samedi barred that exit.

"Why do you protect her?" asked the Baron. "You know so little about her."

"I know she's an innocent woman, and that you're trying to hurt her. That's all I need to know."

"Innocent?" He laughed. "I stand corrected. You know nothing about her."

Samedi came at her with an overhand swing of his shovel. This one wasn't a feint, and Sister Blood crossed her arms in front of her face to stop the shovel from caving her skull in. Her attacker brought his knee up into her gut, but she managed to twist partially out of the way and ended up taking the strike on her hip.

Ignoring the pain, Sister Blood pivoted her twist into a spin and smashed her elbow into Samedi's ear. Dazed, he tottered and fell to his knees. Sister Blood moved in to finish him off.

The Baron's fall turned out to be another ruse. As he fell, he thrust a hand onto the floor and brought both legs up and scissored them around Sister Blood's knees. Before she could react, the floor rushed up to meet her face. In an instant, his long limbs were intertwined with her own, entangling her in a knot of sinewy muscle.

His strength nearly rivaled her own, and being on top of her allowed him to leverage all of it against her joints and tendons. She felt his hot breath on the back of her neck.

"You and me could be having so much fun, my pretty. The pleasure I could show y-urk!"

Sister Blood threw her head back and smashed her skull into her assailant's nose. The momentary lapse of pressure from him gave her the opening she was looking for. Before he could re-establish his backbreaking hold, she ripped her arms from his grasp. She rolled over and kicked him off of her, sending him crashing into the plaster wall.

Samedi reached for his shovel lying in the middle of the room, but Sister Blood was quicker. She stomped her foot down on the handle, daring him to make another move for it. She realized her mistake when a wicked grin spread across his face. The Baron now had a clear path to the kitchen.

Quick as a viper, Samedi launched himself toward the doorway. Sister Blood arrived just in time to have the door slam shut in her face. Flinging the door open only delayed her for a moment, but that was too long. A scream erupted from the darkness and a body flew past her and struck the refrigerator. Sister Blood grabbed who she assumed was Giselle, only to be surprised to find she held Baron Samedi.

"He's not the only one who is proficient in savate," said Giselle from the other side of the kitchen.

Sister Blood flung Samedi back into the living room. She glanced back at Giselle and said, "When you see an opening, break for the door!"

An animal-like snarl drew her attention back to her attacker. He leapt toward her, his shovel held high for a two-handed blow. She went low and caught him in the chest with her shoulder. The two went down to the floor in a tangle.

Both combatants climbed to their feet with their hands clutched around the other's throats. Sister Blood's eyes widened as a change came over the Baron's appearance. His braids no longer smoldered, but were now licked with flames from tip to scalp. The painted flesh of his face burned away to a bare skull, its mouth filled with sharp, pointed teeth. But it was the eyes set into that skull that shocked her the most. The empty sockets opened onto an endless black void that drew her in ever deeper.

After what felt like an eternity, a distant scream echoed in her skull. Her fall through the emptiness slowed. The screaming grew louder, and she rushed back up out of the inky darkness. She snapped out of her trance to find the scream that drew her back was coming from her own throat.

Sister Blood and Samedi still clutched at each other's necks, but the Baron's demonic flames now engulfed both of them. Searing pain overwhelmed the vampire as her flesh turned to ash and flaked away. She longed for unconsciousness to claim her to end this torture. Behind Samedi's leering skull-like face stood the open door to the hallway. *At least Giselle escaped,* thought Sister Blood.

A second leering skull appeared in the doorway. Brother Bones lifted a pair of twin .45s, and the muzzles flashed brightly. Sister Blood felt the thudding impacts of the bullets as they struck Baron Samedi's back.

Now it was the Baron's turn to scream. He dropped Sister Blood and turned to face this new attack. As she fell, another figure appeared in the doorway. The last thing she saw before darkness claimed her was the face of Bobby Crandall.

...HIS FACE BURNED AWAY TO A BARE SKULL...

Paula knew only pain. It consumed her entire existence. She heard sounds, but didn't recognize them as voices. Shapes hovered over her slit eyes, but she never recognized them as faces. Noises came from her throat, but she couldn't form words. The concept of time was beyond her comprehension. The only part of her existence that she understood was the all-encompassing pain.

Eventually, the pain lessened from this maddening level to being merely unbearable. Now she could hear voices and make out words. When people were in her field of vision, she saw their faces. She was coherent enough to attempt to speak.

"Wh-where am I?"

Nancy Hansen bent close to Paula, straining to hear her weak voice. "Paula, did you just say something?"

"Yes," Paula whispered. It hurt to speak, but each word formed easier than the last. "What happened? Where am I?"

"You're at Bobby Crandall's apartment in his bed. Baron Samedi burned you pretty bad, but you're slowly recovering. You look pretty bad, I'll be honest. But you do look better than you did a few days ago when we brought you in here."

"Thought... thought I was dead. So much pain. How am I still alive?"

"You can thank Bobby for that. When Samedi jumped out the hole in our apartment's wall, Bobby rushed over to you. After smothering the flames with a blanket, he opened one of the veins in his arm with a knife and held it to your lips."

"Is he..."

"He's alive. You almost sucked him dry, though. And he would've let you, too, if Brother Bones hadn't separated him from you." Nancy shuddered. "It was a pretty horrible scene all around."

"Police? Landlord?" All this talking exhausted Paula, but she had to find out what the situation was.

"Bobby and Bones rushed you out of there before anyone showed up. The cops determined that we were the innocent victims of a random bombing carried out by a Comintern anarchist." Nancy shrugged. "Who am I to argue with that? Sounds a lot more plausible than a demon and a vampire duking it out over the fate of a human soul."

Paula was too weak to laugh. "And Giselle?"

Nancy shook her head. "No one has seen her since that night. There have been no more murders in Little Jamaica, though, so there's a good chance that she's still alive somewhere."

Paula couldn't keep her eyes open any longer. She managed a quiet "thank you" to Nancy, but any more questioning would have to wait. Brother Bones had some things to answer for, and she wanted to be at full strength before she had that conversation.

Twenty hours later, Paula awoke again. The coppery taste of blood lingered on her lips. She looked over to the chair next to her bed and saw Bobby resting there. His forearm was freshly bandaged. He looked pale, but whether that was from the moonlight shining through the window or from blood loss, she couldn't tell. She slid out of bed and wrapped herself in a robe that was draped over the footboard. Booby's breath was deep and even. *Good,* she thought. *He's asleep, not dead.*

She slipped past Bobby's sleeping form and out of the bedroom. She wandered out into the tiny kitchenette where a cot had been set near the kitchen table. Nancy was sound asleep on it, covered with a single blanket. The faint sound of a raspy voice drifted from behind a closed door. A flickering light shone from beneath. She glided over to door and pressed her ear up against it, but whoever had been talking was silent now.

Paula opened the door, cringing at every squeak of the hinges, and entered the room. She had never been in here before, but she knew it was where Brother Bones spent all of his time when not out hunting the streets of Cape Noire. She also knew that no one but Bones entered this room. Not even Bobby.

Brother Bones was seated in a chair with his back facing the door gazing out the room's only window. The room was dark. The only light came from the streetlamp on the corner. To the left of the door was a bureau and on it Paula made out a single unlit candle. According to Bobby, the only time it was aglow was when Bones' spirit guide summoned him. Next to it was a snow white porcelain skull mask.

"Paula Wozcheski," said Bones without turning around. "You don't belong in here."

"Yeah, well, I have a bone to pick with you, and it can't wait until you decide to come pay me a visit. You owe me some answers." She didn't budge from where she stood, though her weakened legs were shaking.

The undead man sat in silence for several moments. Finally he stood and moved over to look out the window. "Sit down before your legs fail you." He kept his back to her. No one looked upon the Undead Avenger's face….ever.

Too exhausted to let pride stand in her way, Paula sat down in the chair Bones had just vacated. It held no residual warmth form the prior occupant.

"Ask your questions. I will answer them, or not."

She glared at his back. "Where is Baron Samedi?"

"I do not know. I did not pursue him once he left."

"You didn't go after him?" Her voice rose with her anger. "Why not?"

"I was not there to 'go after' Baron Samedi." He looked at her for the first time. "I was there to save you."

"Save me? What about saving his victims? He's a killer! He needs to be stopped!"

Bones kept his back to her. "All is not as it seems, Paula Wozcheski. Your answers will come in due time. Now leave me."

"All right, I'm leaving." She huffed as she stood and started for the door. "But don't think…"

She shook her head and did not finish what she was about to say. What was the point? How do you argue with a dead man?

She exited and the door closed behind her.

Paula held the red silk blouse up and inspected it.

"Thanks for grabbing this for me. It looks good as new."

"I didn't want anybody finding it in what's left of our apartment," Nancy replied. "Sister Blood's outfit turning up at the scene of the crime would have thrown the whole 'anarchist bomb attack' theory right out the window. Well, if we still had a window, that is."

Paula laughed, but that laughter turned into a gasp.

"Oh, don't make me laugh. It hurts too much."

"You're in no condition to be gallivanting about town. I really wish you wouldn't."

"It's been a full week. I'm hungry." Paula glanced over at Bobby's bedroom door. He was sound asleep after letting her "bite" him again. "And I can't keep feeding on poor Bobby. Who knows how this will affect him long term? And have you forgotten about Giselle? I need to find her still."

"But, just look at yourself! I mean, you don't look like a charcoal briquette anymore, but you don't exactly look normal yet, either. You'll still scare the crap out of anyone who sees you."

"Isn't that kind of the point?" Paula picked up the rest of her adventuring gear and headed to the tiny flat's single bathroom off the kitchen. The flat was intended for two people, not four. She and Nancy would have to find another apartment fast. They were all starting to get on each other's nerves far too much.

Her skin burned like fire when she slid the silk blouse over her bare shoulders. Pulling on the pants almost caused her to faint. Her raw flesh felt as if it would tear with each twist or stretch. *There's no way I can turn into my bat form in this condition*, thought Paula. *I barely even have enough energy to walk around this apartment. How am I going to do this?*

"Need help?" Bobby called through the door. She opened it and he stood there leaning against the door frame. His sunken eyes and pallid complexion told Paula everything she needed to know about what he was sacrificing for her. Behind him Nancy looked on anxiously.

"Dear, sweet Bobby." She stroked his hollow cheek with a hand that looked more like crispy bacon than human flesh. "What has become of us?"

A lone tear dripped from her eye and ran down her cheek. Bobby wiped at her face, and when his hand came away she saw only blood on it.

"I know I can't keep you from going," he said. "But at least let me drive you. You need someone nearby in case you get into any trouble."

Paula wrapped her arms about him and held him in a gentle embrace.

"Bobby, there is no one else I would rather have with me."

☻ ☻ ☻

"Okay, here it is," said Paula. "You can park around the corner there." She eyed a familiar building as they drove by it.

"The soup kitchen?" Bobby raised an eyebrow at her. "I know you're hungry, Paula, but I don't think this is gonna help you with that." He pulled the car around the corner and stopped up against the curb.

"It's not soup I'm after."

"Oh, c'mon! Seriously?" Bobby's brows knitted together in concern. "Give these poor guys a break. Don't they have enough to worry about just feeding themselves and their families? Surely you're better than that."

Paula glared at him. "Bobby Crandall, shame on you! You know I don't prey on the innocent."

"All right," he conceded. "Then what exactly are you after?"

"Answers," said Paula. "There's a piece to this puzzle that I'm missing, and I think I know someone who can help me find it." She opened the door and stepped out. "Wait here for me. This shouldn't take long."

"How will I know if you need help?"

"I think I can handle this one alone. This guy is less dangerous than you."

"Gee, thanks."

"Oh, stop pouting. You know you're just too damn cute to be scary." She leaned in the window and kissed a freckled cheek. "I'll be fine."

Paula walked past the soup kitchen's entrance. Half a block down, she stepped into an ally cast in shadow by a corner streetlamp.

If I remember right, he should pass right by me in just a few minutes.

As if on cue, Paula was soon rewarded. She had to wait less than ten minutes before she heard a faint tapping approaching. It grew gradually louder as her target neared, but then unexpectedly stopped. Minutes passed. She grew impatient and peered around the corner and up the sidewalk towards the soup kitchen, only to find the sidewalk empty.

"You are expecting someone, maybe, Sister Paula?"

She spun around and faced Devareaux. "Yes, Deacon, in fact I am. We need to talk."

"Ah, you have more questions for me? I am entirely at your service."

Paula eyed the clergyman, noting how his conservative clerical garb contrasted with her revealing Sister Blood outfit. "How long have you been in cahoots with Baron Samedi?"

The dark glasses hid his eyes, but his eyebrows leapt high enough up his forehead for Paula to see them.

"What makes you think I am working with such a character?" Both of his hands rested on his cane now. He widened his stance so his feet were in line with his shoulders.

Paula noted his change in posture. *He's readying himself for action. He's in for a rude surprise if he tries anything.*

"Well, let's see." Paula held up her index finger. "First, Giselle is attacked outside her home by Samedi just hours after you see her back to her home. How did he get her address?" She held up a second finger. "Then, she is attacked a second time when Samedi blows up my apartment. Right after I tell you that she's staying with me. I don't think either of those encounters was a coincidence."

"You misunderstand the situation, Sister Paula. I do only God's work."

She stepped closer to him, within arm's reach. "I don't believe you, Deacon. In fact I don't believe you are actually a deacon."

"I have lived here nearly all my life. I have known Father O'Malley since before I attended seminary school. St. Michael's paid for my mission work in Haiti. All of this can be vouched for. I assure you, I am legitimately a man of God."

"I see." Paula moved closer still, glaring at her reflection in his glasses. "Can you?" Her hand moved faster than the man could process the question. In a blink, she snatched the Deacon's glasses off of his face. His eyes widened for a moment, then he snapped them shut tight. But not before Paula saw, and what she saw drew a gasp form her.

"Your eyes! I've seen those eyes before, when I was fighting Samedi the first time." The Deacon hid his eyes not because he was blind, but because the swirling gray mists that billowed behind his eyelids revealed his true nature. "You're not even human!"

"I am more human than you, abomination," snarled Devareaux. Or was it Devareaux? As he spoke, his eyes darkened to pitch black pits of nothingness, long, smoldering braids spilled out from under his hat and fell across his shoulders, and his shadow cast on the ground from the streetlamp behind him stretched toward her as he grew taller. His frock coat tore and hung open, appearing now as a tattered coat with tails. His white collar turned liquid and streamed down his bare chest. He spread the white across his torso, forming an upside-down cross, then he held his hand up to his face. When he looked up, the skull-faced nightmare that was Baron Samedi leered menacingly at her.

For the first time since she had become a vampire, Paula felt the chill of fear run down her spine. On a good day, fully sated with fresh blood, she may have been able to go toe-to-to with this demon. This was not such a day, and her flesh burned anew with the memory of Samedi's flames engulfing her. Her legs, already weakened from her injuries, trembled as she backed away from him and into the alley behind her.

"Are you still Deacon Devareaux? Or are you the murdering demon Samedi?"

He advanced on her still, forcing Paula further back into the alley.

"I am both demon and deacon, Sistah Blood." Samedi held his shovel in one hand while he placed a cigar in his mouth with the other. He grabbed one of his smoking dreadlocks and lit the cigar with the glowing embers at the tip. "And I have murdered no one."

"Then I suppose there is some other mystery killer out there preying on the people of Little Jamaica?"

"Yes, someone else out dere who is committing dese crimes." Samedi took a long drag on his cigar. He held his breath for a moment, then blew out a single large smoke ring. "But who dat person is is no mystery to me." He grinned at her, and the smoke ring slid down the tall crown of his top hat like a second brim.

Paula raised an eyebrow. "Is that so? And are you going to share this secret with me, or do I have to guess?"

"Oh, I will be happy to share with you." Samedi grinned again. "But I don't tink you will be so happy to hear it." He took another drag of his cigar and sent a second smoke ring up atop his hat. "You see, I am hunting de same killer you are, Sistah Blood."

"You can't mean…"

The demon extinguished the smoldering cigar with his tongue, took a flask out of his coat pocket, and took a long drink. His eyes turned from pitch black to Smokey gray before he closed them. Slowly, the fearsome form of Baron Samedi dissolved into a cloud of smoke and billowed away, leaving Deacon Devareaux in his place.

"I mean exactly that," said the now-frail looking man. "The Lady Giselle is the murderer you and I are both after."

"That's impossible," said Bobby. The intermittent streetlamps bathed his face in pale light at regular intervals as they drove down the road.

"That's what I said," Paula repeated from the back seat before going back to her meal.

"Be careful back there, would you?" Bobby pleaded while glancing back at her in the rearview mirror. "Bloodstains are a pain to get out of the upholstery."

Paula rolled her eyes back at him. "As if I would let any go to waste." She wiped the gore dripping down her chin with a finger and licked it clean. "I feel almost like myself again. And that's one less thug knifing people for the contents of their billfolds."

"So, you believe the demon… er, deacon… whatever the hell he is?"

"He's both. The 'Demon Deacon'. That's good, Bobby. Has a nice ring to it." She rolled the corpse of the mugger onto the floorboard. "I'm done. We can dump this trash now."

"I'm heading to the waterfront as we speak. But back to Giselle and the Demon Deacon, help me out here."

"I saw the man transform into Baron Samedi right before my eyes. If something like that can reside within frail, little Antione Devareaux, who's to say that frail, little Giselle isn't hiding something sinister?"

Bobby shook his head. "I dunno. How can we take the word of that… that whatever."

"Devareaux controls Samedi; I saw it myself. And even the Baron mentioned that the Deacon keeps him on a tight leash."

"Then why can't Giselle control the demon possessing her?" Gravel crunched under the tires as Bobby slowed the car and pulled off the side of the road.

"Marinette, Devareaux called it. Marinette Bras Cheche. Somehow, this Marinette spirit tricked Giselle into wearing a talisman. I saw her praying with it as if it were a rosary. That talisman gives the devil inside full control over the person being possessed."

Bobby opened up the rear passenger door, and the two of them worked the body out of the back seat. "So, Giselle herself isn't all bad, just the Marinette spirit she's carrying around with her."

"Exactly." Together, they pitched their burden over the seaside cliff to splash into the ocean below. "Which is why I need to find her before he does. Samedi has the power to send Marinette back to whatever hell she came from, but he first needs to get her out of Giselle's body."

They both stared down at the surf crashing against the rocks. "And that requires killing Giselle," Bobby finally said.

Paula looked over at her companion with her jaw set and her eyes glinting with anger. "I won't let that happen, Bobby. Giselle is an innocent woman, and she's not going to die at the hands of the Demon Deacon."

☠ ☠ ☠

The tires squealed as mob goon Frank Brass stomped on the accelerator. The smoke from the burning rubber mingled with the smoke from their tommy guns as they sped away from the street-front restaurant.

"Did we get him?" Brass asked his passengers. "Is he dead?"

"I plugged him a few times, for sure, Frankie," replied the gunman in the back seat. "I saw his head pop like a grape."

"Yeah, I saw a few of 'em go down for good," said the thug in the front passenger seat. "You wasn't supposed to shoot everyone, Sol, just Capo Mazzonie."

"I didn't see you exactly stickin' to the menu yerself, Vick," said Sol. "So a few slobs bought it; shit happens. They shouldn't have been eatin' at a mob-run restaurant anyway, am I right?"

"You sit down to eat with the wolves, you're bound to get bit," said Brass. This elicited laughter from the other two.

A loud thud cut short their revelry. Sol looked up at the convertible top above him "What the hell was that?"

A fist punched through the roof and grabbed Sol by the throat. Brass watched the rear view in horror as his partner was ripped out of the backseat through the torn canvas. Vick, obviously not holding any sentiment for Sol, leaned his tommy gun out the window and pulled the trigger, spraying bullets over the top of the car. The gunfire stopped abruptly as the gun was ripped from his grasp.

"What the hell was that?" echoed Vick.

As if to answer that question, a woman landed on the hood the speeding sedan, her black cape billowing in the wind. The last thing Frank Brass ever saw was Sister Blood's fist come crashing through the windshield.

Sister Blood flapped her great wings and soared higher into the air. *I feel almost alive again!* Her lips stretched over the fangs of her bat-like maw in an approximation of a smile.

She turned and circled low over the wreckage of the getaway car. Sirens in the distance announced the cops that were in route. She gave two more flaps of her wings and caught an air current that carried her up and away from the carnage below.

Rejuvenated with the influx of fresh blood over the past two days, Sister Blood's preternatural senses drank in all the information the night offered. A hunter at her peak prowess, she scanned the streets below for her quarry. Relentlessly she searched, until finally she was rewarded. An almost overwhelming scent of fresh spilled blood alerted her to a grisly scene unfolding beneath her.

She hesitated, almost afraid of what she would find. But the frail form on the ground surrounded by an ever-widening pool of blood was unmistakable. She landed on the ground beside the body and returned to her human form and her costume.

"Giselle," Sister Blood said. A feral hiss from a shadowed figure was the only response. "What have you done?" The vampire stood over what was once a young woman, probably no older than Giselle herself. Her cheap and scandalously revealing clothes left little question as to what trade she plied on these streets. Before she died, that is.

"I know that's you hiding in the shadows, Giselle." Sister Blood walked toward the figure crouched behind a steel drum in the alley. "Or should I call you Marinette?"

SHE GCAUGHT AN AIR CURRENT THAT CARRIED HER UP AND AWAY FROM THE CARNAGE BELOW.

Another low hiss emanated from the darkness. "Putting my name on your lips is a dangerous game, child." The voice, while that of a woman, did not belong to Giselle. This woman's accent was similar to the girl's, but the voice rasped like wind blowing through dead leaves.

Marinette stepped out of the shadows, still crouched low. She more slithered than walked, her thin, almost skeletal limbs writhing snake-like as she moved. A thin crimson shift wrapped her gaunt body, exposing much of her papery, brown skin. Wisps of white paint followed the lines of the bones of her limbs and ribs, accentuating her emaciated appearance. Her face was also highlighted with the paint in a way very similar to Baron Samedi's, different only in the jewel-like accents that decorated Marinette's cheek bones and forehead. A manacle hung from a length of chain still attached to a matching manacle on her left wrist. Her eyes glowed red, like windows into Hell.

Sister Blood recoiled at the sight of those eyes, the memory of her fiery embrace with Samedi still fresh in her memory. "Why?" she asked as she gestured to the body behind her. "Why are you murdering these people?"

"I am Marinette of the Chains." She held up her dangling manacle. "For centuries, the people that worshiped me were bound in slavery." She motioned to the body of the young woman. "She, too, was a slave, though she wore no chains. She was trapped in bondage from which she could never escape." An evil smile spread across her face, revealing sharply pointed teeth. "I freed her."

"But you killed her! There are other ways to help people escape misery without resorting to murder."

The demon shrugged, and her braids crawled about her neck and shoulders as something alive. "Her death nourishes me." She sniffed in Sister Blood's direction, then smiled. "In this, we do not differ so much, eh?" Marinette threw back her head and laughed. Her hair fell away from her face, exposing her neck.

Sister Blood noticed something — or rather the lack of something — when she saw that bare throat. The beaded necklace that Giselle never went without was missing. The talisman was gone!

"Giselle!" Sister Blood called out. "I know you're in there. Fight her! She has no power over you now!"

Marinette hissed, but that hiss died on her lips and the fire went out of her eyes. She moaned, then she was gone. Giselle opened her eyes, her completely human, beautiful brown eyes.

"Giselle, thank God!" Sister Blood grabbed the confused young woman by the shoulders. "Now stay with me. That horrible demon can't hurt you anymore."

Giselle shrugged off the vampire's touch and shook her head. She took several steps back into the shadows. "No... no, you don't understand..."

"I don't understand... what?" Sister Blood took a step toward Giselle, then hesitated. *Something's not right here.*

"It isn't Marinette who is using me, Sister." She smiled, but her eyes glinted of madness, not joy.

As Sister Blood watched in horror, the fire rekindled in the girl's eyes once more. Before she was completely consumed, Giselle said something that froze the blood flowing through Sister Blood's veins.

"It is I who am using her."

☠ ☠ ☠

Bobby Crandall dragged a comb through his hair as he looked at his sallow face in the mirror. "Good lord, I look like one of the walking dead."

"Well, it could be worse," replied Nancy. "At least you're not actually dead."

"Yeah, it's not like I've been keeping my vampire ex-girlfriend alive for the past couple of weeks by letting her feed on me, or anything. That could be harmful to my health." Bobby draped a bow tie around his neck and tried to knot it correctly. "I really wish I didn't have to go into work tonight."

The door to the spare room creaked open and Brother Bones emerged from the darkness. His twin .45s were slung in their holsters that hung from his shoulders, his coat was slung over his arm, and his hat was in hand. Bones strode past Nancy and Bobby and took a seat at the kitchen table.

"Got a date tonight, Boss?" asked Bobby.

"Crandall, answer the door," came the gravelly reply.

Bobby glanced over at Nancy, then back at Bones. "But, there's no one—"

He was interrupted by a knock at the door. Bobby shook his head, knowing better than to question the strangeness that surrounded Brother Bones. "As you say, Boss."

Bobby moved over to the door and opened it. "Well, just when I thought my week couldn't get any stranger."

"Ah, Mr. Crandall, is that you?" asked Deacon Devareaux. "Very good. I wasn't sure if the church files had your current address."

"As much as I'd like to imagine you're here to save my soul from all of the weirdness going on in my life, Deacon, I going to guess you're not here to see me."

"I am always happy to discuss the Salvation offered by our Lord and Savior, Bobby, but you are correct. You are not the person I am seeking."

"Yeah, that's what I figured." Bobby crossed his arms and didn't move out of the doorway. "Well, Paula ain't here right now."

"Let the man in, Crandall," said Bones. "I have been expecting him."

Bobby stepped aside and said, "Please do come in. It appears we've been expecting you." He took the clergyman by the arm and led him over to the table.

Devareaux sat across from the Undead Avenger. They stared at each other for an uncomfortable few moments, as if each was waiting for the other to blink.

"I won't waste time with words, Brother Bones," said the Deacon at last. "I need your help."

"Explain," was the only reply.

Devareaux reached into his frock coat and pulled something out and laid it on the table between them.

"Hey, that's Giselle's charm necklace," Nancy gasped.

"Yes, an… associate of mine obtained it when he visited your friend not long ago." Devareaux smiled at Nancy. "Dreadfully sorry about the mess." Turning back to Brother Bones, he said, "You more than anyone else in this city know how thin the veil is between the spirit world and the world of the living. And how fragile."

The dead man said nothing, his unblinking eyes never looking away from those hidden behind the deacon's glasses.

"The two of them together are too strong for me," the Deacon continued.

"Hey, now wait just a minute," interrupted Bobby. "Bones, you can't seriously be considering helping this guy. That's Paula he's talking about, and…" His protest died on his lips under a withering gaze from the dead eyes behind the skull mask.

"Continue," Bones said.

"I have a plan," said Devareaux. He held up the necklace and pointed to the central charm. "And this talisman is the key."

Bones' gaze drifted to the well-worn charm. He stared at the symbol carved into the metal for long moments before he finally looked back into the dark glasses of the clergyman.

"Tell me your plan."

Sister Blood stared in wide-eyed shock as Giselle faded away and the demonic form of Marinette took over. The vampire swore and reached for the girl's arm, but she wasn't fast enough. Marinette caught Sister Blood by the wrist and flung her like a doll. Sister Blood grunted as she struck the pavement but rolled with the impact and into a defensive crouch.

Marinette screeched like some demonic bird of prey. She lifted her chain and twirled the hanging manacle over her head. The iron shackle burst into flames, leaving a fiery tail as it spun ever faster. With a snap of her wrist, she whipped the weapon at Blood's head.

Sister Blood ducked away from the strike, but flames still licked her cheek as the burning iron hissed past. The cuff struck the wall behind her with explosive impact, showering Sister Blood with dust and shrapnel of shattered masonry. A scorched crater the size of a fist on the brick wall marked where the weapon struck. *That could have been my skull*, thought Sister Blood. *If this flail is anything like Samedi's shovel, I might be in trouble.*

Marinette was swinging her weapon again. The chain snaked out to triple its length as it whirled like a flaming wheel of death. The narrow confines of the alley left little room for Sister Blood to maneuver. Her only way out was up. Blood launched herself skyward as the demon struck again. The manacle hit the spot where she had just been standing, leaving another smocking crater in the pavement.

Sister Blood's leap carried her to the roof of one the neighboring building. The second her feet touched the rooftop, she bounded into the air again. She changed into her bat form in mid leap and took flight. *Gotta get the higher ground, here.* She arched over backwards and looped back down towards Marinette.

The alley was empty.

What the hell? She was right here a second ago! Sister Blood searched the streets below in an ever-widening circle. *Even Samedi isn't that fast. Where is she?*

As if in answer, a piercing shriek came from above. A sharp pain slashed Sister Blood's shoulder and back, causing her right arm to go limp. The great bat wing folded like wet cardboard, and Sister Blood rolled over into a dive. She crashed hard into a rooftop, but she managed to stagger to her now-human feet. *Nothing broken, as far as I can tell.* She glanced over her shoulder at her back and saw thee bloody gashes torn through her blouse. *Nancy's not going to be happy bout that.*

Another screech snapped Sister Blood's head around. She dropped and rolled as a pair of taloned feet swiped at her head. An enormous, black owl — every bit as large as Blood's own bat form — swooped away with the beating of its great wings. It landed on the chimney above her and glared down with baleful red eyes. The beast's knife-sized talons dug into the brick.

Sister Blood tensed, waiting for the next attack. And the owl looked ready to oblige. It opened its wings and lowered its head in preparation of another dive at her. But it stopped, craned its neck, and looked back across the rooftops towards the city skyline. In a silent flurry of its wings, the monstrous bird took flight once more and disappeared into the night.

Oh, no you don't! You've got Giselle trapped within, and I'm not giving up on her so easily. Sister Blood leapt off the rooftop and took to her wings in pursuit.

Bobby and Nancy stood on the sidewalk and looked up towards the rooftop ten stories above. "For this, I missed work tonight," said Bobby as he leaned against his car.

"What exactly are they doing up there?" asked Nancy.

"I'm not sure exactly." Another fireball briefly lit up the sky above the building. "The Deacon mentioned something about setting a trap for Giselle."

"And they're using that talisman as bait?"

"Something like that." Bobby shrugged. "I guess it's important to the demon that's possessing her."

Nancy took a sip of coffee out of a paper cup. "I'm not sure Paula's going to like any of this."

"Oh, I'm sure she won't. She's going to protect Giselle at all costs." He crumpled up his own cup. "I'm out. I'm going to go back across the street and get another cup o' joe. You good?"

Nancy drained the last of her coffee. "I'll join you."

They made it to the middle of the street when a bloodcurdling shriek split the still night air. Bobby reflexively flinched, then he all but dragged Nancy to the far sidewalk and under the diner's awning.

"What was that awful noise?" Nancy's voice was hoarse with fear.

"I don't know, but look!" Bobby pointed to something in the sky. "My guess is that it was that!"

A giant black owl circled the rooftop of the building they had just been watching. The creature landed on the ledge of a neighboring roof and screeched loudly, craning its head back like a wolf baying at the moon. It then spread its wings again and swooped down to the building where Brother Bones and the Demon Deacon laid in wait.

Several explosions cracked like thunder, and flames billowed from the rooftop. The combatants had engaged.

"What's happening up there?" asked Nancy.

Bobby watched the chaos erupting atop the building and shook his head. "I have no idea. But I'm glad we're down here."

💀 💀 💀

Sister Blood strained to keep up with the demonic black bird. Her gashed shoulder screamed in pain with every flap of her wings. Thankfully, the city lights silhouetted it enough for Sister Blood to keep it in sight.

The thing cried out again as it neared downtown, and Sister Blood saw tiny figures scatter off the streets below. Then the night exploded into flames. Whatever Marinette had been making a beeline toward, she found it. And judging by the chaos on the rooftop below, Sister Blood arrived just in time.

She landed in the midst of a running battle. The rooftop was ablaze, bullets whizzed over her head and ricocheted off brick and metal, and shouts and screams rang out over everything else. Sister Blood watched as Marinette whipped her chain around the handle of Samedi's shovel and ripped the weapon from his grasp. It landed at her feet with a clank.

Sister Blood looked down at the shovel, then back up at the combatants. Marinette now had her chain around the Demon Deacon's neck as he desperately tried to fend off her off with his arm.

"Sistah Blood," he gasped, reaching out to her. "My weapon!"

Sister Blood kicked the shovel away. Samedi's eyes widened and Marinette's laughed.

Gunfire exploded from behind her as Brother Bones unleashed his vengeance upon Marinette. "Paula Wozcheski, you need to choose a side."

"I have, Brother Bones. I can't let you kill Giselle." A swift kick struck Bones' arm, throwing off his aim.

The Undead Avenger leveled a gun at each of the women in front of him. He hesitated, as if unsure which to shoot. With her chain still wrapped around the Demon Deacon's neck, Marinette whipped her flaming manacle at Brother Bones. The Deacon struck with explosive force, blasting both men through a brick chimney and knocking Sister Blood to her knees.

Marinette looked at her two downed opponents. Nothing sat between her and her talisman lying in a ring of fire in the center of the roof. The demon threw back her head and let out a shriek of victory.

Sister Blood saw Marinette's braids slither off her shoulders, revealing her bare throat. She knew what must be done. Putting all of her remaining strength into one last burst of speed, the vampire struck like lightning and sunk her fangs deep into the demon's throat.

Though sorely taxed by the battle, Marinette still had fight left within her. Like a cornered animal, she flailed about trying to dislodge her attacker, but Sister Blood held tight with all of her waning strength. The red glow in Marinette's eyes began to flicker, then dim, and then she went limp in Sister Blood's arms.

Sister Blood always sensed the moment when one of her victims gave up their ghost, but the rush she felt now nearly overwhelmed her. She dropped Giselle's body and reeled, trying to regain her senses. Another presence was slithering through mind, one filled with black hate and red hot fury. Sister Blood fell to her knees and screamed as she clawed at the flesh on her own face. The presence sunk itself deep into Blood's psyche, and roots snaked out into every part of her being. Sister Blood tried to fight, but she couldn't tell where she ended and the other began.

As she felt herself fading, another sensation creeped in. The invading presence was now retreating, losing its grip on her. Black tendrils of hate withered, and Sister Blood once again pushed back. She screamed and opened her eyes.

Before her hung a billowing black mass that was both physical and ethereal, and at the same time neither. It billowed like smoke, or it pulsated like a living thing, depending on where she looked.

"She is out!" shouted the Demon Deacon. "Now, Bones, strike now!" He flung the talisman into the air towards the mass.

Brother Bones was on one knee, trying to regain his feet. Without hesitating, he whipped one of his pistols up and caught the glittering metal disk in his sights. The Undead Avenger pulled the trigger, and a single bullet struck true. The talisman shattered in a violent explosion, instantly blowing the mass to nothingness. The shockwave rolled across the rooftop, leveling the three remaining occupants.

All was silent, save for the crackling of the flames.

"Deacon," Bones rasped.

"It is done," Samedi replied. "She has been sent back to Hell."

Sister Blood retched, still trying to expel the last remnants of whatever had invaded her. "What... what happened?"

The Demon Deacon rose slowly to his feet and walked over to lay a hand over Giselle's still open eyes. "Having lost her host, Marinette sought another soul to possess. You were the only one available."

"But, why didn't she? Possess me, I mean. I felt her dominating me, but then she just disappeared."

The Deacon laughed. "Ah, my dear Sistah Blood. Marinette couldn't possibly possess your soul, no matter how hard she tried."

"I don't understand. Why not?"

Brother Bones came over and offered his hand to help her up.

"Because you have no soul."

☠ ☠ ☠

Sister Blood sat alone in the darkness with Giselle's body in her lap. The cacophony of sirens several blocks away showed no sign of dying down, as police and fire department vehicles streamed in from all directions to the site of the battle.

"I'm sorry I failed you, Giselle."

A sound startled her.

"Where... where am I?" Her voice was weak, but it was clearly Giselle.

"You're safe girl, you're with a friend." Sister Blood's cold heart trembled.

"I... I must have died," Giselle said. "I remember standing with Baron Samedi at the gateway to the spirit world."

Sister Blood felt a tear stream down her cheek. A tear of joy.

"He said I wasn't ready to cross over yet, that it wasn't my time. Then he laughed and blew a big puff of cigar smoke at me, and... and here I am."

Sister Blood laughed and embraced the young woman. "And here you are, indeed. Welcome back."

THE END

WRITING SISTER BLOOD

Of all the original characters that have come out of the New Pulp movement (and there have been many fantastic ones), Brother Bones, I feel, stands above all others. In fact, I am convinced the Brother Bones character, had he been created and published back in the original pulp era, would have stood equal with the popular characters of that period, characters like the Shadow, the Spider, or Doc Savage. Brother Bones is every bit as iconic.

One of the key elements to the success of the Brother Bones character is the mythology that has developed around him: Cape Noire, the city he lives in; the cast of supporting characters; and the supernatural essence that permeates everything. All these ingredients enhance each other and, when mixed together by a select few word chefs, have resulted in some pretty fantastic literary dishes!

With all this in mind, imagine my surprise when Ron Fortier, Brother Bones' creator and Airship 27 managing editor, invited me into the Brother Bones kitchen to try my hand at cooking up a story. Are you kidding me? I was walking on cloud nine for the rest of the day! I had a lot in my plate at the time, but there is no way I could pass up such an opportunity.

This anthology called for stories that featured not Brother Bones himself, but one of the many exciting supporting characters. And when Ron suggested I do a Sister Blood story, I agreed enthusiastically. Sister Blood is a strong female character with a fascinating background, a compelling motivation, and some cool supernatural elements.

There are three themes that I felt are threaded to one degree or another through every story set in Cape Noire: religion, the supernatural, and moral conflict (nothing in Cape Noire is black and white, merely varying shades of gray). I took those three themes, tossed them in with the rest of the Brother Bones ingredients, added a dash of my own personal spice, and cooked up the Sister Blood story you hold in your hands. I hope you find it as enjoyable as the rest of the stories in this volume.

ANDY FIX - first discovered heroes such as the Lone Ranger, Conan, Tarzan, John Carter, and Doc Savage as a child. Many years later, he would come to realize that all these characters originated in pulp magazines. Since then, Andy has been a fan of all things Pulp, and he is very excited to be writing New Pulp adventures. Andy is currently working on a cycle of short stories featuring Sir Axel the Axe, Knight of the Round Table, an original character of Andy's creation.

For updates on these and Andy's other writing projects, you can follow him on Twitter (@AndyFixWriter) and on Facebook (facebook.com/Andyfixwriter).

SAFE

by Drew Meyer

He'd had the dream again.

The sweat felt chill against his skin. He had to convince his eyes to open and remain open before he rolled out of bed. The room was dark in the predawn, but a streetlamp below cast just enough light for him to make his bed—which he did with military precision. He walked to the kitchen, filled a kettle, and lit the stove. He cracked a window and let the cold sea air creep into his flat—the frigid dank woke his body with a jolt. Inhaling deeply, he reached for his toes with an exhalation. His breath and the ticking of a clock were the only sounds in the quiet apartment. As he counted down, he tried to remember what time he got in last night. He shivered, not because of the sea air, but because he knew how much paperwork he would have to look forward to today. He was not a man who thrived behind a desk. The shrill cry of the kettle roused him from his thoughts, and he made his way back to the kitchen to start the coffee. As he stirred, so did the sun, which began its daily ritual to banish the clinging dregs of last night's shadows. As always, it won, but as always it had to struggle—after all, this was Cape Noire.

The coffee's invigorating scent filled the room, followed by the rising sun's meager light. The soft morning glow began to illuminate the spartan surroundings. He inventoried the room between push-ups. Not because he feared anything missing, but to shake yesterday's cobwebs from his head. One bed, one chair, one table, one mug (stained brown), one plant (needs water), one dresser and above it, a scrap of newspaper tacked to the wall featuring the *Tribune*'s Sally Paige. Above that, a framed American flag—its forty-eight stars presented proudly. He finished, saluted the flag, and reminded himself that he was lucky to be alive and that countless others didn't share his luck. He opened his sock drawer to rummage for a clean pair, which he found hidden behind the small box containing his Purple Heart and French Medal of Honor. He sniffed the socks to make sure they were clean before putting them on.

He downed his cup then opened the closet, not a single unwrinkled shirt in the bunch. He'd forgotten to stop by the dry cleaners again. He sniffed a few shirts and selected the one with the fewest blood stains and which reeked the least—twenty minutes in the smoke-filled station would mask the offensive odor. He poured the remaining hot water from the kettle into an iron and gave the shirt the once over. Better. He selected a tie and stood at attention at his mirror. He looked tired. It had been a long week.

Before leaving he watered the plant and placed it on the window ledge by the fire escape. He turned it so it could get better light. Sighing deeply, he left the apartment. He might be back in a day or so. Maybe.

His car was still parked in the station lot. It was only a twenty-minute walk to Police Central. The fog hung heavy and smelled of salt and garbage. Few creatures stirred at this early hour, save for the night things, scurrying back into the shadows. The city was waiting for something, and Lieutenant Dan Rains, Chief of Detectives would be ready for it. After another cup of coffee or two.

The precinct looked hung over. The third shift was on its last legs and each eye he met held his gaze, daring him to bring them bad news. He climbed the steps to the second floor and found his office the way he'd left it—like it had witnessed a weeklong stake out. He moved four stained mugs to the small couch in the corner, slid the takeaway off his desk and into the waste bin with the others before he collapsed in his chair. He cracked a window, followed by his knuckles, and then his neck. He closed his eyes and listened to the hum of the precinct, the calls, the foot falls, the messages being taken, the orders being given. Home.

He'd been reviewing case files for an hour when there was a sharp knock on his door. Without waiting for his reply, the large frame of Harriet from the switchboard operator's pool entered and handed him a coffee. Her perfume mixed with the halo of smoke from the cigarette that dangled from her lip. He could see the ash on her blouse… she'd already burned through a few this morning.

"Good morning, Daniel." She was a recent transfer to Cape Noire and had quickly established herself as queen bee of the operators. Older than most of their mothers, but spry enough to cut off the amorous advances of the officers.

"Thank you, Harriet, and it's Lt. Rains." For whatever reason, she'd taken a shine to him. Normally he'd balk at the extra attention, but her coffee was far better than the precinct's usual brown water. "You're here early."

"Well, when you're a widowed woman of years, new to the big city, you're always on the lookout for something to do—and I have no intention to learn to knit. By the way Daniel, you didn't hear it from me, but the Chief was asking for you. You'll be getting a summons any minute." Harriet's grasp of the inner workings of the department bordered on the supernatural.

"Thanks for the heads up." The phone rang and the soft voice of Miss Ray came through the other end, "Thank you Miss Ray, I'll be right up." He closed his office and made his way to the third floor.

Chief Torrance had been transferred to Cape Noire six months ago from back East, replacing Chief Warren. Warren had been a good chief and the news of his retirement came as a surprise to everyone, including him. Torrance was a lean, bitter man with a big appetite, and a constant scowl.

Rains knocked as he entered, and Miss Ray greeted him with a weak smile. She was a new hire, the third secretary since Torrance arrived. She nodded to the open office and the cloud of cigar smoke within. Rains nodded back and made his way to the cloud. He gave a short wrap on the Chief's door.

"C'mon in Rains," the voice was gruff and was more croaked than spoken.

Rains passed on the offered chair. "What can I do for you, sir?"

Torrance scratched his jaw with a tobacco stained hand before sliding a report across his desk to the detective. "CNFD has confirmed that the old Edgewater Library went up this morning. The brigade has it under control, but I'd like you to personally go over and give it the once-over."

"You suspect arson." It wasn't a question, but Rains was surprised that the Chief would even be interested in something like this. The Edgewater was all but forgotten, a throwback to the early days of Cape Noire. It was more a landmark than a functioning library and that section of Old Town wasn't a popular place to check out books. "Wouldn't this be the 27th's case?"

Police Chief Torrance stood and pointedly extinguished the short stub of his cigar, his eyes never leaving Rains. It was a predatory stare. "I'm sending you over there, because I don't think those…*boys* are up for such an important task. Maybe it's arson. Maybe it's not, but you're going over there. Show 'em how the *real* police handle things." His eyes never left Rains. He lit a new cigar and grinned. It didn't take a detective to know when he was being dismissed. "And send in Miss Ray, would you? I have some notes for her."

Rains made his way back to the second floor, passing the break room where a symphony of snores cascaded out with all the delicate melody of a train wreck. Leslie Owens, veteran detective, laid sprawled out on a sofa. Rains was reaching to wake the man, seeing as his shift had ended several hours ago, when he heard a polite cough behind him and turned to see detectives Graff and Barclay. Graff had been with Central for almost ten years; he was older than Rains, a quiet man for the most part. Barclay, the younger of the two, had transferred two years back. Both detectives were good at their jobs, especially when it benefitted them. Today they were sporting new suits; the last six months had treated them well.

Barclay motioned to the veteran. "We're giving Leslie some space; poor bastard's been working Old Town all night. Some of 'Mad Dog' McGinty's boys got shot at yesterday, so they decided to start something with a couple of Iggy Draper's guys over at the Gridiron. The old man there spent ten hours on the scene looking things over while the officers took statements. We figured we'd let him grab some rest before we sent him home with one of the uniforms on their way out to patrol."

Rains looked over the sleeping veteran with a smile. Was this his future? God, he hoped so. The three stepped away from the break room and into the hall. "We hear the Chief's sending you out to the Edgewater fire."

"Word sure does get around fast," thought Rains, then out loud, "I guess he suspects arson, though the state of that place, I wouldn't be surprised if it were just an electrical fault, or a patron getting careless with a smoke."

"I'm sure Torrance has his reasons. Anyway, better you than us." Barclay said it with a smile, but Rains knew neither of the men wanted to spend their day questioning witnesses to a library fire, especially not in that neighborhood. The docks attracted the sort of business that kept it and the 27th busy—it wasn't always fish they were pulling out of the waters up there. The police weren't well respected throughout most of Cape Noire, and the Old Town docks were especially unwelcoming.

"We hear your boy Winstead's already on the scene. Sounds like it could be his big break." Both detectives smiled in a way Rains found annoying. If James were on the scene, maybe it wouldn't be a waste of a trip after all. "Sure, and maybe I'll pick up one of them romance novels while I'm there." Rains got up to leave. As he walked away, he could hear Graff say to his fellow detective, "The only romance novel the lieutenant is looking for is gonna have Sally Paige on the cover." Rains knew they didn't mean any disrespect to Sally. *Let them laugh*, he thought and then, *but still, that'd be a hellava cover.*

"Captain!" Sgt. James Winstead of the 27th greeted Rains with a smile and a salute.

"At ease, sergeant." Rains returned the smile and offered his friend a hand. Winstead had served with him for only a short time, but he had proved himself to be more than capable in a pinch. After the war, Rains had given Winstead his highest recommendation and was crestfallen when his friend had been stationed at the 27th instead of Central Police Headquarters. Winstead was doing a fine job at the 27th, but the precinct was overworked and underfunded.

Rains worked with a lot of good men who genuinely had dreams of seeing this city become a better place. However, money was hard to come by and dreams don't come cheap. More officers than he'd care to admit were in the pockets of the syndicates, but not James; never James. He knew it wasn't Winstead's refusal to take a bribe that kept him from reaching his full potential—all that talent wasted, just because of the color of a man's skin.

"Good to see you, Captain. Shirley was saying just the other night that it feels like years since you came over for dinner."

"You tell that pretty wife of yours the next time she makes her amazing chicken pot pie, I'll be there and eat your ration too." It felt strange to laugh outside the scene of a fire. Several uniformed officers patrolled the area, keeping curious onlookers from getting too close. Even though the blaze had been put out hours ago, a steady stream of smoke rose into the gray morning sky. Bits of charred pages danced in the thick sea air and clung to wherever they landed. On the sidewalk, a bespectacled man in his late fifties was hauling arm loads of wet books into a waiting pickup truck, his face one of grim determination. Another, a younger woman, her prim dress smeared with soot, exited the building with a similar burden.

"The librarians from Mid-Town came as soon as it was safe, trying to salvage what they could. The Fire Chief gave them an hour to take what they can before they close the place for good. Everything on the top floor was lost; it's just a charred husk now, but a few of the lower level sections went untouched from both the fire and the hoses. I didn't know wet books had a smell, but," he inhaled in an exaggerated fashion, "there you go."

"Any idea what started it?" Rains bent down and picked up a book that had fallen from the librarian's recent armload and placed it in the truck on his way to the library's front step. The man gave the detective an appreciative nod before making his way back up the stairs and into the building.

"Well, no one's ruling out arson. The head librarian, a guy named Roland, was the first to sound the alarm and run upstairs. His assistant," he motioned to a younger man straining under a final pile of books, "quote- 'saw a man and a woman rush out the front door.' When Roland didn't return, he went to investigate and found his boss unconscious at the top of the stairs. He was taken to Cape Noire General. One of my guys told me they expect him to regain consciousness shortly. We can head over there together if you'd like."

"Sure. Sounds good. Did you check out the second floor already?"

"We went in as soon as they let us. The staircase is marble, so it didn't burn, but the second floor is pretty treacherous. Aside from a few storage rooms, there's nothing left."

"All right," Rains watched the librarians drive off in the pickup as a man from the fire department closed and locked the doors to the ruined library. He hated to leave a possible crime scene uninspected but if there were any clues within, they weren't going anywhere.

The little man looked almost comical. His head was wrapped in bandages. His spectacles were inserted into the gauze and across the bridge of his nose, so that he had to tilt his head to see anything. He sat upright, both hands wrapped, sipping water from a straw held by a nurse. Both of his eyebrows had been burned off and very little remained of what had once been a mustache.

He continued, "Well yes, I smelled the smoke first you know. It is a smell we all dread, and I was quick to recognize it. The library had recently acquired quite the collection from the estate of a local aficionado. Most of it was non-fiction—some antiques, folios, manuscripts, and the like. I had not gotten a chance to really study it, but it looked promising. We were lucky to receive it; Mid-Town usually gets such donations, but the man had been a patron of our little library for forty years and…" the librarian recognized Rains's look and got back to the point, "I was just about to catalogue the collection on the second floor, where it was stored, when I smelled it. We urge our patrons not to smoke in the library, but so few of them listen…but this was not tobacco smoke. I, myself, enjoy a pipe now and again. I am rather fond of— right, forgive me. I made my way through the stacks trying to identify its source, which grew stronger the closer I moved to the foyer. At first, I did not understand, but then I looked up and saw the smoke coming from atop the stairs. I rushed up to open the doors—"

"And that's when the doors opened, and a large man knocked you down?" Rains sat back as James questioned Roland. "What did this man look like?"

"Now I cannot be sure because he was wearing a mask. Or at least I think it was a mask. His face was definitely covered. Oh, it all happened so fast, but I did see that the man was dragging Miss Lily behind him."

"Miss Lily?" Both Rains and Winstead leaned forward.

"Oh yes, Miss Lily McGinty, the daughter of 'Mad'—I mean Mr. Lawrence McGinty, the quotes are facing the wrong way. It should read the...'businessman.' She's a regular patron. She's there every weekday, usually with a—*ahem*—chaperone."

"Are you sure it was Lily McGinty?" Rains asked suddenly on edge.

The bandaged man *harrumphed* at the question, "Well detective, I cannot see how it would have been anyone else. Miss Lily is one of our finest patrons and the only one who spends time on the second floor."

"Why is that?" Winstead followed along, writing down the facts in a notebook.

Here the man became slightly sheepish. "Hm, yes. You see, the second floor has been under...renovations for quite some time. It is the non-fiction section, and it is not as popular with the patrons as it once was. Usually we would discourage anyone who is not city maintenance from using the department, but Miss McGinty has been such a loyal patron for so long. If it were not for her, the library might have closed its doors years ago. She has as much a right to be on the second floor as any of the staff, and it would break our hearts to deprive her of her beloved books."

Rains stepped in, "And the man you saw her with wasn't her usual 'chaperone'?"

"Oh no, this man was much bigger. The man she usually visits with is —well detectives, I would not say he was the sort of man who looks like he enjoys spending time in the library."

"And that's all you can remember?"

"Yes detectives. I woke up here, less than an hour ago, in this state."

"Thank you, Mr. Roland." Both men got up to leave. Sgt. Winstead handed the nurse a card. "If he remembers anything else, please call the 27th immediately." Rains saw the nurse take the card, but she placed it dismissively on the bedside table.

As the two men walked from the room, they could hear the librarian, "It is such a tragedy. All those books. All that knowledge. Gone. I do not know how this city will ever recover. These are dark days, truly dark days."

☠ ☠ ☠

It was dark, truly dark. She tried to stretch, but it was too cramped to move. The air was stale, and she couldn't inhale deeply. Her first instinct was to shout so that someone would come and let her out. But she dared not. She didn't know who would be listening or what would happen if she was heard. She knew where she was and what it meant, so she waited. In the dark.

☠ ☠ ☠

File in hand, Rains closed the cabinet drawer and made ready to leave. He'd asked Winstead to stay with the car. Given Torrance's clear contempt for the 27th and its officers, he thought it best if the Chief wasn't aware of James's presence. As he stepped out of his office, Harriet appeared at his side, fresh cup in hand. "You didn't hear it from me," she said as she leaned in, immersed in a halo of perfume and cigarette smoke, "but Graff and Barclay were called out to Marlowe Heights to investigate a guy what got 'hamburgered,' maybe an hour after you left for the library. Here's the address." She handed Rains a slip of paper, which he pocketed. "And these are for the road; you're looking thin." She placed the pastry inelegantly in his overcoat pocket before making her way back to the pool. "One of them is for your friend."

☠ ☠ ☠

"So, what have we got?"

Rains's car was just leaving Mid-Town. Traffic was light. Sgt. Winstead rode shotgun, the file on McGinty in his lap. "Not much. According to this, McGinty ran with Jorgensen when Big Swede was small time. Back then he was an enforcer." Winstead sucked in with a whistle. "It says the guy used to use a fire poker on anyone who crossed him. There are pictures, and they are not pretty."

Rains turned onto Central Ave., "I don't remember McGinty being mentioned in any of the reports the night Jorgensen got whacked. In fact, I barely hear about him at all these days. I know he's got offices on Chauncey Ave. and I know he does business across the board, mostly money laundering, but word is he's small-time."

"Looks like the guy settled down after his kid was born. No, wait, here it is, looks like McGinty's wife died a few years after the daughter was born. After that, the guy just sort of faded from the spotlight. Jorgensen rose to power and left McGinty behind. He's been picked up a couple of times, but each time he was back on the street within a day. Looks like he's got good lawyers backing him up. His list of associates is pretty extensive, guy's got connections and manpower. The file estimates twenty goons on the payroll."

It was Rains' turn to whistle, "What's a guy doing with that many guns if he isn't moving in on weaker territory? That sort of payroll isn't going to allow for much of a profit, so if they aren't going on the offense, you have to wonder what he's protecting."

💀 💀 💀

Old Town had its charms but as Rains drove down Chauncey Ave. towards McGinty's territory he couldn't help but think the streets felt different today. The people moved in packs, but with an edgy speed, as if they knew not to be seen. It wasn't the neighborhood; the neighborhood was safe enough. A newsstand sat on the corner, The Three Brother's Pawn behind it. Kang's Laundry filled the alley with the smell of steam and chemicals. McGinty's office sat above Pendycke's General Store across the street from the Wagon Wheel Motel and Bar. Men with heavy coats and suspicious eyes watched as they parked alongside The Wagon Wheel. A group of them broke from the crowd and made their way toward the vehicle. Rains slowly flashed his badge out the window and stepped from the car. Paranoid, check. Well-armed, check. Renowned temper, check. Rains wasn't looking forward to this meeting, but as the Chief of Detectives, it was his job not just to solve crimes, but to prevent them. Lily McGinty shouldn't suffer for the sins of her father.

As James exited the passenger side of the car, one of the men pulled back his coat to reveal a Thompson machine gun. He didn't point it at anyone, but his meaning was clear, *Only one of you gets to come in.*

Rains thought about challenging the man, but time was of the essence.

"James, you going to be all right?"

"Me? I'll be fine. You go ahead. I'll stay with the radio; in case we hear anything."

☠ ☠ ☠

"IT TOOK YOU LONG ENOUGH! What the hell do I pay you for?... oh, it's you." Clearly, Rains was not the police representative McGinty was expecting. Rains had been patted down as soon as he knocked on the door at the back of the General Store. Two soldiers led him up the stairs to the apartments above. Each of them shouldered Thompsons. He had been handed off to another two goons at the end of a long hallway. Maybe this was business as usual, and maybe this was preparing for war. He was led to a large corner office which looked out over the newsstand. From there he could see several men eyeing passersby with suspicion. The air was tense, and the beet red McGinty broke the tension with the subtlety of an artillery shell.

Rains scanned the office while McGinty barked demands, punctuated by jabbing his fingers in the detective's direction. McGinty wasn't a tall guy, so it was easy to get a clear view of the office. Behind him sat an artistically done portrait of an elegant young woman. Rains was no art critic, but judging from the style of the woman's clothes, the painting was at least twenty years old. Perhaps the missing girl's mother? She had piercing eyes and the curve of her lips couldn't hide the hint of a smile. The wall on either side of the large painting showed scuff marks and the detective had no doubts that behind it hid an equally large safe. On the desk in front of him was a framed photo. Rains couldn't see, as it was turned away, but good money said it was of the missing girl. There wasn't much else of note in the office. It felt lived in. It smelled of coffee.

"Let's go over it again from the top" Rains said, interrupting the small man's tirade. The eyes on the man bulged for a moment, but his feverish look settled when met with the steady, confident gaze of the person most qualified to get him what he wanted. Standing beside McGinty was a lean man with dark circles under his eyes. The man wore a grey suit with wide shoulders and worn elbows. There was heavy scarring on the man's knuckles. He held a toothpick in his lips and eyed Rains with all the contempt a shark might have for a meal.

"Very well, Detective Rains. My daughter Lily is missing. No doubt Iggy Draper or one of his goons is behind this. I swear on my mother's grave,

"LET'S GO OVER IT AGAIN FROM THE TOP" RAINS SAID.

I'm going to rip out his throat when I get my hands on him. I'll gut him like a damned salmon! I'll…!" This went on for a while, the small man practically foaming at the mouth as his descriptions got more and more vivid. Eventually, he began to wind down and with no small amount of effort, he stopped and composed himself.

"Mr. McGinty, why don't we try again?" Rains was a paragon of constraint. The little man sat down and made himself comfortable, but the mixture of anxious energy and caffeine kept him fidgeting.

"This morning, my little Lily went to the library." He picked up the framed photo off the desk, stared at it for a moment and handed it to Rains. The photo showed a pale girl of about sixteen holding a book, a dour expression on her face. It looked as though the photographer had interrupted her reading. Rains made note of her appearance and handed the picture back to McGinty, who replaced it lovingly on the desk.

"She's usually there when it opens and stays until it closes around 5:00. She loves books, you see, got that from her mother." He motioned to the portrait behind him. "Then, this morning, I get a call telling me there's been a fire, so I send some of my boys to pick her up, only she ain't there."

"Did your daughter go alone to the library?"

"Are you kidding? Of course not. I usually have a guy with her, mostly Cheeves here, but this morning Mr. Cheeves was needed for…business, so I sent Lily to the library with Lug."

Rains arched his eyebrow. "He's big. It's dumb, I know, but so is Lug. His real name's Jasper Thwait, but we've called him Lug since he got on the pay roll, and that's been awhile. The guy's as loyal as they come, and he'd do anything for Lily—which has me worried. They're both missing, and I don't think he'd let her out of his sight."

"What's this Lug look like?"

"Like I said, he's big. He's a big bald guy. He's a hard guy to miss."

"Lily and Lug in the library, sounds like a children's book." At that, McGinty stopped fidgeting. Behind him, Mr. Cheeves grew tense. Rains realized he'd crossed a line and braced himself for trouble. The little man stood up with grave purpose, rested his white knuckles on the desk and leaned over towards Rains. "This ain't funny detective. My little Lily is out there, possibly in the hands of my enemies." Rains saw something behind the man's eyes come loose at the thought of his daughter in trouble. "Everyone needs to know that I ain't joking around. If I gotta tear this city apart, I will do so to get her back. So help me God, I will kill anyone who lays a finger on her."

Rains waited a beat for McGinty's blood to cool, counted his lucky stars he didn't have a bullet in his skull, and continued. The man's temper lived up to its reputation. "You don't know for sure that anyone has her though. Have you received a ransom? Who do you suspect would do something like this?"

"Detective, I'm gonna assume you ain't an idiot. Just cause we ain't done business doesn't mean we can't come to an understanding. I got understandings with a lot of different families and not everyone's happy about it. There's a ton of guys gunning for my spot. This is prime real estate and anyone in their right mind would be happy to put me in the ground and take it. Hell, someone took a shot at my boys just the other day while they were minding their own business. I sent a couple of my guys out to see what they could find, and one of them didn't come back."

"Who was this?"

"New guy, only been with us a few months." He turned to Cheeves, "You worked with him, what was his name?"

Mr. Cheeves looked bored by the question. "Ogden Presley, out of Chicago."

"Oh yeah," McGinty continued, "nervous kid, I remember he asked a lot of questions. Drove the other guys nuts. Didn't you say you thought the guy went back East?"

Mr. Cheeves shrugged in response.

"Anyway," McGinty turned back to face Rains and took a moment as if he were lost in thought, "I can see it already, someone's itching for a fight, and just because I ain't got a ransom yet, doesn't me it ain't coming."

"And if there *is* a ransom?"

"Then whoever it is has my little girl is gonna get what's coming to 'em. Now, you get out there and you do your job, because if I don't have her back here by sundown, I will take this to the streets and get her back myself." He was breathing hard and spittle had begun to form on his lower lip.

"Before I go, any idea what this 'Lug' was wearing when he left with your daughter?"

"Charcoal suit, yellow tie." Even McGinty seemed surprised at how quickly Mr. Cheeves answered.

"What? Guy had one suit and loved yellow ties."

"Thanks," Rains placed his hat on his head and made his way out of the office—leaving the little man to fume, the portrait of his wife, smirking behind him.

He found two toughs standing by the car, eyeing its occupant, when he returned. They seemed about to challenge Rains when Cheeves leaned out the office window and waved them away.

Sgt. Winstead looked bored. "How'd it go?"

"He's everything the file said and more. How'd it go with you?"

"Oh, they were very hospitable. I got out to stretch my legs and got as far as the back of the Wagon Wheel before they escorted me back to the car."

Rains started the engine and drove up Chauncey Ave. until they were clear of McGinty's territory. He pulled the car over and turned to Winstead. "I don't think McGinty's going to go public with the abduction. It'll make him look weak."

"Who does he think is behind it?"

"His money's on Iggy Draper."

"Draper's one of Wyld's boys isn't he? Think the 'Queen of Crime' has a thing against McGinty?"

"It's possible, but it's a bit heavy-handed."

"We could go ask Draper. The Gridiron isn't far from here."

"If Draper did it, I doubt he'd admit to it. Besides," Rains said, checking his rearview mirror, "there's a chance McGinty had us followed. If we head to the Gridiron, it'll just confirm his suspicions and there'll be bloodshed, here and now. No, our best bets on finding the guy last seen with the daughter. McGinty said his name's Jasper Thwait, but everyone calls him Lug." Rains got on the radio, "All units, this is Chief of Detectives Rains, be on the lookout for a tall, muscular man in a worn charcoal-colored suit, yellow tie. Subject is wanted in question to the Edgewater Library fire; last seen in the vicinity of Edgewater Library, possibly heading toward Little Jamaica."

Rains started the car again and began to drive. "In the meantime, let's go back to the library. Now that we know what and who we're looking for, maybe we'll find something we missed on the first go-around."

Rains was about to pull out and head back to the library when a voice came over the radio, "Lt. Rains, is your subject a bald man?" The voice was of Spencer Simmons, a rookie everyone was calling 'Kid.'

"Affirmative, subject is bald."

Kid Simmons came back over the radio. "I don't want to get your hopes up Lieutenant, but we might have someone here matching that description."

"Where are you Kid?"

"Marlowe Heights."

Graff and Barclay's *hamburger*. Rains fished in his coat pocket and pulled out the scrap of paper with the address in Marlowe Heights. "I'm on my way."

"What do you think sergeant, want to come along?

Winstead thought for a moment, "You take this one." He got out of Rains' car, shut the door and leaned into the window. "I'll head back over to the library, give it another look over, like you said, see if we missed anything. Besides, Marlowe Heights is too rich for my blood."

Marlowe Heights.

The drive from Old Town was only thirty minutes, twenty without traffic, but you might as well be visiting a different planet. The gray three-story businesses with asphalt parking lots made way to three-story mansions with manicured lawns. Instead of fish and smog, the air smelled like money. Rains could work from now until he was a pensioner, save every cent and never be able to afford a place behind these stone walls and iron gates. Half of the residents here belonged behind bars and the other half got paid to keep them out. Most of the city's bosses had homes in Marlowe Heights. In the city they'd be mortal enemies, but here they were neighbors. As he drove past he took the buildings in turn, matching each with the source of its wealth. Lawyer. Lawyer. Smuggler. Doctor. Heroin, probably. Weapons, definitely. Mayor. Lawyer. Judge. Alexis Wyld. He drove past the last house with a shudder, understanding Sgt. Winstead's hesitance to come here. The residents of Marlowe Heights had their prejudices and their secrets, and they'd happily make you disappear to keep both.

Farther past the mansions, Rains pulled down one of Marlowe Heights 'lesser' neighborhoods. This section of town was in its early stages of development. Nice homes, rather than mansions. Plenty of trees. Small private streets that ended in cul-de-sacs. The lots were spacious with views of forested hills where construction hadn't begun. There was room for growth in Cape Noire if you had the money. This neighborhood was uncontrolled by the syndicates, so the homeowners paid officers extra to visit from time to time to make sure no one disturbed their quiet suburban lifestyle.

The address sat back from the street behind an unassuming white picket fence. Rains could see that the yard was well maintained, someone had mowed it within the last few days. The garden was clear of weeds. It wasn't a big place, but it looked cozy. Probably a safehouse. A Packard was parked out front, its trunk open.

Several patrolmen were stationed outside the front door and they nodded as Rains approached. As he entered the building, he heard the *POP!* of a camera flash and saw the police photographer, O'Shea, bent over a large body.

Detective Barclay, already on the scene, noticed Rains and came over. "Central received a call earlier this morning about possible gunshots. Patrols were dispatched to investigate. Officer saw the body through a window and reported back. Torrance called us to do our thing."

"Do we know who called it in?"

"We canvassed the area once we got here. A neighbor up the street saw a large guy pull up and take a girl out of the trunk. The girl looked like she was resisting, and the man held her head as he took her inside. She thinks she heard a gunshot a little while later, but she wouldn't say for sure, says it could have been a door slamming."

"No one ever wants to get involved. What time did she say this happened?"

"Sometime around 9:30, but she didn't call us until after her husband got home for lunch. Apparently, they thought it wasn't any of their business. Like you said, no one wants to get involved." Barclay motioned to the body at his feet, "this stiff got a name?"

"Gentlemen, meet Jasper Thwait, aka Lug. Last seen with Lily McGinty, daughter of Lawrence 'Mad Dog' McGinty." Thwait and McGinty were seen fleeing the Edgewater Library in Old Town right before it burst into flames."

Rains took in the scene. Most of the muscular body lay on a rug in the center of the living room. The large, bald head, haloed by a pool of blood, was face down and he could see even without moving it, that it had sustained damage. The grey suit was stained in blood. One corner of the rug was folded back beneath the body. A ruined yellow tie peaked from under his frame. His legs were splayed as if he had been kicking before he died. He had fallen on his left side and that arm was crumpled somewhere under the mass. However, his right arm was extended outward, over the edge of the rug. His jacket sleeve was slashed across the forearm, the skin beneath revealed a nasty cut. A dark streak followed the hand and in another flash of O'Shea's camera Rains saw the message.

Written on the floor in large, awkwardly scrawled letters, was the word 'safe.' The man's index finger was covered in blood, but there appeared to be no wound on the hand. The thick mitt of the hired muscle smeared the last letter, possibly as the hand went limp—his last act before succumbing to the exertion of death.

'Safe.'

Rains crouched down next to the body, tuning out the hum of the crime scene. He dabbed his pencil into a single rivulet of blood which had made its way from the larger mass. The skin bent inward, then broke, freeing the browning fluid to slowly ooze further across the floor. This guy had been dead for a few hours. '*POP!*' This time the flash caught him in the face, and he grimaced. O'Shea chuckled, 'I'll be done in a moment, Lieutenant."

Barclay crouched alongside Rains. "Looks like this guy got it square in the back with the first blast and the second blew his jaw clean off. Some of it's over there by the plant; the rest is covering the wall. No question the weapon used was a shotgun, and a powerful one at that. We found both casings in the hall."

"Any chance the girl did this, to get away?"

"Seems unlikely. If she came here in Lug's car then she'd probably take his car to leave. The keys are in his pocket, and I'm guessing the Packard with the open trunk out front is his. Also, any weapon that does this sort of damage has got a hell of a kick. I'm not saying a five-foot tall teenage girl couldn't wield it, but...well, like I said, it seems unlikely..."

Rains moved to the wall. Blood coated its surface like a fine mist. It rolled down leaving a waxy shine. Like the blood on the floor, the streaks had turned to rust. There was something about the pattern on the wall, something about the spray. It looked incomplete, like something had been in the way. "What about the slash marks on the jacket?"

"Definitely not caused by a shotgun. Could be a defensive wound? Maybe the girl found a way to fight back."

"Maybe?" Rains wasn't so sure. This wasn't adding up. "Aside from the ones who called it in, have we talked to the neighbors?"

"Most of the men are at work. A few of the housewives we spoke to said they saw a car around the corner in the early hours. There's a small oil stain up the road; it could be from our mystery mobile. We don't have any better description than 'large and black'."

"They're all 'large and black.' If you needed to leave the neighborhood in a hurry and didn't have a car, how would you do it?"

"There's a bus stop no more than five minutes from here. It runs regularly into town in the morning and again in the evening."

"That doesn't seem as likely. What are we thinking 'safe' means?"

"Well, we were just talking about that. Now that we have a name to go with what's left of the face, Simmons thinks Thwait might be referring to the McGinty girl…that's she's safe, though we aren't sure where. I'm more inclined to think he's referring to *a* safe, but we've checked the whole house and haven't found anything."

Rains stood and took the whole scene in, his head filling with more questions than answers. Who shot Thwait? There's no sign of anyone breaking into the safe house, so they would have had to have had a key. That means either they stole one or already had one. He'd have to ask McGinty about that. If the missing car belonged to the shooter, it meant they were waiting for Thwait—which means they needed to know he was coming here. If they were here before Thwait, then that means he passed the car and either didn't notice it or recognized it and didn't register it as a threat. More importantly if he had Lily McGinty with him then where is she now?

He took in the scene again, standing where the shooter had to have been. He raised his arms as if wielding the deadly weapon. Graff watched his superior working out the scenario and stepped near the prone body to help with the visualization.

Rains imagined the gun going off in his hand, the heat and power of it. He saw the coat tear away and spin Jasper Thwait around. The second shot went off and the large man fell to the floor, his massive frame landing face down, his vital fluids leaking into the rug. The large rug.

The shooter must have thought Thwait was dead and left, because he couldn't have held on to life much longer after writing those words on the floor.

"We need to move the body."

"Why?" Barclay stood, confused.

"The shooter must have thought they killed Thwait and left the room. It's the only way they didn't see this. That means either they already had Lily or she wasn't in the house to begin with…or.."

"Or she's in the house and she's…oh, Jesus."

"Move the damn body!"

It took four officers to lift the corpse of the giant man. It peeled off the rug with a sickening sound. Now that the left side of his body had been revealed, they could see multiple cuts in the man's jacket. His left hand had a grisly gash across it.

The rug, dark with blood, lay foreboding in the center of the living room. Rains grabbed a corner, felt it squelch like a sponge and yanked. It jerked up off the floor awkwardly so that the detective had to pull it several times before the large door was revealed.

"Well I'll be damned," muttered Barclay.

Leaning over, Rains found a small depression in the door and pulled. The wooden façade lifted away, revealing the large floor safe beneath.

"That's a hellava safe," Graff said flatly.

Barclay looked down. "So, let me get this straight. You think this Lug guy put Lily in this floor safe to, what—protect her from whoever attacked her at the library? That's idiotic!"

"Lug's wasn't supposed to be the brightest bulb, but his job was to protect Lily."

The group stood, considering the daunting metal door.

"How much air does she have in that thing?" His question was met with blank stares.

Barclay crouched down by the safe and gave it a knock. "Depends on how deep the safe is. From the description we were given, McGinty's daughter is small, barely over five foot; so the safe *has* to be at least three feet deep if she's in there. If the safe is airtight, she's already dead. If it isn't airtight and she's conserving her breath, or unconscious she might have enough air for three, four hours, tops. That means, at best, she has thirty minutes to an hour's air left...but even that's a long shot."

Rains quickly turned to the gathered collection of officers. "You've already canvassed the neighborhood. Get me a doctor and tell him to bring his stethoscope!" He pointed to Kid Simmons, "Get on the radio and tell Central they need to send over a safecracking team. We need someone who can get this open, now!" Officer Simmons ran outside to call the station.

Rains looked at Barclay, "We need to call McGinty and get the combination to this safe."

"There's a phone in the hall, call him from that." Rains ran to the phone.

The operator connected him to McGinty's office, but the line just rang. Rains grew more and more impatient with each ring. The thought of the girl trapped in that safe was making him sweat. The operator came back on the line to apologize, but he was already hanging up.

"I need one of you to get back to the station double-time and get over to McGinty's compound and find out where he is."

"Um, sirs." 'Kid' Simmons stood in the doorway looking pale. "I called the station like you said,"

"And?"

"They want to talk to you, Lieutenant."

Rains ran out to the closest patrol car and got on the radio. Barclay and Graff watched, hearing only his half of the conversation.

"This is Rains. Uh huh. What?!! Jesus Christ. Yeah… yeah, I understand. No… yes." The detectives watched their boss blanch.

"All right men listen up. Central got a tip from someone inside the McGinty compound. Twenty minutes ago, McGinty received a package. It contained a human pinky and a necklace. Our source confirms that the necklace belonged to Lily McGinty's mother and the pinky belonged to Lily McGinty."

"How do they know it was McGinty's pinky?"

"The pinky had a ring that McGinty himself identified. Size and nail polish color were a match as well. From what the source said, 'Mad Dog' lost it and sent his whole crew into Old Town. He's convinced Iggy Draper and his men are behind the kidnapping. So that's at least twenty armed men headed into a part of the city heavily populated with civilians. Police Central has mobilized every available unit. They've called in patrols from Mid-Town and the 27th.

"Do they need us to get up there?"

"Yes, but I'm changing the play. Our number one priority is to get this safe open. If Jasper Thwait put Lily McGinty inside to protect her from whoever assaulted her at the library, then her time is running out. If we can get her out of there and she's alive, maybe we can get her father to stop a war that could pull in every crime family in Cape Noire."

Barclay looked flustered. "But what can we do? None of us are lock smiths and we don't have the combination. Clearly McGinty's out with his men and isn't near a phone. Hell, if the station's empty, there's no way we'll get anyone out here."

Rains weighed his options. "All right. Barclay, stay here with Graff. Call the officers back and get them to Old Town. Central will tell them where they're needed over the radio."

"What are you going to do?"

"We need someone who's good at opening safes, and if the police can't do it, then I'm going to look for another option." He grabbed his hat and left the safehouse. Rains didn't have time. His shadow reached his car long before he did. He could feel the sun going down over his shoulder.

Barclay shouted after him, "Lieutenant, where are you going?"

Rains shouted back over his shoulder, "McGinty's going after Draper, I'm going to see Draper's boss!"

💀 💀 💀

He could see the lights of the city burst into life twenty minutes up the road as he sped through the suburbs. Trees sailed past. Houses that cost more than Rains would make in three lifetimes whizzed by in a blur until there were no houses in his headlights, only mansions. Some of it was old money; some of it was new money. *And some of it*, he thought as his car came to a screeching halt outside of the largest mansion he'd ever seen, *was blood money.*

Stupid. Stupid and dangerous. Stupid and dangerous and stupid and necessary.

Lieutenant Dan Rains, Chief of Detectives for the Cape Noire Police Department checked to make sure his service revolver was in its shoulder holster. He prayed he wouldn't need to use it, drawing it would definitely make matters worse, but there was more than the life of Lily McGinty to consider now.

He pounded on the heavy front door and cursed himself for letting it come to this. He thought about 'Mad Dog's men heading into Old Town, loaded-for-bear. He thought of the potential loss of innocent lives and pounded again. Again, he raised his hand to slam against the door when it opened.

Before him stood one of the largest men he had ever seen. He knew nothing of Lucas Garrett, but Rains was relieved to see him—it meant his master was at home. Garret's expression was passive, but his eyes smoldered. He stepped to one side and spoke in a deep voice simply saying, "Detective Rains." Rains took it as an invitation and entered without opposition.

Each footfall echoed in the opulence of the hall, but he didn't have time to take in the wealth. He knew what bought this sort of lifestyle, and he was neither impressed by nor desired it. As he neared the study, Garrett leading the way, he could hear a voice say "No, that won't be necessary. Yes, I can handle him. I appreciate your call." He heard the phone hit the receiver as he entered the room and saw her.

The whole damn city was about to go up in flames, and there she stood, cool as ice. Alexis Wyld, Cape Noire's 'Queen of Crime' was easily the most powerful woman in the city. The men, the syndicate, and the money she inherited when her father died at the hands of Brother Bones. The intellect and cunning… that was hers from the jump. Men died and killed

HIS CAR CAME TO A SCREECHING HALT OUTSIDE OF THE LARGEST MANSION HE'D EVER SEEN.

at her word. At any other time, on any other day, Rains couldn't have ignored how attractive she was, but in that moment her killer looks went unnoticed. He was here to save lives.

She sat behind a large oak desk, waiting. Another woman, possibly a secretary, stood next to her. Garrett placed himself between the detective and his mistress, outwardly passive, yet full of intent. The man looked twice as tall and six times as vicious as Rains was willing to deal with.

"Mr. Rains," her tone was playful without a hint of alarm. She motioned to a comfortable looking high back chair in front of the desk. "You look... tense. Ms. Wesley, fetch Mr. Rains some tea. Chamomile is just the thing to calm your nerves."

"Detective." His answer was short and sharp, and she arched an eyebrow in response. "I'm on the job, and I don't have time for tea, just answers." Though his expression remained passive, Mr. Garrett's shoulders tightened.

"What can I do for you... *detective*?" Mr. Roland could have refilled a library with that pause, but Rains' book report days were over.

"I need you to stop this."

"You're referring to Lawrence McGinty's little incursion into Old Town." Not a question.

"He's moving against Iggy Draper. Someone's been taking potshots at his boys and McGinty suspects your man. McGinty's daughter's gone missing. Some sicko sent her pinky to McGinty in a box!" Her eyes widened at this, possibly in surprise. "Draper's holed up near the Gridiron, that's a populated area. It won't just be your men getting shot. There are civilians to think about. Whether you like it or not, you and your men are about to get tangled in the biggest blood bath Cape Noire has seen in years, and it doesn't have to go down like that. You can call them off. Work *with* the police. No one else has to die!"

"You're assuming there's something I *can* do." She stood and deliberately made her way to the front of the desk. "If Lawrence McGinty wants to make a move against Draper then that's a matter for the police. Draper and I have had our business dealings in the past, it's true, but he's an enterprising man and we parted company last week. So, you see, my hands are tied."

She leaned back against the desk; her eyes never left Rains. He felt like he was at the Y playing chess with the afterschool youth. He had made his move, she countered. He decided to change tactics.

"If you can't help with 'Mad Dog' McGinty, then maybe you can help his daughter. We have reason to believe she was pursued by an assailant and was taken to a safe house not far from here. Her bodyguard gave his life to protect her, but he locked her in a large floor safe. My men are there now trying to get it open, but it might already be too late. Please, someone you know has to be able to help get it open. If she's in there, even if she's dead, we can let McGinty know, maybe before another innocent life is taken."

Rains had never met Wyld before tonight, but he had encountered her handywork. He knew she wasn't one to trifle with and her reaction could have been anyone's guess, but the veteran detective did not expect her… to smile. It was an amused smile, not cruel, not macabre, but amused. He was in no mood to be laughed at and he shook in anger. He couldn't look her in the eye. He stared instead at the floor with a gaze that could have burned a hole in the expensive rug she stood on. Possible next moves went through his brain when he heard a creak. He looked up and saw her slinking toward him.

"Detective, I appreciate all that you boys do over at the precinct, I really do. So *many* of you are *very close* to my heart. You're asking me to get involved in a war I have no part in. You come into my home and demand I solve your problems for you."

Closer.

"I can help you Detective Rains. I can bring Draper and McGinty to bear. I can make a call and send an expert to your safehouse. But…"

Here it comes…

"But if I'm going to help you, you have to do something for me.' She was looking him dead in the eye. She was inches away. Lilacs, she smelled of lilacs. Rains had been too flustered to notice before. Her scent was intoxicating. She moved closer.

'What do you want?'

She was against him now. He could feel her breasts against his chest; feel the heat from her body against his. He wanted to back away, but her look locked him in place. She craned her neck so that her soft lips grazed his cheek slowly and her whisper poured into his ear like poisoned honey. "I want Bones."

"What?" Rains didn't know what he had expected from Wyld, but it wasn't this. She drew away from him. "The 'Undead Avenger' is a scourge on Cape Noire. That vigilante has racked up a bigger body count than any 'criminal' you've put behind bars and not one of you has done a thing to stop him. Promise me Brother Bones, detective. Give me your word of honor that you'll work with me, for me, to bring that man… that *thing* that killed my father to justice. Help me bring Bones out of hiding, so I can deal with him myself. You swear to me right now, and I'll do what you and the police can't."

"I can't."

"Can't or won't?"

"Can't. I have no control over Brother Bones! I don't know who he is. I don't know where he is. I can't just call him. For god's sake, innocent people are going to die tonight if you don't help!"

"Well then *Detective* Rains," she walked behind her desk, and sat, "I believe our business is concluded for the evening. Mr. Garrett will show you the way out."

Rains pressed the gas so hard his ankle hurt. In a blur, the quiet security of Marlowe Heights made way for the present danger of Old Town. Over the roar of the engine, he could hear the reports coming in like chapters in one of those radio crime dramas, but this wasn't fiction. Twenty strong, McGinty's men had stormed Old Town. Somehow, Draper's men knew they were coming and met them in the street. Words were exchanged and shots were fired. Draper should have been out gunned, but a third group arrived. Officers on the scene identified them as small-time enforcer Casper Murnow and eight guns—more than McGinty's men were expecting, more than McGinty's guys could handle. McGinty's men were forced to retreat back to Chauncey Ave. Not satisfied with simply routing the force, Draper and Murnow pressed their advantage and followed the retreating men back to their compound. Chauncey Ave. was a war zone, with combatants on either side. McGinty's forces holed up in their offices with Murnow and Draper assaulting from the Wagon Wheel. The CNPD engaged but were taking fire from both sides. Rains could hear the calls coming in over the radio for more men, heard the other precincts responding.

By the time Rains arrived on Chauncey, the police had set up barricades on either end of the street trying to contain the bloodshed. He found Sgt. Sean Duffy and Kid Simmons a block from the action.

Sgt. Duffy greeted his friend with grim news. "Not sure how many of McGinty's men are left. Draper and Murnow left seven in the street outside the Gridiron."

"Any sign of McGinty?"

"None. Officers were on the scene right after it began, but no one has any confirmation that McGinty even showed up to the fight. Dan, we lost a couple of our own when the shooting started. Mathers took one to the chest and Williamson was rushed to St. Mary's with a bad one to the shoulder. We can't move on the compound with Murnow and Draper firing from across the way."

"All right, we need to take out Murnow and Draper first, then we can take the compound. If we let this go on too long, the other bosses are going to join in. I'm surprised Beest hasn't sent his goons in to take out the competition."

"How'd it go with Miss Wyld, Lieutenant?" Kid Simmons looked hopeful.

"Well, Wyld's not backing Draper. Sounds like they had a falling out a week back, so she's letting him hang."

Duffy nodded, taking in the new information. "If we can take them out we can stop this, but most of Central's men are at the other barricade. Some of our boys are a block over, trying the contain the fighting, if they move, things are going to get worse."

From behind, Rains heard a welcome voice. "Captain!" Rains looked up. Several patrolmen from the 27th were making their way towards his group, ducking behind cars to avoid the crossfire, Sgt. James Winstead in the lead.

"Good to see you, James."

"These are officers Jennings and Gore."

Rains gave the officers an appreciative nod. "This is Sgt. Duffy and Officer Simmons. We have an unknown number of shooters on street level holed up in the Wagon Wheel, and it looks like there's at least a few more upstairs on the second floor."

"I heard a group from Central planning a van breech at McGinty's if there's a break in the gunfire."

"Yeah, that'll get men in, but we need to figure out how to keep them from being mowed down before they get there."

"I saw a back entrance along the next alleyway during our brief visit today. We can get in through there if they don't have it covered."

"Sounds like a plan. If we take the backstairs, we can avoid the fire from McGinty. All right, Kid and Gore, you're with Sgt. Duffy. Once we're in, you three head upstairs and see what you can do about the second level shooters. James and Jennings, you're with me. We'll clear the lobby. Let's go!"

The small group made their way along the back alley and to the rear entrance of the hotel. A single shotgun blast took care of the locked backdoor, courtesy of Sgt. Winstead. They could hear the sporadic *pop pop pop* of gunfire coming from upstairs.

They found the back stairs and Duffy took the lead, his Thompson at the ready. Rains and his men made their way through the restaurant's kitchen. They paused at the service doors. They waited for a break in the gunfire from the other side.

"Hey Rains," Sgt. Winstead whispered as he leaned against the wall, preparing to take the door, "reminds you of France doesn't it?"

"James," Rains face showed no trace of levity, "I never want to be reminded of Argonne." Pistol in hand, Rains pushed his way into the lobby.

Immediately, they came under fire. The two toughs, who had paused to reload from the cover of the restaurant's booths had been facing the kitchen and turned their guns on the police. Sgt. Winstead leapt to one side, rolling behind the dining counter. Rains and Jennings ended up on the other side as the bullets sent a cascade of glass from the decimated bar above. Winstead gave the signal, and on three, the police rose from their positions and opened fire. The room exploded as a half dozen guns went off. When the smoke cleared, only the police were standing. The sound of gun fire echoed outside the restaurant, but inside was still.

Rains moved to the bodies to see if he recognized anyone. Elmer 'Whiskey' Meers and Figaro 'Ten Pin' Welch, both small-time, both Draper's men. He'd seen them in the precinct more than he cared to.

Having cleared the lower level, the group moved to the front of the restaurant. The restaurant's front window was a snarled mouth of sharp glass and gun smoke. The newsstand across the street had been reduced to splinters. From their vantage point they could see the second story of McGinty's offices. The windows had been shot out and the blinds were a mangled mess. There was movement from inside and Rains could hear shouting.

Shots like thunder echoed overhead. More glass fell. Two forms came crashing down. Casper Murnow's head burst on the sidewalk like a ripe melon with a dull *plop!* His leaden body was followed quickly by Officer Simmons, who bounced off the newly made corpse with a wet *smack* before rolling into the street with a groan. Luckily for Simmons, he rolled toward the restaurant. Winstead stepped forward and fired two shots sending shooters on McGinty's side of the street back and giving Rains enough time to drag the stunned rookie into the relative safety of the diner. '*At least the kid was alive*,' thought Rains, handing the stunned man to Jennings who helped Simmons up and got him out the back of the restaurant.

From the cover of the booths, Rains yelled to the ceiling "Sean, we got Simmons, he's good. You guys okay?"

There was a pause before the muffled voice of his friend shouted back, "Top floor's clear! We got Draper. He took one to the leg, but he'll live. We're coming down!"

From their vantage point they could see the barricades on either end of the street. The young black officer returned and informed Winstead the van was ready for the breech; they just needed cover.

Once Sgt. Duffy and officer Gore had rejoined them, the group signaled to the breech squad. Using the hall from the kitchen as a line of sight, the officers gave Rains and company the countdown. Once the signal was given, they opened fire and kept at it for what felt like an eternity.

Loyal soldiers. Ridiculous odds. Blood in the streets. Rains had been here before, and he hated it. This didn't feel like police work. This was war. He had hoped this was behind him. He thought of Sally Paige. He thought of old Leslie Owens and his comfortable couch in the Central lounge, and he kept firing.

The police van sped past the restaurant, hopped the curb, and crashed through what was left of the Pendycke's storefront. Three officers rolled out, their weapons lighting up the room. Rains and his group, still firing, ran into the street. They held their position as twenty uniformed officers, their way now clear, filed in.

It was over in minutes.

What little resistance they met with either gave up or was gunned down. After it ended, Rains read the report. Seven of his brothers had lost their lives, four from Central, three from the 27th. Over a dozen ended up in St. Mary's.

☠ ☠ ☠

McGinty's body was found hunched over his desk, his throat slit ear to ear. The coroner's report would later state that McGinty had been dead for hours, well before Draper and Murnow brought the fight to his doorstep. A safe was found behind the large portrait of McGinty's deceased wife. When opened, it was revealed to be empty.

Several of McGinty's men, those who surrendered, helped the police to identify their fallen comrades. Of the small army once wielded by Lawrence 'Mad Dog' McGinty, only Mr. Cheeves was unaccounted for.

Those same men recalled Cheeves receiving a small package by post and delivering it to McGinty. They recalled the cries of despair behind closed doors when the contents of that package were revealed. They recalled a red-faced McGinty ordering them to arms, a bounty on the head of Iggy Draper. They recalled Mr. Cheeves exiting the office, barking orders, a shotgun in one hand and a large bag in the other. Several of them saw Cheeves getting into a car headed in the same direction as the rest of his crew, so they assumed he was headed to Draper's. None of them recalled seeing him when the fighting began.

¤ ¤ ¤

Rains didn't learn any of this until later. As soon as he was sure his men were all right, that Officer Simmons was in good hands and that Duffy and Winstead and the rest were safe, he made his way to his car. Past the medics. Past the handcuffed mobsters with minor injuries yelling for their lawyers. Past the curious spectators who gathered in droves by the barricades once the shooting stopped. He found his car, crawled inside, and lit a cigarette. God, he needed a cup of coffee. Even more so, he needed a win. He needed to know that Lily McGinty had been saved, that they got to her in time. That he had made the right choice leaving her fate in the hands of Graff and Barclay. He took a drag and let it settle. He cleared his head and got on the radio.

Barclay answered. "Dan, what the hell happened? We could hear it all the way in Marlowe Heights. It sounded like a thunderstorm."

"Just tell me, did you get the safe open? Did you find the girl? Were we too late?"

"Dan, we got the safe open, but it's not what you wanted to hear."

His shoulders sank with his heart, "Did you find a body?"

"We did, but it wasn't Lily McGinty's."

A glimmer of hope. "Whose was it?"

"According to his wallet, his name was Ogden Presley. He'd been dumped in the safe, at least a day before. His throat was slit. Other than the body, the safe was clean. If there was anything in it before, it's not there now."

Rains hung up the radio and stepped out of the car. He stood amidst the smoke and wreckage of a warzone, the flashing police lights casting shadows across the buildings. God, he *needed* a coffee. He closed his eyes and tuned out his surroundings—the shouts of the police, the murmur of the gathering crowds. An ambulance, on its mission of mercy, faded in the background. So much happened today, there was so much to answer for, but Lt. Dan Rains, Chief of Detectives had only one question. "So, where is Lily McGinty?"

☠ ☠ ☠

Lily McGinty's joints ached and her eyes watered. She'd been inside for too long. Had she been forgotten? There was a dull thud on the other side of the door and suddenly she was bathed in light, so quickly she had to shut her eyes. The stale air fled, and she inhaled deeply. She smelled the perfume before she heard the voice. Lilacs. A hand, smooth and warm, grasped hers and pulled her steadily to her feet. Still holding the warm hand in hers, she felt a cool glass placed gently in her other, bandaged hand. She raised the glass to her lips and let the cold water sooth her parched throat.

Lilacs.

☠ ☠ ☠

Lily McGinty, daughter of the late Lawrence 'Mad Dog' McGinty sat in the comfortable high back chair, wearing a blood-stained dress. Her bandaged hand rested on a satchel in her lap. She took in the large office and looked as if she didn't have a care in the world.

"So," Alexis Wyld cooed approvingly, "how'd you do it?" The teenage girl turned and looked her in the eyes. Not everyone was willing to keep the gaze of the 'Queen of Crime.' Even fewer were allowed to do so a second time.

"As you know, my father laundered money for Big Swede for almost twenty years. He talked a big game, but never made a move to increase his position in the syndicate. He was reliable enough to be kept in the loop, but never over-extended his reach and so never drew unwanted attention. Of course, he was taking a small percent off the top from every transaction. Never enough to be noticed. He never told his lieutenants; never put it in a bank. He just stored it away in a safe for years. I think once mom died, he just didn't have anyone left to impress.

"I wasn't allowed to be independent. He always had someone with me. He never had time for me but wouldn't let me leave the city. Wouldn't let me go to school with kids my age and there was no way he'd consider sending me to college, even though I begged him. I was tutored at home, three rooms down from his office. I watched suit after suit walk past my study, rarely with even a nod. I wasn't worth their attention. So, I read.

"When I was old enough, I began to visit the library. First once a week. Then every other day. Eventually, I was there five days a week, open to close. Of course, I was always under escort in case my father's 'enemies' decided to strike. I think everyone but him knew I wasn't a target. No one was out to get me; or him for that matter. Now, if they knew how much he had stored away over the years, I'm sure someone would have made a move. As it was, he was left to dwell in the delusion of his 'shadow enemies'."

The imposing form of Mr. Garrett approached her then as Alexis Wyld interjected, "Miss McGinty, if you would be so kind as to give Mr. Garrett the needed address."

The young girl broke from her reverie with a start. She reached inside her bag with her bandaged hand and gave a small scrap of paper to the enormous black man. He quietly examined the scrap and handed it back to her with a nod before turning and leaving the room.

Alexis Wyld waited until the door closed with a *click*. She motioned to Miss Wesley to bring a pot of tea before she turned back to Lily McGinty. "Please, continue."

"The few librarians left me alone. The city had long since reduced their funds to nearly nothing and that beautiful old building was falling apart. I began using my allowance to keep the doors open. I'd slip money in the books I returned and in return, Mr. Roland granted me access to the library's entire collection. Nothing was denied me. And, as long as I was reading quietly, whoever was watching me would leave me alone.

"We stayed exclusively on the second floor. Cheeves said this was for 'strategic purposes,' but I think he just wanted to be able to sit and listen to the Knights games on the radio. It suited me fine. All the fiction was downstairs, so I spent the better part of a decade devouring history and sciences, philosophy and languages. Five years back we put up a 'closed for renovations' sign on the second-floor entrance and never took it down.

"A few years ago, I discovered the library's 'special collections.' I asked for the key and they gave it to me. I think they'd given up on maintaining the records, they were just happy to have jobs. Most of what they considered valuable had been picked over and sold years ago. But they were wrong, or at least, not very creative."

"I had access to city records. Documents dating back a hundred or more years. Shipping records, donations, family histories. A forgotten treasure trove of information. It's possible that I know more about the history of this city than anyone else who lives here. My money, my father's money, granted me access and privacy."

"Which now," Alexis interrupted "sadly, has all burned down."

"Yes," the young girl continued, "that broke my heart. So much lost. But, I saved what was important." She hugged the satchel closer to her then and gazed off for a moment.

"Six months ago, I began mulling over a plan. If I'm being honest, I'd been thinking about it for years—but, it was purely hypothetical. That changed on my eighteenth birthday. I had dismissed my tutors months ago. Father didn't even notice they were gone, and they were happy to continue getting paid for a job they were no longer doing. When asked what I wanted for my birthday, I told my father I wanted to go to college. I suggested Italy. It was old and full of knowledge and none of his 'enemies' would even think to go looking for me there. Of course, he said no. For the usual reasons.

"He told me there was 'no need to leave Cape Noire. No need to *ever* leave the city. Everything I needed was here.' He said it with his back turned to me, as he opened his safe and added money to his growing collection. He heard me crying and handed me a handkerchief to dry my eyes.

"'I know you are disappointed'" he said, "'But I know what's best for you. I have to keep you close. I *need* to protect you. I won't lose you like I lost her. I would do anything, trade everything to see you safe. I would go to war to make sure no one harmed you.'"

"A sincerely loving father would have hugged me or shown me any kind of affection after saying something like that, but I know he saw me as the ghost of my mother. He was haunted by her and chose me as the instrument of his own torment. So, I found an instrument of my own."

Alexis Wyld leaned forward just slightly. She eyed the leather bag on Lily's lap. *This is where it's going to get good,* she thought to herself.

"Mr. Cheeves was an impulsive idiot. Not like Lug, who clinically was an idiot. Cheeves excelled at violence, but had no ambitions of his own. I think that's why dad chose him to guard me. The man was a shark and it killed him to be stuck with 'baby-sitting duty,' as he calls...called it. I knew he'd never hurt me if I tried to run away, but he definitely would hurt anyone who tried to help me. So, if I was going to escape my father, and that was the plan, I needed Cheeves on my side.

"He liked to gamble, but he was terrible, no head for numbers. He was losing hundreds of dollars a week to erratic betting and it was getting to him. One day, instead of reading, I sat next to him while he was listening to a game. I suggested he bet in a certain way. He wouldn't listen to me, so instead, I asked him to place a bet for me. I think he thought I was being funny. I made $80 that afternoon and another $100 the next day. That got his attention.

"Over the next week, he begrudgingly came to me for advice. Not all my picks paid out, but enough of them that I earned some respect. We didn't always talk sports. I nudged the conversation to my father's organization. I've been keeping my ears open for years and learned a thing or two. Cheeves filled in the rest, and I had a plan.

"As I said, Cheeves wasn't interested in power. He didn't care about rising in the ranks. He just wanted to make money and hurt people. I told him I knew a way he'd never have to worry about debt again, and he listened.

"I told him just enough of the plan to pique his interest and left the unpleasant parts for him to come up with. I nudged him in the right direction a few times, and by the end, he'd contributed enough that he was pretty sure it was all his idea in the first place."

Alexis Wyld leaned back with grin, there was so much more to this girl than met the eye. She looked her over again. She was pale and bookish with a fashionable haircut that hadn't been properly maintained. Her clothes were new but worn without care. Wyld had never been impressed with Lily's father, but whoever her mother was, she'd been a looker.

Lily continued. "For the plan to work, we needed to convince my father that I had been kidnapped. For that to happen, we had to make sure the threat was believable. Since my father's enemies were non-existent, we had to make some. I heard from Cheeves that Iggy Draper had recently left your employment. I didn't see the bigger picture at first; I just needed someone my father could feel threatened by.

"Cheeves strong-armed another of my father's soldiers into taking pot shots at a couple of the guys a few days before, to get their hackles up. It worked; father increased the guard around the house. Of course, Cheeves then had to get rid of the guy so he wouldn't talk. He suggested to my father that since Draper was so close to Chauncey Ave, I was safer at the library than at home. He then suggested that Lug should take me to the library by himself so that Cheeves and a few of his guys could chase down a lead in the shooting. Cheeves partnered with Presley and that was that.

"I told Cheeves I needed to start a fire. Unsurprisingly, Cheeves had a penchant for arson and sent me to the library this morning with accelerant.

While Lug was on 'look out,' I made my way to the special collections room. I lit a fire, tore my dress, and screamed.

"I told Lug someone had attacked me, that I had barely escaped and that we needed to leave. Sweet predictable Lug saw the smoke, took me by my wrist, and led me downstairs. To protect his face, I gave him a piece of my torn skirt. By the time we got to the doors the fire had spread, and smoke had filled the halls. Mr. Roland came up the stairs just as we were leaving, and Lug knocked him down. I reached out to him and jerked as if Lug were pulling me. Clearly the near-sighted old man didn't recognize my 'assailant' and was far too meek or injured to go after us. Then again, there was the fire. It spread so quickly."

She paused, her eyes reddening at the thought of the lost books. Wyld knew this story ended with several dead bodies and no tears would be shed for them. *This girl had her priorities.*

"From the library I had Lug drive me to the safehouse. I told him to put me in the trunk so no one could see me. It was not a pleasant experience. I've never liked feeling trapped."

"The property was quiet and out of the way and it would be the last place anyone looked. Having a safehouse outside our protected area was a risk, but my father liked the idea of hiding in plain sight. This way, if he ever made an alliance with a bigger family, he could offer cross-town territory.

"Cheeves was already there, waiting. I stayed in the trunk until we arrived. When Lug got me out, I pretended to be disoriented, in case anyone was watching. The poor sweet idiot kept reassuring me and stroking my hair trying to calm me down."

"Once we were inside, I led him to the living room where Cheeves attempted to slit his throat. That did not go well. Cheeves' betrayal caught him off guard, but once he was on the defensive, he put up a fight. I yelled his name from across the room and when he turned, Cheeves took him out with a shotgun he found stored in the safehouse. I barely stepped aside in time to avoid the spray." She looked at the blood stain on her dress with mild disinterest. "I guess I didn't avoid it completely.

"I had hoped to get rid of Lug quietly. The plan was to wait at the safehouse while Cheeves went back to Old Town to rile my father into action. Now, it was only a matter of time before the police arrived.

"Both Cheeves and I knew about the safe in the floor, so I left a message with Lug's finger. A 'clue' like that was sure to keep the cops occupied."

Alexis was impressed. *It seems 'Mad Dog's' little pup has bite.*

"Cheeves was smiling as he cleaned his knife and turned to me. 'You

SHE PAUSED, HER EYES REDDENING AT THE THOUGHT OF THE LOST BOOKS.

ready for the next part?' I honestly think he took enjoyment in what happened next. I knew my father would be incensed by my 'kidnapping', but I couldn't guarantee it would be enough to get him to go to war. It was Cheeves who came up with this part of the plan."

She held her bandaged hand up and examined it. "We did it in the back of his car. He gave me his belt to bite on and held my arm so I wouldn't struggle. In one quick motion he cut off my pinky. I don't know what I expected, but I didn't expect it to hurt so much—or bleed so much. I almost fainted. He wrapped my hand, put the pinky in a box for my father, then drove me here and dropped me off."

There was a soft knock at the door and Mr. Garrett entered holding an exceptionally large canvas bag which he placed at Wyld's feet. She leaned down slowly, without a care in the world, unzipped it, and examined its contents.

She smiled and tuned to her bodyguard. "And the man who had this?"

"The man now rests in the harbor. He will not be found."

"Thank you, Mr. Garrett. That will be all for tonight." He left, as quietly as he entered closing the door with a *click*. "Ms. McGinty, please continue."

"As I said before, Mr. Cheeves was motivated by money and violence. In order to get him to go through with such a plan, I had to promise him plenty of both. So far, I had made good on half of that promise. It was time for the other half.

"No one but my father knew the combination to his office safe, and he wouldn't have opened it in front of anyone, especially not Cheeves, unless it was under the most dire circumstances.

"I can only imagine the exchange. Cheeves delivering the package along with the ransom note, my father must have gone red. Maybe he suspected something, maybe he didn't." She eyed the sizeable bag at Wyld's feet, "clearly he was willing to pay the ransom.

"I told Cheeves to do it quietly, not like Lug. I gave him a bag for the money. He didn't think he would need one that big. I'm sure he was pleasantly surprised."

"So,' Wyld continued the story, "your father opens the safe, Cheeves kills him with, presumably the large knife he just used to cut off your pinky, filled this bag with everything he could carry and then leaves the compound...what, under the pretense of joining the ranks in the upcoming fight?"

"I gave him a number of good excuses, depending on who stopped him, but in the heat of battle soldiers rarely ask questions. He had an address and instructions to wait until I came to get him. I told him I would have even more money for him if he pulled off his part."

"So, while Cheeves enacted your plan to open the safe, murder your father for the money, incite a war which would wipe out two well established syndicates, you spent the better part of the day in a cramped space beneath my floor hiding out in case your plan failed. Though, by the sound of machine gun fire in the distance, I'd say it worked perfectly."

"It wouldn't if you hadn't helped me." Lily paused. "Out of curiosity, why *did* you help me?"

The corner of Wyld's mouth curled ever so slightly. "Because you intrigued me. It's not every day a teenager knocks on my door, demands to see me, and tells me that if I hide her in my home and don't interfere in a war between her father and one of my ex-associates, a war she put into motion, she'll 'tell me a tale I won't soon forget' and I'll be 'rewarded beyond my wildest expectations.' That took brass. What did I have to lose? That's why I helped you," she narrowed her eyes then, "but you knew I would. What made you so sure?"

"Because my father feared you. I'd hear him, talking to his men about your rise to power. How you effortlessly took over your father's empire, how you took...whatever you wanted. I knew you had no love for Draper and that my father's business interests only benefitted your enemies. Getting rid of them both would create a vacuum which you could fill with a loyal lieutenant or anyone you chose. I knew you were smart enough to see that, and," she motioned to the bag packed with money, "I lived up to my promise."

"You certainly did."

"And since the only other person left alive who knows the entirety of the plan is you, I will be free. I can make up any story I like as to where I was during all this. Though," she bit her lower lip "there's still Detective Rains. He may not have all the pieces yet, but he's not stupid. I've read the papers, the guy's a knight. He won't stop until he finds out what happened to me."

"Oh, I wouldn't worry about Rains." Wyld smirked and finished her whiskey. "Before we got you out, I put in a call to Chief Torrance and made it *very* clear that I didn't approve of City detectives waltzing into my home without a warrant. Torrance knows how the game is played. I don't imagine he can fire Rains, but he can keep him busy long enough for you to invent whatever story you choose."

Wyld considered her empty glass for a moment. "There is one thing I don't understand. I don't see why you had to set the library on fire. It sounds like this Lug would have followed your lead if you simply told him you'd been attacked. You clearly loved that place, why burn it down?"

"Because, after this I can't go back there. That's not me anymore and if I am going to change my life, that means severing old ties." Lily McGinty stared defiantly at Wyld, the two women locked eyes for a moment.

"You're not a very good liar, are you?' The lethal beauty moved from where she had been leaning on the desk and made her way to the drinks cabinet. She poured two glasses. She returned and held out one. Eventually, even hesitantly, Lily McGinty took it. "Don't worry, you may have fooled a greedy thug and a simple bruiser, but when I'm through with you, you'll be able to lie directly to Dan Rains' face. So, why'd you burn the library?"

"Like a lot of this, it wasn't part of the original plan."

"There's nothing wrong with being able to think on your feet. It's a talent I appreciate in my associates." She raised her whiskey in salute before placing it to her lips.

"I needed to destroy the evidence."

Wyld raised an eyebrow. "What evidence? There was no assailant. What crime was committed…aside from arson?"

"Theft." The waifish blonde moved to the satchel on her lap, undid the clasp, and pulled out the oldest book Alexis Wyld had ever seen. Its binding was covered in stains. Dark stains. Spattered dark stains. The name along the spine had long since worn away. The paper was yellowed and a faint odor she couldn't quite place filled her nostrils. As the girl placed the book lovingly on her lap, Wyld could swear the room got colder. She felt a tickle race up her spine and the goose pimples raised the hairs on her arms. She involuntarily took a step backwards and found herself against the desk.

"This was donated to the library by the estate of a recently deceased collector. Mr. Roland was planning on selling it, though he didn't recognize its true worth. So, I took it. No one else had access to that collection, he eventually would have noticed it was missing, and he would have figured out it was me. It's a shame to have lost so many wonderful old books, but none of them… not the entirety of the library's collection comes close to the value of this book."

"Lily, what book is that?"

"This?" She traced her bandaged hand across the book's worn cover. "This is a legend, a treasure, hidden among garbage. To everyone else this was just another donation to be examined, cataloged, and shelved. I knew what it was the moment I saw it sitting in a pile on Roland's desk.

"This is the single most valuable book in the world. *This* is what you've been waiting for, the second half of the promise I gave you when you took me in and hid me. A reward beyond your *wildest* expectations."

She stood, cradling the ancient text in her injured hand, and calmly walked to the large bag full of money. She reached in and removed a small box. She pulled a severed finger from inside, removed the ring, and tossed the finger in a waste bin. Somewhat awkwardly she placed the ring on her uninjured hand. She reached into the box a second time and retrieved a necklace. It was a simple silver chain affixed to a pendant shaped like a snake's head. The eyes were two tiny red rubies. She held the necklace out to Alexis Wyld before turning her back to her. She lifted her hair as the most powerful woman in Cape Noire fastened the clasp around her neck.

Alexis Wyld, Cape Noire's 'Queen of Crime' stepped back and took in the view. No longer was the person standing in front of her someone to be protected. For the first time, she saw her for what she really was.

Lily McGinty, sheltered daughter of Lawrence 'Mad Dog' McGinty stood now a changed woman. The book in her injured hand glowed with an undulating light, ancient and powerful. "My whole life, my father tried to keep the memory of my mother alive in me. You think I killed him for money, but my father died with my mother, many years ago. I just had Cheeves finish the job. And it wasn't for money; it was for freedom."

Before Alexis Wyld's eyes, the book's glow intensified. It clung to Lily McGinty's hand and seeped like liquid into the bandages. "Lily," she gasped.

"My father called me Lily," the bandages fell to the ground revealing her perfectly healed hand, "but my mother named me Lilith."

"This is the sole copy of the *Eschatonicon*, the Book of Endings. With this," again her eyes met Wyld's—this time with no deceit, "with this, you can kill Brother Bones once and for all. And that's just the beginning."

EPILOGUE:

Dan Rains stood in the smoky office, shifting from foot to foot, as Chief Torrance looked over reports, absently chewing the cigar stub in his mouth. Torrance pushed the files away from him and leaned back in his chair locking eyes on Rains. Neither man spoke for several seconds. Finally, Torrance addressed his subordinate—calmly, even coldly.

"No."

"What do you mean 'no'? Chief, Lily McGinty is still out there somewhere. All I'm asking for is some time and some men to help me look for her."

"No."

"Fine, I don't need the men, I'll go myself. Give me a week. I'm sure I'll be able to…"

"No."

"But Chief!"

"*Detective* Rains, I have a half dozen police funerals to arrange and twice as many men at St. Mary's to look after. Three city blocks of Old Town are in ruins, some of it is still on fire. We made close to twenty arrests, all of whom still need to be processed. The paperwork alone for this debacle will take a month to clear up, and I expect you to do your share of said paperwork. Starting today."

"What? Chief, what about Lily McGinty? What about Mr. Cheeves or Ogden Presley? If we don't act now, the trail will go cold. I think we should get a warrant and visit Alexis Wyld to find out what she…"

The chief slammed his fist into the desk. "That is EXACTLY what you are NOT going to do! I've been getting calls from men in *very* expensive suits, all of whom want to talk about your unlawful visit to Miss Wyld."

"Unlawful?"

"Did you have a warrant to enter her home? Were you invited in?"

Rains thought for a moment "No, but…"

"You screwed up Rains. I ordered you and your men to get back to Old Town to handle the McGinty situation. Not only did you fail to find the daughter, but you delayed the arrival of key officers. Who knows how many of ours could have been saved if you hadn't made your little stop to harass Alexis Wyld."

"Chief, she's a known business associate of Drapers. She had connections that could have helped us with the case."

"Since when does the CNPD need help from civilians? I may be new here, but I think I see where Warren fell down. He didn't reign in your department tight enough. You're off the McGinty case; you're a liability to the investigation. You've forgotten your priorities."

"Chief, I'm trying to save a life and solve a crime!"

"AND I AM TRYING TO RUN A POLICE FORCE! It's bad enough this city has a vigilante, nix that, vigilan*tes* running around killing people. It makes this force look like a joke. Six months I've been here, SIX MONTHS and I have yet to see a single file from your department regarding this Brother Bones. Or do you not think a masked man killing citizens is worthy of the great Detective Rains? From now until I say so, your job is to find this Brother Bones character. I want to know who he is and where he lives."

"Chief, I can't do that."

"You don't want to do paperwork. You don't want to follow your Chief's orders. I don't see what use you are to this force. I'll tell you what detective, I'm putting you on indefinite leave as of today. Take some time and figure where your priorities lie. We'll see where your head's at in a month."

"A month?! Are you kidding me? What am I supposed to do for a month?"

"I don't know, and I don't care! Maybe you can learn how to properly speak to your superiors. Leave your badge and gun. You're dismissed."

"But…"

"I said dismissed, *Mister* Rains."

☻ ☻ ☻

Torrance watched the smoke swirl about the room before he slid the badge and gun from the desktop to an open drawer. He closed and locked it with a smile.

"Miss Ray, why don't you go ahead and take your break now?" He waited for the pretty secretary to leave before picking up the phone. He dialed a direct line, no operators.

"Miss Wyld, it's done. I've just made sure Rains won't be bothering you or your associates for the foreseeable future. Oh, and that *mister* Rains bit really shook him."

The voice on the other end of the phone was calm and collected. "Thank you, Chief Torrance. As always you have my gratitude for your cooperation—especially today, your work was invaluable. And please, send my thanks to Detective Graff for his quick thinking in alerting me to Rains' arrival. I hope he put the combination to McGinty's safe to good use. I'll make sure a nice donation will be added to each of your retirement funds. Until next time."

She hung up the phone and turned to the young woman sitting in the corner, reading.

"So, Lilith, where do we start?"

THE END

BEING SAFE

To date, *Safe* is the single most stressful writing challenge I have ever attempted. I love pulp fiction. The hyperbolic action! The supernatural suspense! The sensational prose! The open license to use exclamation points! Pulp worlds, by their very nature, invite invention and I love spending time and playing in those worlds. I was a part of the creative team that put together the *Ron Fortier's Cape Noire RPG* sourcebook. In order to make playing in the world as immersive and as authentic as we could, I read and reread every Cape Noire story, multiple times. In doing so I found myself coming up with MANY 'what if?' scenarios. I pitched several of these scenarios to the rest of the creative team as potential adventure supplements. Since only one adventure module could be included in the sourcebook, those other tales were set aside. So, when Ron approached me to write a story for this anthology, I already knew what it needed to be and who it needed to be about.

To me, Dan Rains is a compelling character because he's a normal guy living a city filled with technological wonders and supernatural horrors. He's a genuinely good man who makes tough choices in his pursuit of justice. But where did he come from? Who was he before he became Chief of Detectives? I had the idea to explore Rains' military history. What was he doing during the first World War? I had my own ideas, but this was Ron's character, so I sent him my thoughts. I was very relieved to discover Ron and I were on the same page. He answered all my questions and helped me fill in the blanks. Ron also reminded me that Rains was an officer of the law and as such, part of a larger team. Some of those team members were on the side of the angels, others were on their own side, and still others...well.

So, I knew I wanted to write a Dan Rains story, which needed to include other members of the CNPD. Originally, I conceived of *Safe* as a race against time. Each story break would begin with a clock which would gradually count down as the victim's air supply ran low. I also knew I wanted to include a scene where Dan Rains met Alexis Wyld for the very first time. I wrote the story I envisioned, but it just didn't fill the required word count. I tried padding the story, but padding is boring and none of it felt earned. The finished product felt disjointed.

I decided to try again and this time, I wanted to focus on the characters themselves. How their choices made the story more compelling. And I wanted to make sure the most important character was Cape Noire itself. The second draft of *Safe* weighed in at a whopping 21,000 words! It was still a race against time. It still had Rains meeting Wyld. But now, it was told in three intersecting parts, featured over twenty new original characters, and covered every inch of Cape Noire (including a lengthy section devoted to Cape Noire's Chinatown). I printed a massive copy of the map found in the RPG sourcebook and hung it on my wall to better plot accurate locations and location specific story events. It was a logistical nightmare. A truly muddled mess. My beta readers couldn't make head nor tails of it. The narrative was lost in the minutiae. Once again, I became frustrated with the story.

Part of the problem stemmed from my inexperience writing mysteries. *Safe* is my second prose story set in Cape Noire, but it's also my second published work of prose period. I've worked on a half dozen roleplaying games and twice as many essay anthologies, but I had never tackled a mystery. I grew up on a steady diet of Sir Arthur Conan Doyle's Sherlock Holmes stories as a kid and in 2019 discovered and enthusiastically consumed the works of Agatha Christie. Here I was, a fledgling author, foolishly attempting to ape the storytelling styles of the masters and failing miserably.

I was already VERY behind on my deadline when we found out we were moving. The next few months were completely devoted to packing and selling our old house, finding and buying a new house, leaving an old job and finding a new job, and settling into a new home in a new state. In that time, zero creative projects were even attempted. I'm not ashamed to say I fell into a funk that was very difficult to pull myself out of. Every attempt at writing met with failure. It felt like I was repeatedly digging a hole, deeper and deeper. Knowing I'm behind in a deadline can elicit two distinct responses in me: it can galvanize me to get the work done or I can throw my hands up and wallow in self-pity. I was in the throes of the latter.

Around the time everyone began quarantining, to combat the threat of Covid-19, Ron wrote to check up on me and see how I was and how the story was coming along. It wasn't, and I wasn't much better. My days were spent in a cycle of depressing news articles and videogames. It wasn't a great place to be, but I genuinely wanted to make it better. I took inspiration from those who sought to make the world a better place through art and through action. From the heroes on the frontlines, helping everyone by putting others before themselves. So, I started over by starting over. I began by outlining the story elements that HAD to be included and throwing the rest out. That meant letting go of some moments I really loved. I eliminated all but the most essential characters. I knew I needed Rains to be the main protagonist. I knew a young girl would be in trouble. I knew Alexis Wyld was involved somehow and that Rains and she would finally meet. And that's it. I just started writing—chunks of scenes, character moments, bits of dialogue. All new. The piece grew to almost 19,000 words and as I paired it down the story took shape. My very patient wife listened to my ideas while we went on our nightly walks and each night after work I wrote.

I forget sometimes that writing isn't romantic. It's work. I worked very hard on this story and I hope it isn't apparent. I hope it seems effortless. I hope it's fun! I hope you like its hyperbolic action and its supernatural suspense! I hope you'll enjoy the sensational prose! Most of all, with everything going on in the real world—as you spend time in the world that Ron Fortier created and allows us to play in—I hope you're safe.

DREW MEYER - is a library assistant and educator who moonlights as a podcaster and independent game designer. He's written for a number of anthologies including 2015's *Legends of New Pulp Fiction*. He currently lives in Lynchburg, VA with his talented and patient wife and their impatient cat. He may or may not have a beard.

DARK REAL ESTATE

By Ron Fortier

1877

The fire swept through most of the Warrens alongside Carlyle Street burning all the buildings facing the docks. It was pushed along by strong winds whipping off the Pacific and all of the city's fire brigades responded within minutes of its eruption. Yet their equipment was too old and inadequate the stop the inferno that consumed one block of buildings after another. The heat was said to have melted the iron handles on business establishments.

As the brave firefighters did their best to wash down those structures yet to be touched by the hungry flames, they became aware of the rats that scurried across the paved roads around them. At first it had only been a few dozen, but with each passing minute more and more of the rodents appeared until they became an army of thousands.

Savagely they descended upon the families who were fleeing for their lives, having abandoned all their belongs, hopes and dreams to the devouring holocaust. Firemen turned their hoses on the maddened creatures with some success. They swept the rats off the wharves into the churning salt waters.

It was then that Lilith Delamore walked onto the scene. Reports would later claim she simply emerged from the wall of fire totally unscathed, her black dress whipping about her body, her laughter seeming to feed the blaze.

Lilith was a witch and the leader of a coven established in the nearby town of Castle Harbor. The week before, several Christian pastors had raided her Satanic church and burned it to the ground after having given Lilith and her Sisters fifty lashes of the whip. They had then ordered her to leave or else suffer the consequences. Undaunted by their threats, the badly beaten woman had cursed them; vowing she would have her revenge on all of Cape Noire.

"I am the Devil's daughter," she had declared, "and all of you will burn."

Those words echoed in all who witnessed her impossible appearance that night.

"Rats and bats, snakes and lizards," she cried out. "Lucifer's own born of Hades and here to do my bidding."

Several brave coppers drew their pistols and confronted her.

She laughed at them, her black eyes reflecting in the flames. "You fools!. Your doom is upon you." With that she raised both hands and cursed in a foul, ancient language.

Lightning seemed to spring from her finger tips and strike the officers. Their bodies shook in a grotesque dance until they all fell lifeless to the ground.

At this sight, their companions began firing at the laughing witch only to see their bullets evaporate into smoke puffs inches from her body. Lilith's laughter seemed to swell at their helplessness. One by one the firefighters and policemen began to back away. From the crumbling warehouses even more rats sprang forth, all of them surrounding the all powerful Witch Queen.

It was then that the old man walked on to the scene. He moved through the press of fleeing people, his stoic face locked on Lilith. He wore simple clothes, boots, jeans, a blue cotton shirt and his long, iron gray hair was tied with a red bandana around his head.

"So, what have we here?" Lilith glared at the solitary figure. He was an Indian, which was evident by his leathery, red skin and chiseled features.

"I am Cheveyo," the Indian replied calmly. "I have fought your Master many times, demon bitch. And I have always defeated him."

Lilith's brows arched. "No, that is impossible."

"Is it?" Cheveyo swept out with his right hand. "I am here. Where is your Master?"

"He doesn't waste his time with puny fools like you," she retorted. "I am more than capable of carrying out his wishes.

"Are you prepared to die, old man?"

"Whenever, witch. Stop wasting my time."

Lilith screamed, raised her arms and once more sent out bolts of electricity.

At the same time, Cheveyo waved his own hands in a circle before his chest and every charge was deflected. Sparks rained about him, but he remained unharmed.

Surprised by his power to thwart her, Lilith renewed her attack. She poured every ounce of black magic she possessed into her assault only to see it rebuffed.

"You are powerful, old man," she conceded. "But you can't kill me."

"That was not my plan," Cheveyo said patting the amulet hidden under his shirt. "I leave that to him." He pointed to one of the dead police officers.

Lilith watched in silence as the dead man began to tremble as if awakening from a long sleep. The burned corpse awkwardly rose to its feet, revolver still clutched in its right hand.

"Shoot her," Cheveyo commanded.

The dead man's hand snapped up and he pulled the trigger. The bullet hit Lilith in the head just between her now startled eyes. Her body fell back to the pavement and didn't move. A second later, the vermin dispersed and the threat to Cape Noire was over.

Cheveyo dropped his tired arms to his side and looked at his new avatar. "Hello, Dead Sheriff. It has been a while. Hasn't it?"

Two days later Siras Dawling sat back against his rickety wheel cart on the small rise that was the apex of Cape Noire's Potter's Cemetery. In the cart was the canvas wrapped body of the witch, Lilith Delamore. Looking back at the city, the dark black pall that had remained there after the awful fire was now slowly dissipating. Northerly winds pushed the ugliness to sea revealing crystal blue skies in its wake.

Dawling reached into his back pocket for a flask of whiskey and took a long pull. Smacking his lips he looked down at the oblong hole he'd just finished digging. Now it was time to dump the body, cover it with dirt and go home. As he began to tug on the stiff wrapped legs, he felt a presence and turned to find two women standing before him.

"*Jeezuz Christ*," he yelped. "Where da hell did you two come from?"

Both woman wore gray cloaks, the hoods concealing half their upper faces. One was a few inches taller than the other. It was she who spoke.

"Forgive us. We did not mean to startle you."

"Whatcha doing here?"

"The person you are about to bury has something of ours and we would like to retrieve it before you put her in the ground."

"Oh," Dawling scratched his bristly chin. "And what might that be?"

"A necklace. It would still be about her neck, as she died with it on."

"Yeah. Is it valuable?"

"No. Not to you."

"What's that suppose to mean?"

The shorter of the two ladies reached into a pocket and pulled out two twenty dollar gold pieces. "It means this is for you, if you'll kindly give us our sister's necklace."

Sunlight glinted off the coins and Dawlings quickly figured out how many drinks forty dollars would buy him.

"Alright then," he reached for the coins. The woman yanked her hand back.

"After you give us the necklace," the taller reminded him.

"Sure, sure," Dawlings groused. He turned around, pulled the body closer to the lip of the cart and then peeled the top flap open slightly. He stuck his hand inside, felt around for a second and then pulled it free. Clutched in his dirty hand was a silver chain necklace. It held a snake-head pendant; with two tiny red rubies as the reptile's eyes.

"This what yah want?" He held it up.

The short sister handed over the coins and took the necklace from him. "Thank you," the tall woman said. Then she and her companion turned and walked away through the lane of wooden markers.

Dawlings clinked his coins together and chuckled as he put them away in his pants pocket. Then he took hold of the Lilith's remains and yanked them out of the cart and into the grave with a thump.

Down the path, the senior acolyte said to her fellow witch. "With this, and the lost Book of The Death, our Lilith will return."

"So sayeth the Master. Amen."

Today

For many, many years the criminal element of Cape Noire existed in an unchanging world of routine thanks to two powerful men, Topper Wyld and Big Swede Jorgenson. Each was relatively content in owning their half of the giant northwest metropolis' criminal operations. What crumbs were left were divided and often fought over by the various smaller outfits. It was an unholy alliance of sorts and worked rather well. Even the police, which itself was corrupt, accepted the status quo. As long as everybody got their share and more importantly, were happy with them, then things ran smoothly.

Then one day, for no reason other than pure, simple greed, Topper Wyld woke up one morning and decided it was time to take everything for himself. Where this grandiose scheme came from no one ever knew. Perhaps he thought he'd reached an age when complacency wasn't enough and he wanted to leave a real empire to his only heir, his beautiful daughter

Alexis Wyld.

Within weeks, a Wyld owned bordello was attacked and all the girls and their rich powerful clients were brutally murdered. Wyld let it be known that Jorgenson had orchestrated the foul deed, when in fact he was the manipulative master mind behind the strike. Once word hit the streets of Cape Noire, Big Swede had no recourse but to defend himself against a swift and deadly reprisal. Which did in fact occur, but in the process something totally unforeseen also happened.

In the midst of the bloodletting, a supernatural avenger suddenly appeared. Cloaked in black clothes, and wielding twin silver-plated .45 automatics, he called himself Brother Bones. He was in fact the resurrected body of a slain assassin named Tommy Bonello and he hid his hideous dead face behind an ivory white skull mask.

With Jorgenson removed from the field, Topper Wyld remained the only mob boss with enough power and influence to control Cape Noire for years to come.

Unfortunately even Wyld could not escape the justice of the Undead Avenger and was gunned down in his own home only weeks after launching his mad scheme. With his death, Cape Noire instantly became a no-holds barred urban nightmare with dozens of various factions vying for supremacy.

Among the two most notorious were Wyld's daughter, Alexis, who quickly proved herself a skillful leader with a heart of stone. Some believed she was even more cunning and ruthless than her old man.

The other figure to rise to power was the grotesque Harry Beest. A one-time Wyld torpedo, Beest had incurred his boss' wrath by seducing the teenage Alexis and so was punished. Wyld had him drugged and delivered to Cape Noire's mad scientific genius, Prof. Bugosi, who cut out Harry's brain and put it in the head of a six hundred pound silverback gorilla. When he recovered from the operation, Harry Beest learned that his own human shell had been destroyed. Thus he would remain trapped in his new gorilla body until that day Prof. Bugosi chose to repeat the operation and give him a new human anatomy.

In the following years the city endured one bloody gang war after another, all the while the exploits of Brother Bones grew ever bolder. The mere mention of his name caused hardened killers and petty crooks to tremble. When the Undead Avenger set his sights on someone, they were doomed. He was unstoppable. In fact a saying was born on the streets of Cape Noire, "How do you kill a dead man?"

Still, despite his prowess, Alexis Wyld became obsessed with bringing down Bones as a personal vendetta to avenge her father. Yet for all her wealth and prestige, all of her agents and mad strategies failed time and time again. Until the last one resulted in the death of Prof. Bugosi, a shocking development with tragic repercussions for Harry Beest.

Once again gang warfare has erupted throughout the city with several new players about to write the next bloody chapter in Cape Noire's future.

The conference room on the second floor of City Hall was jam-packed with reporters from both the newspapers and radio stations. All were gathered for an early morning briefing by Chief Torrance of the Cape Noire Police Department. What with the recent violent gang activity of the past few weeks, the Mayor had come under severe criticism and ignobly passed the responsibility of placating his constituency to the Chief.

The Tribune's ace crime reporter, Sally Paige, elbowed her way through the throng of her hard nosed colleagues to reach the front of the assembly where the raised stage was located. At its center was a four-foot podium with several wired microphones jutting upwards. Cables extended from them to the floor and off to the either side of the room where several sound technicians from station WXYZ wearing headsets were adjusting a small control panel for sound quality.

The lovely, long-haired brunette was pulling her dog-eared notebook and a pencil from her purse when a familiar face stepped up from behind her carefully holding an expensive flash camera.

"Hey, Sally," Jim Finlay greeted. He was one of the Tribune's top photographers and often shared assignments with the pretty newshound."

"Jim. About time you got here," she teased. "Show's about to start any minute."

Finlay adjusted the lens on his camera and then noticed his friend's haggard look. "You look like shit, partner."

"What you get for being up three days in a row chasing down gunfights and what not from one end of the city to the other."

"Yeah, I hear you. I just came from midtown where those buildings were destroyed by fire. Apparently the Draper mob stored their TNT in the basement. When the fire hit it….kablooey! Gonna take them weeks to clear that end of the street of debris."

"I know," Paige sighed tiredly. "Morgue's got bodies on stretchers in the halls throughout the basement while more stiffs are packed away in a trailer truck parked out back."

"My old man use tell me about the gang wars of the late 80s. Who'd have thought we'd ever get to see those again, eh, Sally."

"What can I say? Welcome to Cape Noire."

One of the radio techs left his station, darted across the stage and cracked open the rear door. He said something to the people waiting there and rushed to his equipment to give it a final quick inspection. All eyes in the room turned to the open portal and from it appeared Deputy Mayor Lou Mougin, followed by a big, burly fellow Paige surmised was the new Chief of Police and behind him were two other men she recognized immediately. Captain Lu Chang, in full uniform and with him Detective Ralph Graff; a stout figure with a noticeable pot-belly.

The Deputy Mayor took the podium while the others lined up behind him.

"Good morning, ladies and gentlemen," Mougin patted down the thinning hair atop his head as he peered through his round, wireless glasses. He was a mousy sort and no matter how expensive his clothing, they always looked as if he'd slept in them.

"Thank you for being here at such an early hour of the day."

"So, where's the Mayor?" a voice called from the back of the room.

Mougin looked up but couldn't tell who had interrupted him. "Please, if you'll allow me to continue. Due to the recent rash of violence throughout the city, the Mayor has been occupied with overseeing the safety of all our citizens. To that end, he could not be here this morning but rather has asked Chief of Police Edgar Torrance to address you and report what is being done to curtail that violence."

Mougin turned and nodded to Torrance. "Chief, if you please." Then he stepped aside and Chief Torrance took his place behind the microphones.

Immediately several reporters began shouting questions. Torrance, looking annoyed, lifted his rock-like jaw and remained silent. More questions flew at him and still he didn't say a word.

Paige leaned over to Finlay, who had already snapped his first picture of the new Chief. "This guy's a cool cucumber," she whispered.

Minutes passed and the voices ceased. That was Torrance's cue. He took hold of the podium with a tight grip.

"My name is Edgar Torrance. It is regretful that our first meeting has to be under such circumstances. As the new Chief of Police, it's my job to see that Cape Noire will abide by the rule of law and those who break those laws will be apprehended and brought to justice."

A reporter for the Evening Star shot up a hand. "Chief, all well and good, but…"

"What is your name?" Torrance demanded immediately pointing down at the sandy haired journalist.

"Ah…Peter Johnson, with the Even…"

"Is it acceptable at your paper to interrupt people when they are speaking, Mr. Johnson?"

"Ah…well..no."

"Then you will kindly keep your mouth shut until I have finished. At which time you, and your colleagues may ask your questions. In a polite and civil manner. Fail to do so and I will personally throw you out of here myself."

Tension settled among the now chastised members of the fourth estate.

"Is that clear enough for you, Mr. Johnson…of the Evening Star?"

"Ah…sure, Chief. Whatever you say." Johnson glanced around at his colleagues nervously hoping for some show of support. Instead they wisely avoided making eye contact with him. No one else wanted to share the chopping block with him.

"Good," Chief Torrance smiled coldly. "As I was saying, I take my job seriously as do all the men and women in the ranks of the Cape Noire Police.

"The past few weeks has seen a dramatic escalation among the various criminal elements that has led to multiple confrontations and a tragic loss of life, both among our men and innocent civilians caught in the crossfires.

"We immediately responded to each incident with all the resources available to us and as of yesterday afternoon, all precincts have witnessed a complete cessation of these bloody encounters. In other words, the streets are quiet once again.

"I plan to see that they stay that way."

Sally Paige jotted down his words making sure that when she wrote her piece, she would quote him accurately word for word. At the same time, sensing a pause, Jim Finlay and the other photographers were popping flashbulbs like popcorn.

"Allright," Torrance took a breath. "I will now entertain your questions. But one at a time. No yelling or shouting…or this meeting ends now."

Paige's hand shot up. Time to take the bull by the horns.

"Yes," Torrance acknowledge her.

"Sally Paige, Tribune. Most reports indicate all of this began two weeks ago at the home of the late Professor Bugosi and subsequently culminated in the mansion being destroyed. Is that true?"

Torrance never blinked. "Yes, Miss Paige. The first outbreak occurred on the Bugosi estate and when our men arrived on the scene, they discovered the bodies of known felons including that of mob boss Ace Bricker."

"So that was the spark." Paige looked down at her notebook. "Was there a direct connection between that incident and the recent war between Mad Dog McGinty's crew and those of Iggy Draper?"

"We are still gathering the facts," Torrance replied. "Criminal campaigns like these are nothing new to any of us. The men you mentioned were among the worst lowlifes in our society and I doubt seriously any of us will mourn their passing."

Peter Johnson found the nerve to try raising his hand again and praying for the best.

"Yes, Mister Johnson," Torrance's glare was harsh.

"How about the Beast Man? Was he involved with any of this?"

"The who?"

"Harry Beest, the guy with the gorilla body?"

Chief Torrance shook his head. "Are you purposely trying to annoy me, sir?"

"Ah..no... I just want..."

"Have you ever seen a gorilla gangster, Mr. Johnson?"

"Well, no, I haven't personally..."

Torrance pointed a finger at the assembly. "Has anyone here ever seen this so called Beast Man? Anyone?"

No one replied.

Okay, this is stupid, Sally Paige thought. She raised her hand. "But Chief, everyone in the city knows the story of Harry Beest and how that madman Bugosi took out his brain and put it in the body of a gorilla."

"Everyone knows a fairy tale, Miss Paige," Torrance retorted. "And I and my men don't deal in fairly tales. We deal in cold hard facts. There is no Gorilla Man and if there are no other such inane questions, this meeting is concluding.

"Good day."

As Torrance and the others quickly exited the stage, Peter Johnson looked over at Paige and shrugged. She nodded and began filing out with Finlay beside her.

"So what did you think of the new chief, Sally?"

"He's obviously a by-the-books type. I know one thing is for sure, I don't ever want to be on his bad side."

"Amen to that."

They were moving through wide corridor heading for the stairs to the first level when Paige spotted Sgt. Sean Duffy off to the side talking with a female clerk.

"Go on, Jim. I'll meet you back at the newsroom."

He waved good-bye and she went over to the red headed detective. Duffy's own conversation was ending and the young lady walked off.

"Hi Duff."

"Sally, how are you?"

"Busy like everyone else. I just came out of the new chief's press conference."

"Right. Guy's a stickler. Old school."

"Agreed. Say, have you seen Dan? I was hoping to interview him about all this but haven't seen him around the station at all."

"That's because Torrance kicked him off the force."

"What?"

☻ ☻ ☻

It was not unusual for Countess Selena to have early morning visitors. The brown hued gypsy seer's door was open to all who required her counseling regardless of their race or social standing. Still, the blind black fellow seated across the round linen covered card table from her this morning was a surprise.

"Thank you for seeing me sans appointment," Deacon Antoine Devereaux said as he made himself comfortable on the padded chair. He wore dark glasses to hide his eyes; a simple black suit and held a wooden cane on his lap. Somewhere in the room scented candles gave off a delicate sweet smell and bright sunlight captured tiny dust motes floating through the air around them.

"It has been too long, my friend," Selena shuffled the tarot cards in her hands. "Would you care for some tea?"

"Perhaps later, Countess," he fidgeted. "After you have read de cards."

Selena smiled knowingly. "Father O'Malley is a fine, tolerant and holy man, but I doubt he would be pleased if he knew you were here."

She referred to the pastor of St. Michael's Catholic Church, one of the oldest religious houses in Cape Noire and the parish where Deacon Devereaux served.

"He is truly a good priest, madam and a devoted servant to the Mother Church. Whereas I remain a son of the islands and cannot ignore those things I was taught as a child in Little Jamaica. The vodou will always be a part of me flesh and bones."

Selena patted the oversized rectangular cards on the table top. "What is it that concerns you, Deacon? Why have you come to me?"

"While at mass this morning, a shadow fell across my very soul, Sistah. I looked about me and no one else seemed bothered. Father O'Malley continued the service and all seemed normal."

"And yet you knew it was not."

"Madam, you and me, we feel what others do not. Something touched me this morning. Something very, very bad."

"All right then, let us see what the cards will tell us." She set the deck in front of the cleric and he cut them evenly. She put the bottom half on the top, brought them back to her side of the table. "Ask your question, *mon ami.*"

Deacon Devereaux cleared his throat and then asked, "What kind of bad juju did I sense in church this morning?"

Countess Selena flipped over the center card. In her reading it would signify her friend. Then she methodically placed a card above it, one below it and then one to either side. The blind man waited. He could hear the fortune teller's breaths and when she made a gasp, he knew she had seen something in the cards.

"You were correct, Antoine. There is an evil present but it is not directed at you personally. Rather, it threatens all of us. It seeks unholy vengeance… and…"

"And what Madam. What else do the cards tell you?"

"There is danger, darkness and terror…and comes in the form of a woman."

"A woman?"

"Yes…she is the Devil's own daughter."

The Wooden Spoon diner was bustling with the last surge of the breakfast crowd when Sally Paige squeezed her way into the busy eatery. She was instantly assailed by the familiar smells of bacon, hotcakes and pungent coffee, while the crowded booths and bar stools were filled with chattering customers. Elbowing her way past two uniformed street cops,

"AND WHAT MADAM. WHAT ELSE DO THE CARDS TELL YOU?"

she rose up on her tiptoes and spotted Lt. Dan Rains seated at the far end booth alone. She put her head down and pushed onward.

Upon reaching him, Paige halted and glowered down at him. Swallowing a mouthful of eggs, the handsome chief of detectives, looked up at her surprised.

"Good morning, Sally," he said while wiping his lips with a napkin.

The sassy reporter put her fisted hands on her hips. "When were you going to tell me you got kicked off the force?"

Rains did his best to stifle a grin and indicated the seat across the table. "Come on, Sally, sit down and please, lower your voice will yah."

Paige tossed her purse onto the seat and then sat, with her arms folded over the formica table top. Set before Rains was a plate filled with bacon, three eggs, and hash brown potatoes. Next to that was a half finished cup of coffee.

"I don't believe it," she declared. "How the hell can you eat at a time like this?"

"Sally, calm down. In the first place, I did not get kicked off the force. I was put on a temporary leave of absence."

"By who?"

"The new chief."

"Torrance?"

"Yes. You familiar with him?"

"I just got out of his press conference at City Hall."

"Aha. I heard that was going to happen. Our beloved Mayor is taking a lot of heat these days."

"As he should. You, better than anyone, know what's been happening these past few weeks. The gangs going after each other like wild dogs."

"Right. And we lost a lot of good men in the process," he added, a somber look masking his rugged features. "So what was Torrance's line on all of it?"

"Only that he and his boys in blue have got a handle on it and the good people of Cape Noire can now rest easy."

"Well, that sounds about right."

Paige was ready to ask him another question when a pretty blonde waitress popped up next to them like a jack-in-the-box.

"Can I get you something, Miss?" she asked politely. The name tag on her breast pocket said her name was NANCY. She looked strung out, a pencil snagged over her left ear and a notebook in her apron pocket. Both of which she grabbed the second she'd made her query.

"Just a cup of coffee for me," Paige replied.

"And I'll need a refill," Rains added.

"You got it," the girl pivoted and vanished.

"She's new," Paige observed.

"Yeah, and so far pretty efficient."

"Okay, so let's get back to the matter at hand. Why exactly did Torrance give you the boot." Rains started to raise a hand and Paige corrected herself. "Give you a vacation? Is that better?"

"Well, it's what it is." Rains looked around at the patrons and then said, "Sally, what I tell you has to be off the record. You understand? This is not for your paper...or any other paper for that matter."

Sally Paige and Dan Rains had known each other for several years and there was a genuine attraction between them. Still, she hated it when he skillfully outmaneuvered her as he had just done.

"For heaven's sake, Rains, I'm a reporter. You can't do that to me."

"Take it or leave it, Sally. Off the record or this conversation ends now. What'll it be?"

Before she could give him answer, the blonde waitress reappeared holding a white coffee mug and steel pot of coffee. She set the mug before Paige and filled it to the brim. Then she twisted slightly and refilled Rain's empty cup.

"Thanks," he got out just in time to see her back vanish back into the kitchen.

"All right," Paige grabbed the sugar dispenser. "Off the record. Now give, what the hell happened?"

☠ ☠ ☠

Meanwhile, in a swank brownstone on Allard Street, Rita Mayfield sat listening to the radio newscaster on her late employer's expensive three foot cabinet radio. "And that was the new Cape Noire Police Chief, Edgar Torrance, recorded during his press conference earlier. And now a word from our sponsor, Wyld Ale, the taste that can't be tamed."

The statuesque blonde jumped up and crossed the room cursing. "No such thing as a gorilla man, heh? Well he certainly doesn't have a clue." She turned the knob and shut off the power. Then she grabbed the pack of cigarettes on the glass coffee table and lit one with the sterling silver lighter beside the black ashtray.

Inhaling deeply, she hugged herself with her left arm while nervously replaying the events of the past few weeks in her thoughts.

Rita Mayfield had been attorney Albert Carrington's live-in mistress for the past year after starting out in the secretarial pool in the law offices he shared with his partners, Ramona Saunders and Huey Blankenship; the latter also recently deceased. Upon Blankenship's sudden demise, Carrington had informed her that he and the Saunders woman would divide Blankenship's clients among themselves equally. As it turned out, one of the half dozen names Carrington inherited was that of mob boss, Harry Beest; the supposed Beast Man.

At the time, the ambitious Carrington had assured her the stories about Beest being anything but human were mere fabrications created by his people to frighten opposing gang leaders. Albert was so convincing, she'd seen no reason to doubt him. After all, the debonair, lawyer had given her a life of riches and luxury unlike anything she had ever dreamed of. She wasn't about to upset that apple cart. Up to that point, Rita Mayfield relished her fancy upper crust life.

Thus when Carrington departed for his first meeting with his new client, she had no reason to worry. When he failed to return that evening, concern began to edge its way slowly into her thoughts. Had anything gone wrong? At first she chided herself for being so easily flustered. Carrington wasn't any naïve shyster. He was a street smart fellow who knew the ways of Cape Noire as well as any other native born resident. Mayfield assumed his dealings with that Beest guy had merely proven to be complicated and told herself that was the reason behind her lover's absence.

Still, he could have called her, she mused, rather than keep her in the dark like that.

Had she known what awaited her, she reflected in hind sight, she would have packed her bags and grabbed the next train out of town. But she hadn't and instead was totally surprised when on the fourth day of her solitude, two brutish thugs showed up demanding she accompany them.

And thus began her nightmare.

She had been reunited with Carrington in the mansion home of Cape Noire's resident mad scientist, Prof. Bugosi. She later learned Bugosi was long dead and another guest at the domicile was one of his former colleagues, Prof. Aton Petrus. All of them had been gathered there by the horrific Harry Beest. The very same gorilla mobster Chief Torrance had claimed was only an urban legend.

Mayfield shivered and took another drag on her cigarette. There wasn't anything fairy tale about Beest. No sirree Bob!! She'd stood nose to nose with the gorilla man, his ugly hair-covered puss and beady black eyes only inches away. Hell, the guy even put on airs, acting like a gentlemen in his hundred dollar, custom tailored, three-piece suit. He'd actually taken her hand upon their first meeting and kissed it with those big, cold, rubber like lips of his.

Eventually, via both Carrington and Prof. Petrus, Rita Mayfield was filled in on the situation she found herself in. With Bugosi's death, Harry Beest required another mad genius to duplicate the incredible brain-swapping operation and his people had found Petrus in California. He'd been persuaded, gangland style, to accept Beest's invitation. Shortly after arriving at the mansion, Petrus confided in Carrington and Mayfield that he had created a synthetic drug as powerful and addictive as heroine. The savvy lawyer realized such a drug massed produced would make them all rich.

Which was when one of Beest's rivals, Ace Bricker, showed up at the mansion with his gang bent upon revenge for past wrongs. In the ensuing assault, Bricker and the majority of his men were slain. Poor Albert Carrington was another casualty of the gun battle and before dying, directed to Mayfield to take Petrus and run.

She didn't have to be told twice and so, while Harry Beest and his men were busy dealing with their enemies, she and the professor escaped via a back exit only minutes before chemicals stored in the mansion's cellar ignited an blew the entire building to kingdom come.

That had been over a week ago. Once far from the burning mansion, Mayfield had come to the realization that there was no better place for her and Petrus to hide out in other than the very brownstone where she'd been living the past year. It was her hope that Harry Beest had no idea about the Allard St. home and would eventually come to believe that they had left the city entirely.

When the lower south-side gang wars started up days later, she welcomed them rightly assuming they would stymie any kind of search the gorilla monster might have initiated. And now, according to what she'd just heard on the radio, things were going to get back to normal real soon. Meaning, their safe house might not be so safe any longer.

Tapping her right foot on the floor, she took her last drag and then crushed the butt of her smoke into the ashtray.

"Rita," Petrus called out from the back room kitchen. "What was that on the radio?"

The anxious blonde went to join him. The kitchen was a large, square room containing the finest modern appliances money could buy from a fancy ice-box to a new gas-stove. But little of any of it had ever been used. Neither Rita or Carrington had been inclined to cook and though the pantry did contain some meager staples, they generally ate out all the time. If they entertained, Carrington hired a local chef from a nearby five-star restaurant.

She found the slender scientist at the kitchen table running a hand through his straight brown hair. His eyes, behind rimless glasses, were studying papers scattered all over the table top, along with a beat-up black briefcase in which they had been crammed. These were all the notes and records from Bugosi's private files Petrus had time to collect before he and Mayfield had fled for their lives. Now they were all that remained of the mad scientist's life-long studies.

"It was a report from downtown," Mayfield said as she came up behind him and placed her hands on his shoulders. She could feel the tightness is his muscles. "That stupid police chief was telling people Harry Beest is just a fairy tale. Can you believe that? That guy's a moron."

At first, when he didn't respond, she wondered if Petrus had heard at all. Then he shook his head and cursed. "It's a crime, Rita. Everything's gone! Everything Bugosi achieved in his lifetime and this is all that's left to show for it."

"Whoa, relax there, honey," she cooed, beginning to massage his shoulder muscles. "You're way too wound up. Let me loosen you up a bit." She continued to knead his stiff muscles.

"I just can't reconcile the injustice of it," Petrus leaned back enjoying her attention. "We can't stay here, Rita. Surely you understand that."

"Right, Prof. But where else are we going to go?"

"Back to California. I still have a few friends there who can help us get established."

"And do what? From what you told me, you aren't exactly a shining star at Cal Tech these days. You said they booted you out. That they didn't have your vision in regards to re-animation."

"The frontiers of science are not for the meek, my dear. Those fools simply could not fathom the wonders that lay ahead if I continued my work.'

"And you want to go back there?"

"I'm sure I can find another research facility that isn't aware of my past." He reached up and took hold of her hands. Anton Petrus wasn't use to feminine companionship, especially with one so beautiful as Rita. He realized had it not been for fate throwing them together, that in any other encounter, the alluring blonde wouldn't have given him a second glance.

"Why are you unwilling to consider my plan?"

"You mean my formula for synthetic drugs?"

"We could offer it to big mobs right here in Cape Noire. They'd pay an arm and a leg for what you can give them for peanuts."

He was about to utter his same argument about the risks involved with such a venture when the doorbell rang. Petrus looked up at her. "Who can that be?"

"I don't know," she answered moving around the table.

"Maybe one of Carrington's friends?"

"Maybe, but at this hour of the morning? Naw, that doesn't make any sense."

They shared a worried look and then Mayfield turned and exited the kitchen.

What the hell, she thought as she went to the front door. *If its Beest's men and they found us, so be it. I'm sick of this hiding out.*

She unbolted the door and pulled it open to be confronted by the biggest, tallest brown man she had ever seen. He stood above her wearing a very clean and pressed gray colored chauffer's uniform. Under his arm, captured against his side was the matching cap.

"Good day, Miss Mayfield," he announced in a deep bass voice. "I am Lucas Garrett and my mistress, Miss Alexis Wyld, requests the presence of your company. You and the professor, that is."

There was no smile with the invitation. Rita Mayfield knew a command when she heard one.

Damn it, here we go again.

☠ ☠ ☠

"So let me get this straight," Sally Paige grilled Lt. Dan Rains after he had related the events of the past week. "All this, to include your dismissal, was about Iggy Draper kidnapping Mad Dog McGinty's daughter?"

"Lily," Rains supplied. "And yes, that's about it. Both had been pushing for a fight for about a year with each making small incursions into the other's territory. Like all mugs, they eventually got tired of waltzing around with each other."

Paige drained the last of her coffee and set the mug down. "But kidnap someone's only child. That's personal."

"Exactly. McGinty went ballistic and as you've already seen, Cape Noire lost half a dozen good men and two whole city blocks."

"But what about Lily?"

Rains' eyes darkened. "We...I....never found her. You can add her to the list of innocent victims to all this."

Nancy the waitress materialized again as if by magic with her bottomless pot and refilled Paige's. Rains put his hand over his own cup. "I'm done, kid. Thanks. Just bring me the check."

"You got it, handsome," she flirted before disappearing again.

"But I'm still confused as to how all this relates to your situation?" the brunette reporter reached for the sugar jar. "I mean, did Torrance can you for not being able to find the girl."

"No, Sally. It's a little dirtier than that."

"What's that suppose to mean?"

"Well, when the trail started getting cold on us, I tried a one more gambit in hopes it might not only find her but put an end to the whole stupid war. I went to see Alexis Wyld."

Paige stopped stirring her coffee. "The Queen of Crime! Holy smokes. Now that's a meeting I want to know to about. In detail, Lt. Rains."

"Honestly, there isn't much to tell. In the end, she was exactly as I'd imagined; a calculating, cold-hearted bitch."

"Go on."

"She seemed to be amused by the whole thing. Including the girl's disappearance. When I asked for her help, she all but laughed in my face. Then she said if she did this favor for me, I'd have to do one for her in return."

"What did she want?"

"For me to help her track down Brother Bones."

"Bones! You're kidding."

"I wish I was. No, Sally, she was adamant. In fact when she mentioned him, a change came over and I could tell it was more than a casual thing. The woman is obsessed with getting vengeance for her old man, even now, years later."

"That's nuts," Paige commented. "What did she think, you had some kind of connection with our Undead Avenger?"

"Apparently so. Of course I told her such was not the case and her request was impossible for me to ever carry out. And that was the end of our conversation. She told me to go and I didn't waste any more time with her.

"Three days later, Torrance calls me into his office and tells me she filed a complaint saying I'd barged into her home and harassed her. That unless I was reprimanded in some fashion or another, she'd get her lawyers to sue the city."

"Damn, and Torrance went along with this travesty."

"I don't think he had much choice, Sally. I mean, I don't think she was bluffing about suing the city. That would have brought the Mayor and Police Commissioner down on his head for sure."

The two sat silent for a few minutes. Paige felt helpless and that bothered her a great deal.

"Dan, let me a write this up." He started to interrupt but she kept talking. "Hold on, I won't mention you or any of this. Promise. I'll use the old my-sources routine. Something not even a judge can get out of me. Once the public gets wind of this, Torrance will have no choice but to reinstate you."

"Sally, please don't do anything."

"But Dan..."

"Sally, I think he's crooked."

"Huh...what? Who?"

"Torrance, I think Alexis Wyld has him in her pocket. Deep."

For once, Sally Paige didn't know what to say next.

The young woman formerly known as Lily McGinty admired herself in the full length mirror of one of the many guest rooms of the Wyld Mansion. After she had been accepted by the mistress of the house, Alexis Wyld, and demonstrated her arcane abilities to Cape Noire's Queen of Crime, she had been welcomed with open arms. She'd allowed Miss Wyld to witness her transformation and rebirth then had explained to the older woman how her arcane powers would grow ever more powerful with each passing day.

Wyld had only one obsessive desire; the total destruction of the skull wearing vigilante known as Brother Bones. At that, Lily, now calling herself Lilith, had laughed merrily.

"Miss Wyld, leave that to me. It shouldn't take me more than a few days to find him and then erase him from this reality as if he had never existed."

At that Alexis Wyld's cold green eyes had gleamed relishing the dream that had eluded her for the past few years. "If you can do that, I will give whatever you want, Lil...ah, Lilith."

"For now a place to dwell in privacy and security is all I require. After I have dealt with this Bones person, we'll discuss my future plans."

And with that Wyld had her personal secretary, Amanda Wesley, escort Lilith to the lavish third floor suite which would become her personal sanctum for the foreseeable future. The shy, thin woman had shown her the giant closet filled with dozens of dresses and gowns; all of which were hers to wear and enjoy. She'd been given a tour of the adjoining bath with its sunken tub and long vanity desk. Whereas the bedroom itself was spacious, with a poster bed, reading end tables and another writing desk equipped with paper and other paraphernalia. All in all it was a room fit for a princess.

Which is exactly what I am, Lilith thought as she spun around in front of the mirror to marvel at the silver satin gown she wore. It had puffed sleeves that kept her forearms bare and on her feet were matching silver shoes.

Around her neck was the snake-head necklace. She dared not ever remove it.

As Lily McGinty, the daughter of the late Mad Dog McGinty, she had always sensed she was different from other girls. Since her early teens she had felt an inner darkness that wrestled constantly with her soul. By the time she was sixteen her dreams were filled with dreams of other places beyond this world; exotic dimensions in which bizarre, horrifying creatures dwell. But what was odd was the fact that they did not scare her. At times she even seemed to recognize them.

Having no one to discuss any of this with, Lily began spending time at the library and there discovered the section on occult lore. It was in those old dusty books untouched in centuries, that she ultimately discovered the history of the Witch of Old Town, Lilith Delamore. The story behind the satanic priestess who called herself the Devil's Daughter mesmerized Lily. Was it possible that she, a gangster's daughter was the resurrected Lilith? The answer to that would take another year of research until two crucial events occurred within days of each other.

One Spring afternoon, the librarian, Mr. Roland approached her holding a heavy, leather-bound book and carefully set it on the table before her. Knowing of her fascination for the occult, he told one of the library's janitors had recently discovered the tome in a hidden cellar maintenance closet. Perplexed at how the book had come to be hidden away like that, Roland had examined it and though not fluid in ancient languages, he was able to decipher the book's title, Eschatonicon.

He told Lily McGinty from his own studies, he believed the language was early Egyptian and the title translated roughly to, The Book of the Dead.

As it did not appear to have any intrinsic value, he thought she might enjoy looking at it. The girl, like Roland, was intrigued and thanked him for his thoughtfulness. After he had left her, she took hold of the cover and lifted it up to reveal the first yellowed page with the barely visible hand written script. Under what she assumed was the title, was a detailed drawing of a stylized snake's head with two gems in place of its eyes.

Now what could that mean? Never one to shy away from a mystery, she set about finding someone who could help decipher the text and unlock the book's ancient contents.

Exactly one week later, while visiting the Antiquarian Book Shoppe, one of Cape Noire's quaint little stores she often frequented, Lily walked past a tiny glassed in jewelry shelf set against the wall by the cash register. As her only interest when visiting the business was to find old books, this time Miss McGinty took a peek at what was in the display. It was obvious most of the few items resting on a black velvet mat were cheap, plated costume pieces. She was about to turn away when her eyes saw the snake-head pendant fastened to a silver chain.

She felt her heart stop. The pendant was the exact double of the drawing she had seen on the title page of the Eschatonicon.

She waved to the blond clerk April Moon.

"Hi Lily," Miss Moon smiled greeting her regular customer. "See something that caught your eye?"

"That pendant there, shape like a snake's head with the jewel eyes. Is it expensive?"

Carefully, the helpful clerk lifted the glass front and picked up the necklace. She handed it to Lily. "Not really. This is just junk stuff Mr. Sinclair found in the shop when he first bought it. You can have it for a dollar."

Lily McGinty was having a hard time understanding April. The second her fingers had grasped the necklace, a surge of electricity has shot through her body. It was all she could do not to gasp. There was power in the object. Much power.

Turning to her bodyguard, she instructed him to pay the clerk. Then she thanked her, slipped the pendant into her jacket pocket and ran out of the store. Whatever had caused her physical reaction when making contact with the necklace was as yet another oddity she would have to solve by herself.

Eventually, via her studies and of Lilith Delamore and her daily handling of the mysterious necklace, Lily McGinty came to the conclusion that she was in fact a living reincarnation of the long dead witch and only by placing the necklace around her neck could she bring about a complete reawakening.

Which is exactly what had happened but only after the girl had faked her own death and caused her father to go to war with the rival Draper mob. When both bosses were felled in bloody gun battles, Lily went to Alexis Wyld and here she was, Lilith Delamore returned from the dead.

The metamorphosis had somehow merged both their identities while aging her body to Delamore's adulthood. The Devil's Daughter looked in the mirror and liked what she saw. Possessing the child's memories, as well as her own, she thought she resembled the movie star Clara Bow, with her curly sunflower hair. That was a nice change from the black locks she'd had in her past life. Happily, her voluptuous body was the same in all its curves; the better to mesmerize the opposite sex into doing her bidding.

Yes, I definitely like the new me, Lily. Thank so very much. But now it is time to go to work.

On the table next to the bathroom door was the magic book opened. She sat on the stool in front of it and let her fingers caress the brittle page. Another result of her rebirth had been her ability to now read the long forgotten language. She could not help but marvel at the arcane formulas and spells within its covers. Here was unlimited power at her fingertips.

Sitting back enjoying that thought, Lilith brought her hands up and speaking several words created a tiny fireball that floated in the air between her two palms. It revolved like a miniature hot globe and she peered into its flame.

How would she go about finding Brother Bones? In the fire she beheld a section of Cape Noire that didn't seem to have changed much since the city's founding. What was it the citizens called it?

Ah, yes. Rat Haven. It was an area most avoided because of the large rat population that congregated in that one city block. No one knew exactly why and apparently no one had ever been able to clean it up.

She would start there.

Through his alcoholic stupor, Morris Langier, held up his bottle of Four Roses wine and saw it was almost empty. Only a tiny splash sat at the bottom of the glass bottle. He tilted it up towards his grease-covered lips, making sure not to spill a single drop. Who knew when he would be able to scrape up another few bucks to get another bottle? He tilted his head slightly only to have the bright noon sun blind him as it reflected off the bottle's bottom. His bloodshot eyes squinted and he cursed, almost missing his mouth.

The cheap sweet wine washed over his tongue and down his throat. He smacked his lips and wondered what it would be like to drink the good stuff. Seated near the end of the alley, he could see traffic moving up and down Thatcher St. A few people crossed his line of sight but never bothered to look his way. Then again, nobody looked down dark, dingy alleyways. Especially in this neighborhood.

The old wino heard a loud commotion coming from the wall of overstuffed trash cans to his right and looked to see what was going on. He'd been sharing the spot with a mangy looking tomcat for the past few hours and now he could hear it screeching. More steel cans rattled and the cat screeched louder.

"Atta boy, you show them rats what's what," he mumbled tossing his empty bottle where the noise was coming from. He made out several shapes converging on the spot and suddenly one of the waste containers fell over, spilling half its foul-smelling content across the alley's tarred surface.

The cat then bolted out of the cluster of cans and ran past him as if fired from a canon. Behind it a dozen rats appeared, each the size of a small dog. The old man's eyes doubled in surprise. He blinked several times, believing he was hallucinating again; which was nothing to new to his addled mind.

But this time he wasn't seeing phantoms, only what was actually there. Their sharp teeth chattering, the pack of vermin fell upon him before he could even scream.

Less than three hundred yards away, rookie police officer, Spencer Simmons asked his mentor, Sgt. Dave Thompson, "So why's it called Rat Haven?"

Behind the wheel of their squad car, Sgt. Thompson kept his eyes on the road when answering. "The entire block has always had a rat problem, Kid. Going back since the damn city was founded. No one knows why and no administration has ever been able to deal with the problem.

"Maybe they should just tear the block down," Simmons suggested. He didn't mind the nickname Kid, it was a precinct thing. With almost six months under his belt, he was slowly proving his worth as a reliable, gutsy lawman.

"Folks who own the buildings are afraid the city will screw them in the end and sell the empty lots to new developers for big bucks."

Kid Simmons merely nodded, his eyes moving constantly as he'd been trained to do at the academy. Good cops were always aware of their surroundings at all times.

But the last thing he ever expected to see was a man come running out of the alley to their right. The man, yelling and flailing his arms wildly, dashed into the middle of traffic right in front of their car. Sgt. Thompson mashed down on the brakes.

Through the windshield, Kid Simmons could see the man was covered by rats, at least a dozen, all over his body. Blood smears covered parts of his legs and torso as he twisted about. Two were clamped on his face tearing into it with their teeth.

"Holy shit!" Simmons flung his door open and jumped out. Pulling his service revolver from its holster, he rushed towards the Morris Langier.

"Don't shoot!" Thompson cried out as he rushed in from the other side of the car. He took hold of his own pistol by the barrel and then began swinging the butt at the savage rats clinging to their wailing victim.

Kid Simmons did the same and the two carefully bashed away, doing their best not to hit the man. The rats refused to let go and it took several blows to each to make them fall broken to the road. One, holding on to the Langier's belly, turned and leaped for Sgt. Thompson's face. He batted it away with all the strength he could muster and it hit the side of a milk truck with a plopping sound.

The cops kept hammering away, one rodent at a time. Finally their efforts were slowly having effective results. Then, just as Kid Simmons, his face covered with sweat, thought they might have a chance, one of the last crazed rats tore open the wino's throat and blood erupted outward spraying the young cop in the face. Some entered his eyes and mouth and he frantically tried to wipe it off with his free hand. He watched in horror as the old man stared back at him, the life ebbing out of his eyes in shock and then he collapsed.

There was a loud shot, and Simmons looked to see Sgt. Thompson now shooting the last few rats trying to scramble off the now lifeless body.

One minute later those not beaten or shot, raced back into the alley. They left behind the two heavy breathing cops. Both were too numb to move. They stood facing each other, then down at the remains of Morris Langier.

"Rat Haven," Sgt. Thompson muttered. "Shit-hole Rat Haven."

☻ ☻ ☻

Blackjack Bobby Crandall sat up on the old cot and ran one hand through his wild red hair. The kitchen clock over the stove told him it was almost noon. Normally, he slept till mid-afternoon, being that he worked nights at the Grey Owl Casino. But ever since his girl friend, Paula, and her roommate Nancy had moved in, he'd volunteered to sleep on the hard canvas cot. His second story coldwater flat had two small bedrooms, a bathroom and tiny kitchen/dining area.

Crandall's room, which he'd given over to the girls, was to the right of the bathroom. The one to the left was occupied by a dead man; Brother Bones.

With his bare feet on the cold linoleum floor, dressed in pants and a tee-shirt, the freckled face card dealer, began pinching the inner corner of his eyes to rub the sleep out of them. He stood and felt a stab of pain in his lower back.

If I don't get my bed back soon, I'm going to be crippled for life, he mused as he walked around the small square table in the middle of the room. He filled the empty black pot with water from the sink, placed it back on the stove and got a fire going under it. He would feel better once he'd had his coffee.

Leaving the stove, he again circumnavigated the table and walked into the bathroom. As he did so, his face plowed into something wet.

"Agh!" He fell back a step switching on the light. A small rope extended across the facility from over the bathtub to the left and right wall above the sink. On this makeshift clothesline hung several feminine pieces of underwear including the brassiere that he had walked into.

"Damn it!" He pushed the still damp bra aside, closed the door behind him and went over to the toilet to take care of business. That done, he went to the sink, now cluttered not only with his own soap and toothbrush, but two others and along with a can of talcum powder. As he brushed his teeth, glaring at himself in the mirror, Bobby Crandall was decidedly not happy.

He rinsed his mouth out, wiped it dry with a hand towel and stepped back into the kitchen to his second surprise. Paula Wozcheski was on the other side of the door and he jumped. "YAHH!!"

The tall, beautiful brunette with the crystal blue eyes couldn't help but start laughing.

"That's not funny," Crandall barked. "You could have given me a heart attack."

"Oh, Bobby," she was wearing an old pink cotton bathrobe. "I'm sorry."

She stepped up to him and draped her arms around his neck pressing her full, womanly body against his. "Really, I am."

He was unable to resist her. It had been that way from the start when they had first met at the club. Paula had been hired as a cigarette girl and seeing her in that sexy outfit of high heel shoes, fishnet stockings and satin bustier had frozen lots of men in their tracks. At the time she'd been married to a longshoreman. He was dead now.

As her lips touched his, Crandall reflected, *Longevity isn't a Cape Noire normal.*

He couldn't help but wrap his arms around her waist and pull her in tighter for the kiss, her ample bosom crushing into his shirt. He was nuts about her and his hungry lips made that abundantly clear.

Even after Paula Woscheski had become a vampire, Bobby Crandall refused to let her break off their relationship. He didn't care that she fed on the blood of others to survive. She was his one true love and his devotion to her would never end.

"Hey, easy, tiger," Woscheski laughed, breaking their embrace. "Kind of early for romance, don't you think?" Then she nodded her head towards the closed bedroom door. "And don't forget him."

"Bones, ah, you don't get it. He doesn't give a damn about anything, Paula. Really. He is dead. Well, at least as dead as any zombie that gets its marching orders from the spirit world can be."

Steam poured out of the pot and began whistling loudly.

"Sit down, Bobby, I'll get it." She removed two cups from the overhead pantry and filled them with brewed coffee. She then took the chair opposite Bobby's and handed him the green porcelain cup. Both of them like it black. That wasn't anything special with him but it remained an intriguing wonder for her.

From the books she'd read as a young girl back in Poland, Paula Wozcheski had believed when anyone became a vampire they lost all appetites for anything other than human blood. Whereas she'd been one such toothy undead for almost a year now, she had noticed no diminishing of her earthly pleasures; both from enjoying food and drink to the more erotica dalliance. In fact her vampirism had actually augmented her

HE COULDN'T HELP BUT WRAP HIS ARMS AROUND HER AND PULL HER IN TIGHTER FOR THE KISS...

passions in those intimate categories. Bobby Crandall having become the primary benefactor of those heightened sensibilities.

"Have you and Nancy made any progress with finding a new place?" He asked, after tasting the bitter elixir. As ever the caffeine began to have its desired stimulating effects.

"Nancy says she's gotten a few good leads at the diner."

As if on cue, there was a clinking of a key at the front door and it opened pushed by the blonde waitress from the Wooden Spoon, Nancy Hanson. She was mildly surprised to see both Paula and Bobby awake.

"Hi all," she greeted, pulling her purse off her shoulder and dropping it on the nearest chair before her. "How's everyone doing today?" The petite blonde was a bubbly soul and always maintained a cheery disposition.

"Considering I may need back surgery soon," Crandall said straightening up and raising his hands to the ceiling to pop his back joints. "Everything is just hunky-dory."

"Don't listen to him," Woschesky laughed. "He's just got up on the wrong side of the cot is all." She pointed to the pot. "The pot's fresh, if you want some."

"No thanks, Paula. I had lunch before leaving the diner. I need to wash up a little and get some rest."

"Did you hear any more about possible apartments?"

"Yes, in fact the cook told me about a place only a few blocks away that sounded perfect for us and affordable. I have the address in my bag."

"See," the sexy vampire slapped one of Crandall's hands. "I told you we'd be out of your hair in no time."

"Thank God for little favors," he chuckled touching the stubble on his chin. "I'm gonna need to shave later."

"No worries," Hanson assured him. "I just need to brush my teeth, throw some water on my face and then I'll be out of your way." She started for the open bathroom door when she remembered something and turned to her brunette pal.

"Oh, I almost forgot, I saw that lady reporter from the Tribune this morning."

"You mean Sally Paige." Woscheski had met the spunky newshound a while back in her guise as Sister Blood. "She stopped in for breakfast?"

"Actually she was there to find her a detective from police headquarters. Some guy named Rains."

At that Bobby Crandall interrupted. "Dan Rains? Big guy with square shoulders and a rock hard jaw."

"Yeah, that's him. Still, he's kind of cute if you like them like that." The girl grinned. "Then again, who doesn't, hey Paula?"

"You know him?" Woscheski asked her freckled face lover.

"I don't. Personally that is, but he and Bones have had run-ins before. On the whole of it, Bones says he's one of the few honest cops in Cape Noire."

"Interesting. Maybe this guy and Paige are friends," the blue eyed beauty surmised.

"It looked like it," Nancy Hanson continued. "I mean, it was obvious they were acquainted, but I also got the feeling something wasn't right."

"How do you mean?" Crandall pressed.

"Oh, I don't know. He was already eating his meal when she showed up. And from what I could tell, she was kind of upset with him. But then he got her to calm down."

Both Crandall and Wozcheski waited for more and the tired waitress concluded. "That was it. I wasn't about to snoop. Now if you'll both excuse me." She went into the bathroom and closed the door behind her.

"Hmm, so what do you make of that, Bobby?"

"Could be nothing, Paula. Maybe Rains and Paige are just friends. Or she was there about a news story. It could be lots of things."

"Right, but with all these gang wars lately, I hope she isn't in some kind of a jam."

"Look, Paula. Best to just leave it alone. You don't need to go looking for trouble."

"Maybe you're right, sweetie." Paula Woscheski drained the rest of her coffee while thinking, *Still, maybe I should pay Miss Paige a visit.*

☠ ☠ ☠

Alexis Wyld sat behind her massive office desk studying her guests seated in the comfortable padded chairs before her. To her left was Rita Mayfield, a platinum blonde woman clearly wary of being in her presence. Occupying the other chair was the gaunt, pale scientist from California, Anton Petrus. Unlike Mayfield, Petrus looked bored, sitting up straight, his hands resting on the arms of the chair.

Behind the both of them, leaning back against the wall by the room's only door, was Wyld's bodyguard/chauffeur, Lucas Garret. His cap was held loosely in his hands as he silently awaited any further instructions from his mistress.

"Welcome to my home," Wyld began with a smile. "Thank you for accepting my invitation."

"Did we have choice?" Petrus asked the obvious question.

"You did, sir," Wyld responded amused. "Whereas you would not have enjoyed the consequences of any other decision. As I'm sure Mr. Garrett would have made clear."

Refusing to be toyed with, the professor opted to forego senseless banter. "With respect, Miss Wyld, why are we here?"

"Easily answered, sir. I wish to know why Harry Beest is tearing the city apart looking for the two of you?"

"You are well informed," Petrus commented.

"Ten to one she paid off one of Beest's men," Mayfield interjected. "Am I right?"

The two women locked eyes. Wyld nodded. "Perceptive—Miss Mayfield, isn't it?"

"Yes, Rita Mayfield. I was Albert…"

"I know who you are, Rita. It is your friend who is the mystery to me."

"I am a Doctor of Applied Physics, Miss Wyld," Petrus declared boastfully. "And a one time colleague of the late Prof. Bugosi."

Wyld's reaction was immediate. "Aha, and now this begins to make sense. I had assumed Harry would try and find someone else to replaced Bugosi. Someone who could replicate what he had done and thus put the old boy's brain back into a human body.

"Correct?"

"Yes, madam. Mr. Beest sent several of his employees down to California to bring me here with that express purpose in mind."

"So what happened?"

It was Mayfield who answered. "Before the prof here could fully study all the data that was in Bugosi's place, it was attached by a rival outfit with a grudge against the gorilla goon."

Wyld snapped her fingers. "Ace Bricker!"

"That's the name I heard," the blond confirmed. "In the shootout, my guy was gunned down but not before telling me to take Anton and get lost fast."

"And as I eventually deduced, you wisely played it safe by staying in Carrington's home." Alexi Wyld's admiration of Mayfield went up several notches.

"Well, I wasn't all that smart. You found us, didn't you?"

"Come, Rita. Give me some credit. I'm not surprised poor old Harry never put it all together. That's why what's left of his gang is still running around town without a clue as to where to find the two of you. I find that really funny."

"Be that as it may," Petrus shrugged. "What happens to us now? Are we your prisoners, Miss Wyld? In which case we seem to be no better off than before."

"On the contrary, Prof. Petrus, you and Rita are free to leave at any time. In fact tell Mr. Garrett where you would like to go and I will have him take you there."

No one spoke for the next few minutes and Wyld's visitors digested her words. Seeing they were staying silent, she continued.

"On the other hand, I would very much like to make you an offer, Professor."

"What kind of offer?"

"Decide to remain here in Cape Noire and allow me to be your sponsor."

"Sponsor?"

"Patron, whatever word you prefer. Look, what I am suggesting is this. In the past I maintained a very profitable relationship with Prof. Bugosi. At the same time I kept him relatively safe from any of Harry's threats. You have to understand, Harry knew his only chance of ever being human again was to see that no harm ever befell Bugosi."

"But when Bugosi was killed, all that went to hell," Petrus put the pieces together.

"Exactly," Wyld applauded him. "Now I find myself without someone of those skills and Beest is going bananas, if you'll excuse the puns. Which isn't good for any of us."

"Agreed, Madam. So in what shape or form would this sponsorship take? I have no funds, no means to build a working laboratory."

"You leave all that to me, sir. That is the crux of my offer. If you agree to remain here in Cape Noire, I will find a suitable place where you and Miss Mayfield can reside and where you can build your laboratory. To that end I will fund every nut and bolt you require to build such a scientific facility with no questions asked."

"You will be free to work on whatever projects you desire with no interference from me?'

"But what do you get in return, Miss Wyld?"

"Only your promise to assist me whenever I have a problem requiring your particular skills. If you agree to those terms, then I assure you both of us will benefit greatly from such a partnership."

"And what of Mr….ah..Beest?"

"Again, you leave Harry Beest to me. I will deal with him and as long as our partnership remains in place, you will never have to worry about him ever threatening you again."

Petrus ran a hand through his hair in contemplation.

"Whoa," Rita Mayfield's voice rose up. "What's any of this got to do with me?"

"That's entirely up to you," Wyld replied smoothly. "If you want to leave, there's the door. For whatever reasons, Rita, you became a part of this and I think you've got a really good head on your shoulders. I would feel much more confident knowing the good professor here had someone as strong and quick-thinking as you by his side."

"Well, thanks. I guess."

"And I'll pay you."

"You will?"

"Of course. If I'm going to bankroll his new lab, it's only fair you get something out of the deal. Say yes and you are on salary as of right now."

"Well, hot damn." Rita Mayfield turned to Petrus. "What do you say, Prof?"

The scientist shrugged one more time. "I suppose it's a reasonable plan. All right, we will accept your offer, Miss Wyld."

Alexis Wyld stood and reached out her hand. The thin Petrus went over and clasped it.

"Mr. Garrett," the Queen of Crime ordered. "Get us a bottle of champagne. We have some celebrating to do."

☠ ☠ ☠

While Alexis Wyld and her company enjoyed their drinks, upstairs the reincarnated Lilith Delamore reveled in her rebirth. After sending out her psychic command to the furry rodents of Cape Noire, the powerful witch returned to trying on more of her host's elegant gowns and dresses. The hours flew by but she didn't tire, twirling around the richly adorned suite like a little girl playing in a giant dollhouse.

Meanwhile across the giant seaport, the rats of Cape Noire scurried through the maze of sewers and gutters that stretched for miles below the busy streets. From the commercial city center to the outlying blocks and into the far off suburban neighborhoods, the millions of furry creatures went about their one singular task; find the one who wore the white skull mask and then relate that location to their master.

It was after two in the afternoon when Wyld's aide, Amanda Wesley, knocked on the bedroom door.

"Come in," Lilith said, as she fastened a small leather belt about her trim waist.

Miss Wesley entered and took in the chic green dress and white blouse Lilith modeled in front of the full length mirror. "That looks lovely on you," she offered politely. It was a far cry from her own conservative gray slacks and blouse.

"Yes, it does, doesn't it," the haughty witch agreed without even glancing at the secretary.

"Miss Wyld asks if you would join her for a late lunch in the dining room?"

"Hmm," Lilith looked at her dazzling reflection and patted the soft blonde curls over both her ears. "I am a bit hungry. Yes. I'd be delighted to join her." She turned to the efficient young woman and waved her hand towards the hall. "Lead the way, Miss Wesley."

Ten minutes later, Lilith was seated across a long, beautiful polished mahogany table that was the centerpiece of the richly decorated dining room. At the center of the long rectangular table was a small bouquet of freshly cut flowers with two silver candelabras placed to either side of them. Alexis Wyld had been waiting at the head of the table which was near the door to the kitchen and at her invitation; Lilith had taken the seat to her immediate right.

"That outfit was made for you," Wyld complimented as she picked up a bottle of red wine and poured each of them a glass. "I'm told we're having roast beef with potatoes au gratin. I believe you'll enjoy it; my chef graduated from a fine culinary school in Paris."

"It sounds wonderful," Lilith took a sip of her wine. "Mmm, if it is half as tasty as this wine, I'm sure it will be delicious."

Wyld took the folded cotton napkin next to her plate and snapped it open before placing it over her lap. "Have you made any progress in your task to find Brother Bones?"

"Some," the beautiful sorceress admitted as she too laid her own napkin over the top of her dress. "I feel confident in saying that by day's end, I will have that information for you."

"And then?"

"And then, Miss Wyld, with your help, I will go and destroy him."

"Marvelous, my dear. That's exactly what I'd hoped you'd say."

The door behind Wyld was pushed open and a maid appeared pushing a cart before her. She was followed by a round little fellow in a white chef's outfit.

"Ah," Wyld sniffed. "That smells divine. Now let's eat."

It was shortly after six o'clock when Brother Bones the Undead Avenger watched the sun sink into the Pacific Ocean. As ever, his dead eyes merely beheld the event without any actual emotional reaction. After all, how much beauty can a dead man appreciate? No, his lot was merely to sit in his chair in the apartment's corner bedroom and look out the window at the same scene day and night. He could see Whittington park only a few blocks away toward the northeast and while straight ahead were the warehouses of Old Town and the docks.

The window itself was open half-way and a cool evening breeze ruffled the curtains. The same breeze washed over his dead countenance, as his almost jet black eyes continued to stare forward. Bones had been dead for several years while his body had decayed to a certain point of decomposition and then became frozen. It was as if it had been allowed to rot so far and then the supernatural forces that animated it had reached a specific status and thus ceased all normal activity.

And so the dead man sat. Never sleeping, never dreaming. Never thinking. He just sat until the cosmic forces that had created him required his services. At which point, he would rise up and go forth bringing gun-blasting justice to the savages of Cape Noire. And that was the irony of his very existence for in his own time of living, Brother Bones had been Tommy Bonello, a heartless killer employed by Topper Wyld. Now he was nothing more than a weapon to be used in righting the karmic unbalance that existed in the hellhole that was Cape Noire.

As darkness descended on the streets outside, a tiny flame flicked to life on the long single candle resting on the bureau behind the seated corpse. Bones turned his horrid face and registered the dancing flame. With stiff precision, he rose up from the chair and walked to the bureau. His dead eyes looked into the small red and yellow fire and within seconds the image of a pretty teenage girl materialized.

The girl had been one of Tommy Bonello's last victims; a young prostitute whose short life had ended with her being at the wrong place at the wrong time. Tommy had shot her, along with everyone in that doomed bordello. Now, she existed in a place of limbo chosen by cosmic fates to be his spirit guide. It was she who delivered their messages and gave the Undead Avenger his marching orders.

"A powerful evil has come to Cape Noire," she told him in her sweet voice. "It is an old evil with its roots deep in the city."

As she spoke, a thin wispy figure began to take shape over the bed that was never slept in.

"See the evil's first new victim," the female guide told him. Brother Bones looked at the ghost of an old man, who moaned from an almost toothless mouth. "He was eaten by her pets, an army of rats."

Bones watched in silence as the last lingering representation of Morris Langier faded away from this reality.

"Justice must be served," the girl repeated as she had done with all her previous appearances. "But there is more, Bones. Another spirit rises forth. One you must heed completely...or else you will perish."

With that the familiar face of the girl vanished only to be replaced by that of a young man with a red bandanna wrapped around his forehead. He was an Indian with long black hair and sharp facial features. As ever, Brother Bones remained attentive.

"Greetings Bone Man, I am Cheveyo," the Indian announced. "But you can call me Sam."

☠ ☠ ☠

Sally Paige rubbed her eyes and yawned. The Tribune's open city room was almost deserted with most of the staff either having departed or in the process of doing so. A few desks on either side of the main aisle had their lights still on.

"Hey, Paige, you ever go home?" Dominic Collier asked as he shut his own desk light off. The senior sports writer had his fedora on and his sports jacket draped over one arm.

"Almost there, Dom," she fired back stretching. "I need to have this follow up piece on the boss' desk before I head out." The boss was Managing Editor Hank Anderson whose office was located at the end of the hall. He'd left hours ago saying he had a dinner date with the publisher.

"Well, get it," Collier added. "You know what they say about all work and no play." He tipped his hat and then meandered off towards the elevators.

Paige took a deep breath, and then rolled out the last sheet of her story from her Smith Corona typewriter. She added it to two other written pages sitting atop a copy of the Tribune's evening edition that had hit the newsstand an hour earlier. Across the front page was the bold heading, POLICE CHIEF ASSURES SAFETY.

"You know, your friend is right," a voice spoke from behind Paige. Startled, she swung her swivel chair around to peer into the shadowy area between her desk and the front wall. From the inky black spot between two tall windows a masked female figure appeared.

Dressed in riding boots, jophur pants, a bright red blouse, opera cape and a delicate lace mask over her eyes, Sister Blood was as always a very dramatic sight.

"Good evening, Miss Paige."

"Sister Blood," the reporter rose to her feet. "To what do I owe the pleasure?"

"Simple curiosity, Sally," the vampire replied.

"About what?" This was the second time the undead lady had come to see Paige.

"I'm told you had a heated conversation with someone at the Wooden Spoon diner earlier today."

"Huh?" Paige cocked her head. "You mean my meeting with Dan Rains?"

"Yes."

"How'd you know about that?"

"You were served by a blood waitress."

"Nancy," Paige recalled. "Her name was Nancy."

"She is a friend. As I believe you to be."

"So what did she tell you?"

"Only that you met and talked with this police detective."

"And that concerns you how?"

Sister Blood smiled and stepping around Paige, leaned back on the edge of her desk. "The last time we met, I told you my purpose was to protect the women of this city."

"I haven't forgotten."

"Then know, when I learned you were having what my friend called a purposeful conversation with a police officer, I was naturally curious as to why. My concern, as you ask, is only for your continued well being."

"You needn't worry about that."

"Good to know."

"But it's Dan Rains I'm worried about."

"Why?"

"He was just put on temporary leave by the new police chief, Edgar Torrance for no other reason than he had the nerve to question Alexis Wyld about a kidnapping."

"Wyld, the so called Queen of Crime?"

"One and the same. After Rains visited her place, she filed a complaint with the Chief and he follow up by taking Dan's badge."

The sexy blood-sucker studied Paige's facial expressions. "There's more, isn't there?"

"Maybe, though Dan was a bit evasive, he seems to think it was all a set up. That Torrance is on Wyld's payroll and crooked. He just can't prove it."

"Can you?"

"I don't know. Maybe with some digging I can find something. Still, in the meanwhile one of Cape Noire's only honest cops sits on the sidelines twiddling his thumbs. It's just not right."

"No, Sally, it isn't. Then again, maybe there's something I can do to speed things along."

"What? No! You wouldn't?"

"Oh, please, nothing so drastic as that. But maybe it wouldn't hurt if I had a little chat with the new Chief. You know, just to persuade him to change his mind."

Sally Paige had to admit, she liked what Sister Blood was hinting about. She grinned and said, "Well, a little talk wouldn't be so bad."

They both started laughing together.

☻ ☻ ☻

Back at the dingy cold-water flat, the spirit of the half-breed Indian continued his tale for the Undead Avenger.

"For many years, I traveled the western states accompanied by another like you."

"Like me?" Bones' voice was chilling to hear. It sounded like a rasp devoid of any true warmth or emotions.

"A dead man who walked," Sam elaborated. "I had the power to animate the dead and so controlled a dead lawman to fight the outlaws and collect the bounty on their heads. It really wasn't a bad life. We even had a fancy Boston newspaper man who rode with us and chronicled our adventures. Maybe you read some of them?"

At that Bones had no comment.

"Naw...probably not. Well, our travels led us here to Cape Noire long

"FOR MANY YEARS, I TRAVELED THE WESTERN STATES ACCOMPANIED BY ANOTHER LIKE YOU."

ago. The town wasn't very old at the time and just as wild and crazy as any other frontier hellhole. Still, by then I was older and tired. We had plenty of money by then and decided to quit and settle down.

"Which was great for a long time until that bitch Lilith Delamore arrived. She had a coven up at Crystal Cove and the town leaders tried to shut them down. All the preachy folks really didn't like the idea of a witch cult operating in their back yard.

"Of course Lilith didn't like that one little bit and one night, starting on the busiest shipping dock, she showed up with her army of rats and tried to burn down the entire city. Which is why I had to come out of retirement and end her madness."

"How did you do that?"

"Magic, my dead amigo. You see the same magic that let me control and manipulate a dead man also let me do lots of other things. So there I was battling with Lilith and I kept her busy long enough to have one of the dead cops she had killed get up and shoot her in the head. And that was it. One shot and the end of Lilith.

"Or so I thought."

"What does that mean?" This was the longest story Brother Bones had ever listened to. He didn't like long stories.

"Well, it wasn't till days later that I learned most of Lilith's powers came from a snake-head pendant she wore around her neck. When I went to where she'd been buried, I learned that several members of her coven had already gone there and had retrieved it.

"For the longest time, I wondered if any of them would take up where she'd left off but that never happened. Until now."

"Get to the point, Sam."

"Hey, take it easy, Bone Man. I haven't had so much fun since I died. Now that's a story you…"

"Stop! What about this witch? Was she responsible for the wino's murder."

"You betcha, Bone Man. Somehow Lilith has come back through the use of another body."

Brother Bones groaned.

"Yeah, I thought that would get to you," Sam commented. "All too familiar, isn't it?"

"Not about me. What is her plan now?"

"Well, the same as ever, I suppose; to destroy the city."

"She'll have to get through me first."

"I think that is her plan. And remember, Mr. Undead Avenger, she wields magic. Something I'm told can easily defeat you."

"That is true. How do I defeat her?"

The ghostly image of young Indian scratched his head and then asked, "I suppose you wouldn't have any magic of your own would you?"

Brother Bones sighed and then a glimmer sparked his black eyes from the candle glow and he replied. "Maybe I do."

"Then good luck, Bone Man," were Sam's parting words. His face was consumed by the flames. Then a gust of wind from the open window extinguished the candle. A curl of smoke wafted upwards and in the darkness, Brother Bones laughed.

Normally Blackjack Bobby Crandall's shift at the Gray Owl Casino ended between one and two a.m. Whereas the recent city shootings had spooked many of the club's regular clientele and so the place had been half full the past few nights. In frustration the owner opted to shut the place down as midnight arrived. Crandall was only too happy to oblige. Maybe he could get a few more hours of asleep on the old cot once back at the apartment.

Usually Paula Wozcheski rode home with him, but this night she'd told him she wasn't ready to do so. She said the hunger was upon her and she had some hunting to do. Watching the sexy vampire walk away down the street, Crandall shuddered at what those words actually meant. As he pulled his roadster away from the curb, he felt some pity for whoever entered the path of Sister Blood.

Of course he knew she had always kept her vow to only feed on the city's lowlife scumbags, he could still imagine their fear when she fell upon them.

God, this city is sick, he thought as he drove the few blocks to the apartment complex where he and the Undead Avenger resided. *Guess that includes me. I'm in love with a vampire. Now that's anything but normal.*

Crandall always parked on the side street next to their building. It was near impossible to find an empty space on the main avenue. He made his way up the cement steps to the front door, entered and then jogged up the wooden steps to the second floor. Their flat was located to the left of the landing.

He used his key, unlocked the door and walked in switching on the kitchen light as he did so. And there was Brother Bones in full attire, seated at the kitchen table facing him.

Crandall's heart did a skip.

"Shit," he yelled. "Will you stop doing that! It scares the crap out of me."

"Quiet," the Undead Avenger spoke through his white skull mask. "You'll wake the girl."

Crandall looked at the closed door to his bedroom remembering Nancy Hanson. He approached the table and whispered. "So what's going on?" For the first time he noticed the small lacquered rectangular box on the table in front of Bones.

"I have been summoned."

"Okay." Crandall knew what that meant. "So where to?"

Brother Bones pushed his chair away from the table, and adjusted the slouch hat on his head. As he did so his jacket opened and Crandall saw his twin .45 automatics in their under-the-arm leather holsters.

"Whittington Park. It is there our evil witch will find us." The Undead Avenger picked up the box and joined Crandall as he opened the door wide.

"What's in the box?"

"A gun," Bones replied and started for the stairs.

"Whittington Park? Are you positive?" Alexis Wyld asked Lilith Delamore. She was seated behind her desk, wearing a dark blue silk robe having been roused from her bed by Mr. Garrett upon Lilith's request. Garrett, as ever, stood against the back wall, fully clothed. For a moment, Wyld wondered if he ever slept.

"Of course," the smiling Delamore affirmed as she sat in one of the plush chairs. "My little pets saw him entering the park not ten minutes ago." Upon receiving the message they had all been waiting for, the blonde witch had dressed hurriedly and summoned Mr. Garrett, per his mistress' standing orders. She had wanted to be notified the minute Brother Bones had been found.

Now Wyld looked to her bodyguard. "How long will it take to get there?"

"It is a fifteen minute drive, Miss Wyld."

"All right, then, as soon as I get dressed…"

"Excuse me, Miss Wyld." Lucas Garrett never interrupted his boss.

"Yes, Mr. Garrett. Is there something else?"

"I don't think you should go. The park is a not a safe place, with its proximity to Old Town, and if Brother Bones is indeed present then it will be dangerous as well."

Alexis Wyld clasped her hands together and thought over what her man had said. Mr. Garrett was not a person given over to unfounded anxieties. If he thought it unwise for her to go to the park, then she had to reconsider.

"Mr. Garrett, I am not afraid of Brother Bones."

"Of course not, Madam. But my concern is for your well being only. Allow Miss Delamore to confront Bones and complete his destruction. I'm sure she is more than capable of seeing this through. And I will be present to offer her any assistance she may require."

"All I need, Mr. Garrett is transportation to the park. Once there, I am more than capable of dealing with that white masked fool." Lilith clutched the pendant hanging around her neck to remind Wyld of her powers. "From everything you've told me, this entity has no way to match my powers.

"I will dispatch him hastily and then bring you back his head; tied in a pretty bow if you'd like?"

Wyld looked from Garrett to the witch. Though her demand for vengeance continued to push within her mind, she hadn't built the city's powerful criminal empire by acting rashly. In the end, she quieted that inner turmoil and acquiesced.

"Very well, Mr. Garrett. I will accept your judgment on this matter." Then she turned to Lilith. "Do not fail me, Lilith. I am sick and tired of this game. Tonight Brother Bones must die…permanently."

☻ ☻ ☻

Chief Edgar Torrance often fell asleep in the comfortable reclining chair in his living room. As he had done many times since moving to Cape Noire, the head cop would have dinner at a nearby restaurant, then retire to his small Cape Cod style bungalow located at the southern tip of Baker St. It was a quiet residential area that suited him well as he lived alone. He'd been married once, back when he was only a Lieutenant Detective in Chicago. Problem was Torrance had a roving eye for the ladies. He couldn't keep his hands off them, regardless of the wedding ring on his finger. After three years of abuse and neglect, Mrs. Torrance packed her bags, filed for a divorce and bid him farewell.

Though it didn't do his public image any good, Torrance found he enjoyed being a bachelor again and promised he'd never saddle himself with one woman ever again.

After his shower, he'd donned his white with blue stripes pajamas and soft slippers to relax and listen to the radio. It was the first chance he'd had to open the bottle of expensive Scotch that had been delivered to him at headquarters that afternoon. There was no note attached, but he knew it was from Alexis Wyld. It was her way of repaying him for the little favor he'd done her.

The first drink went down so smoothly, he decided to have a second. And then a third..and then he put down his empty glass. His eyelids were heavy and he drifted off, his head falling to one side.

He was snoring when a noise abruptly ended his slumber. Torrance's head jerked up and he looked around. Buzzing sounded from the radio to his right. It was the off-air signal the station sent out when it ended its broadcast day.

"My, my, don't you look all comfy cozy," a female voice declared.

Torrance looked to the dark hall between the living room and the kitchen, which he rarely used. "Who's there?" he barked, his right hand slowly dropping to his side. Under the seat cushion was a snub-nose .38 caliber police special.

"I am," Sister Blood said stepping out of the shadows into the lighted area provided by the stand-up lamp to the left of Torrance's chair.

Torrance sat up straight, pushing the foot-rest part of his chair back into its resting slot. He slowly inspected his unexpected visitor from the tip of her black riding boots to the pale face and satin mask wrapped around her eyes.

"And who the hell are you, missy."

"I'm called Sister Blood, Chief. I thought it was time we got acquainted."

"Is that so?" Torrance's right hand reached under the cushion to find the revolver's grip. "And to what do I owe the pleasure?"

"Oh, there isn't going to be any pleasure. At least not for you."

Torrance got to his feet quickly while at the same time whipping his arm around and pointing the gun at his garishly dressed intruder.

"Freeze right there, lady," he ordered.

"Oh, I knew this was going to be fun," Sister Blood licked her lower lip with her tongue. She raised both hands palms out. "Shall we dance?"

Before Torrance knew what had happened, Sister Blood was directly in front of him.

"Boo!" Startled, Torrance pulled the trigger; the gun barrel was only an inch from her stomach. The sound was deafening.

Edgar Torrance had shot many people in his eighteen year career. He knew first hand the affects of a shot at close range and he was ready for this woman's body to go flying backward.

But that never happened. It was as if the bullet had gone right through her abdomen having no effect on her at all.

She looked into his eyes and smiled. "Ouch." Then before he could fire another round, her hands grabbed his robe tightly. She picked him up off his feet and threw him effortlessly into the gray couch to his right. Like a leaf caught in an autumn gale, Edgar Torrance's body soared through the air and slammed into the sofa. It shook under him, the impact cracking one of the wooden legs so that one end collapsed.

Dazed, Torrance tried to stand. The gun was still in his hand. Sister Blood was coming for him. He aimed at her chest and fired two more rounds. But just like that, she wasn't there. Like a puff of smoke, she just wasn't there. He blinked, looked down at the revolver as if it was defective somehow.

Sister Blood kicked his hand and he felt bones break. The gun was sent spinning into the hallway. Then she was picking him up again. Her finger nails had become claws that tore into his chest as she raised his head towards the ceiling.

"NOOOO!!" he cried. "NO!"

"Aw, you're no fun at all." She threw him across the room and he hit the bookshelf against that wall. He dropped to the floor hard, the wind knocked out of him.

Sister Blood pushed aside another padded chair to reach him. Once more her hands took hold of his shoulders and he was yanked to his feet. The motion caused his broken wrist to send a jabbing pain up his arm. He tried to cradle it, as she shoved him against the broken shelf.

"No more, please. No more."

"Listen to me carefully, Chief, because I am only going to say this once. Tomorrow, after you've had your busted up hand taken care of, you are going call Lt. Dan Rains and tell him he is back on the force."

"What? Rains?" Torrance was scared, hurting and confused all at the same time.

Sister Blood slapped him across face. "Shut your mouth and listen, you dump ox. You are going to lift his suspension. Do you understand that?"

"Yes...but Alexis ..."

"Alexis Wyld be damned." Sister Blood leaned closer and opened her mouth. Torrance saw her upper incisors as they began to grow into long, sharp points. "I am what you need to worry about now."

"What...are... you?"

Sister Blood didn't answer. Instead she used her right hand to push his head to the side, exposing his neck. Then she bit into it and began to drink Torrance's blood.

He wanted to scream, but from the second her fangs ripped into his vein, he was helpless. It was as if his nervous system had been shocked. Every inch of his body was burning from within and he couldn't move a single muscle.

Sister Blood continued to drink feeling her own energy being renewed as she took in Torrance's lifeforce. She hadn't drunk in several days and now it took all her own resolved not to kill the man. She lifted up her head, blood smearing her lower chin and she took a step back. She continued to hold him up, though now he was weak and barely conscious.

"Pay attention, Torrance," she warned him. "I could have drained you completely. Do you understand me? Do you?"

"Yes," his voice was a murmur.

"Which I will do if you do not comply with my wishes. And there is nothing you can do to stop me. Remember that."

She let him go and Edgar Torrance sank to the floor in a heap. Head lowered, he began to weep. He disgusted her. *Maybe I should have finished him. Still there's no guarantee his replacement would be any better.*

Sister Blood wiped her chin and licked the blood off her palm. She walked out of the room and back into the night she loved so much.

💀 💀 💀

A dense fog had descended over the city by the time Lucas Garrett drove the silver Rolls Royce through the southern entrance of Whittington Park. On the trip through Cape Noire, they had encountered almost no traffic except for an occasional taxi, city bus or black and white patrol car. The sidewalks were mostly deserted and the further he went from downtown, the more limited was their view.

The fog was a blanket that hugged the dew wet ground and hid so many shapes, including the road lanes that wove through the thirty acre park.

"This is far enough," Lilith Delamore said from the back seat. "I will get out here, if you please."

Garrett brought the expensive automobile to a stop near a solitary lamp post and shut off his headlights. In doing so it seemed like the white pea-soup pressed in closer. He jumped out of the front seat and opened the back door to the witch queen.

"Are you sure you don't want me to go with you, Madam. With this fog, it's almost impossible to see the trails that crisscross the grounds."

"Are you suggesting I might get lost, Mr. Garrett?" Delamore wore only a short woolen jacket over her dress and yet did not seem bothered by the chill in the air. With its proximity to the ocean, Cape Noire's temperature was always on the cold side, especially its nights.

"I didn't mean any disrespect, Madam."

"Mr. Garrett, I walked these trails long before your grandparents were born. There is nothing here that can either surprise or harm me."

With that she brought up her hands, said a few words he could not understand and then both hands were encompassed by balls of light. It was as if they were encased in empty, hot snow-globes.

She held them up to him. "I am ready for your Brother Bones. Rest assured, this will not take long. Try not to fall asleep while I'm gone."

Before he could assure her that was unlikely, Delamore walked off into the thick fog, her glowing hands the last two points of her presence disappearing down the worn dirt path. Garrett worried about her overconfidence but it was not his place to argue. He got back into the car and sat back to wait.

As Lilith walked along, she began to hear the tiny rodents race along the grassy plains and knolls all around her. She stopped for a second and mentally called to them. One by one, hundreds of rats began to appear circling her slowly, their small furry shapes coming only so close. Their tiny eyes all looking up at her awaiting further commands.

"Ah, my babies," she cooed. "You've done such a fine job thus far. Now, take me to the one with the skull mask. Take me to Brother Bones and we shall end this."

As one, the rat army moved and scampered off ahead of her. She laughed and hasted her pace to keep up with them.

Up and down, around ponds and children's sand boxes, the path wove through the gloomy park. The fifteen-foot-tall lampposts were set at twenty yard intervals but on this night, their glow was ineffective in repelling the inky blackness that enveloped the terrain.

Lilith walked past several huge granite boulders that led to a beautifully ornate carousel that was the heart of Whittington Park. It was here, during the warm days of summer, that the children of Cape Noire came to await their turns in riding the brightly painted horses, lions, tigers, and bears as they whirled around to the loud calliope music.

Upon reaching the three-foot-high locked gates and empty ticket booth, the rats came to a halt and began chattering in their squeaky voices.

The witch felt a supernatural force before her. She stopped and raising her hands, made the light from both increase in brightness. She sent their light into the carousel.

"Come now, Brother Bones. I know you are there. Let us not delay this any longer than we have to."

The Undead Avenger had been standing in the middle of the round wooden base, near the engine block that powered the ride. He now stepped between several stationary horses and out into the light of Lilith's illuminating hands. His white porcelain mask glimmering from that eerie light, his black eyes visible beneath the wide brim of his slouch hat.

"At last, the savior of Cape Noire," Lilith mocked, bending over in a slight curtsy.

"I am no savior," Bones retorted stepping onto the ground without any thought for the gathered vermin. When his shoe touched down, those nearest squealed and rush away. As did more when the second foot landed. Methodically he stepped through the furry brown army and they fled him hastily.

"I'm impressed," the resurrected Daughter of the Devil nodded. "You do have some supernatural force within you after all."

"That, or your rats just don't like dead meat."

"Perhaps. Then again, maybe they prefer their meal properly cooked."

She began to wave her hands about her once again mouthing ancient phrases.

Before she could finish, Brother Bones pulled opened his trench coat and whipped out his .45 automatics.

"By the way, Cheveyo sends his regards."

Lilith's eyes widened. "Cheveyo!?"

Then Bones blasted away with both guns. Half a dozen slugs were shot at Delamore but none ever reached their target for in a split second, the glow about her hands ballooned outward surrounding her entire body. The bullets hit the yellow shield and melted instantly.

"Ha, ha, ha," she cackled. "So you thought to startle me with mentioning that old Indian. Pathetic."

"It was worth a try," the Undead Avenger shrugged.

"Did Cheveyo tell you it was only by luck that he defeated me?"

"He said his magic was stronger than yours."

Lilith Delamore once again waved her hands about and from them a bolt of lightning shot forth hitting Bones in the chest. He fell on his back hard. Then the same bolt wrapped around him and at her direction, lifted him up into the air where he remained suspended; unable to move a single dead muscle.

"Magic that you obviously do not possess," she concluded. "You're certainly no shaman, zombie. You're nothing but a walking corpse. After I burn you to ash, you will be nothing but a memory."

Floating stationary four feet off the ground, Brother Bones prepared his final gambit.

"Before you light me up, I should tell you a little story."

"What kind of story?"

"The one about a Chinese assassin named Leo Sinj."

"What about him?"

"Many years ago, he came to Cape Noire on a mission of murder for his Tong masters back in China."

"And no doubt you ended up confronting him," Lilith surmised aloud.

"I did. You see, Sing shot his targets with a special Colt .45 Peacemaker. The kind they used in the west after the Civil War."

"This is boring me, Bones. What is your point?"

"Well it wasn't the gun that was special. You see, Sinj had bullets of green jade made especially for the Peacemaker...and they were magic."

"Really." Despite herself, Delamore was now curious. "Meaning he could have ended you if he had shot you with one of these Jade bullets?"

"Right. But in the end, I beat him to the draw and he missed me completely."

"I see. How charming. What has all this to do with me?"

"At the moment, everything."

Blackjack Bobby Crandall, who had been hiding behind one of the massive boulders came around it holding the Colt Peacemaker in both hands. He then shot Lilith in the back.

The magic jade bullet pieced her heart before she could even scream. Then it tore through her chest. At that instant, with a look of total disbelief on her beautiful face, the Witch Queen of Cape Noire died once more.

Her body collapsed as did Brother Bones. Only she did not get up again. He, on the other hand, stood, dusted off his jacket and walked over to her body lying face down in the grass. He put away his twin automatics and motioned Crandall over.

Shaking nervously, the freckled-face card dealer came to join his ally, the heavy revolver still in his hands.

Brother Bones took the gun from him. "Good shooting, Crandall. Now,

"AFTER I BURN YOU TO ASH, YOU WILL BE NOTHING BUT A MEMORY."

turn her over."

Crandall bent down, took hold of the dead woman and flipped her over onto her back. As he did so both of them saw the snake head pendant resting on her chest. Bones reached down, grasped it and pulled it off her.

He stuffed the necklace into one of his pockets and then said, "You might want to look away, kid."

Crandall did as directed while the Undead Avenger of Cape Noire pointed the gun at Lilith's head and fired two more magic bullets into it. Her head exploded into hundreds of pieces.

"All right, Crandall," the Undead Avenger tapped his shoulder. "Let's get out of here."

Together they strolled off into the fog.

Once they were gone, the witch's army of rats reappeared. They circled her remains, their pointed snouts twitching. Then they swarmed over the lifeless sorceress and began to feed.

☻ ☻ ☻

Instead of going home from the park, Brother Bones had Bobby Crandall drive them to the docks of Old Town. Once on Harbor Boulevard, they drove north to Chaney Avenue and there veered right to where dozens of massive seagoing tankers were anchored. Between them were several piers that jutted out into the lapping waters of the Pacific.

Onto one of these Crandall carefully drove his roadster. Within a hundred yards of the pier's end, he touched the brakes.

"Keep the engine running," Brother Bones told him as he grabbed the passenger side door and climbed out. He shut the door behind him and then began walking towards the water. High tide was rolling in and he could hear the slamming of the pylons beneath his feet as he walked across the thick wooden planks.

When he reached the end, he looked out at the mighty sea; or else all he could see of it. The fog was still present and somewhere miles out away from land he could hear gulls crying as they flew over the waves.

He reached his right hand into his coat pocket and pulled out the necklace he'd taken from the fallen witch. He looked at the small jeweled snake eyes and could feel the power the pendant contained. Power that could, if allowed, revive Lilith's black soul again.

"No," he said to himself. "Not again, bitch. Give hell my regards."

He pitched the necklace with all his strength and after several seconds heard the splash it made upon hitting the water. If he had any imagination left in his lifeless brain, he would have seen the thing sinking deeper and deeper until it was lost in the murky mud below.

Back at the car, Bones climbed in and told Crandall they had one more stop before their night was over.

From the pier, he guided the young redhead along a row of giant, boarded up warehouses until they came to one at the furthest end of the cape itself.

When Crandall's headlights fell over the building, he saw a cardboard sign that read FOR SALE and under it a realtor's telephone number.

"Why are we here?" he asked Bones, shutting off the engine.

"Look closely, Bobby Crandall. This is where it all began."

"It? What are you talk…" Even as he uttered the words, Crandall's eyes were examining the warehouse's outer façade. Then, bit by bit it came back to him. All of it. The horrible night he'd been kidnapped by Jack Bonello, along with his then boss, Big Swede Jorgesnon. It was here they had been taken and it was here Jack Bonello and two of his pals had doused Jorgeson with gasoline and set him on fire. He would never forget the man's awful screams until his seared lungs gave out and he died hanging from chains fastened to the roof rafters. His body smelling so rank, even after all these years, the memory of it made him want to vomit.

He also recalled how the spirit of Brother Bones had appeared out of the ether and taken over Jack Bonello's body thus saving the young man from certain death. Yes, it was in this place that Brother Bones had been born and Blackjack Bobby Crandall's life changed forever.

"God damn it, Bones, why are we here?"

"Because the city has become too crowded for us. Tomorrow, I want you to call the realtor and find out what they are asking for it. I believe we have enough stashed under your bed to cover the cost."

The Undead Avenger was referring to the monies he had taken from all the dead gangsters they had put down in the past few years. Ill-gotten gains that Bones always said would eventually put to use. And now it appeared that time had come.

"Wait a second, you want us to live here." Crandall pointed at the warehouse. "In there?"

"Yes. The upstairs floor has several office spaces we can turn into rooms for your convenience. All I'll require is a chair and bureau."

"But what about my apartment back in town?"

"Give it to Sister Blood and her companion. They have use of it. We do not any longer."

There were hundreds of things Bobby Crandall wanted to say as to why this was a totally crazy idea. But looking at the Undead Bones sitting beside him like the lifeless thing he was, he let them go unsaid. He'd learned early on that when Brother Bones put forth a plan, there was no talking him out of it.

He turned the key, got the motor running and backed away from the building. Then he turned the front end around and stepped on the gas.

What tomorrow would bring was beyond him? It appeared his wild adventures with Brother Bones were just getting started.

☻ ☻ ☻

EPILOGUE

Two days later, Harry Beest sat behind his office desk having finished his breakfast of two dozen banana pancakes with lots of butter and maple syrup. He was wiping his gorilla mouth with a cloth napkin when the phone jangled.

Beest hated to be disturbed this early in the morning.

He snatched up the receiver and held it to his ear. "Yeah! Who is it?"

"Hello, Harry," a soft, tantalizing female voice said; a voice he knew all too well.

"Alexis?"

"How are you, Harry? Still enjoying your breakfast bananas?"

"Hardy-har-har. Very funny."

"Oh, come on, Harry. Don't be so serious all the time."

The gorilla man scratched an itch over his flat nose. "Why'd you call, Alexis? I'm busy."

"Of course you are," she agreed. "We all are. I called because I want you to help me hunt down and destroy Brother Bones."

"That old record again. Give it a break, Alexis. Besides, I don't have any beef with the Undead Avenger. You do. It's your vendetta. Not mine."

"But I have something you want, Harry. Maybe we can come to some understanding."

"Oh, yeah? And what's that?"

"I have Prof. Anton Petrus."

THE END

WRAPPING THINGS UP

Over the years, since creating Cape Noire and its most unique citizen, Brother Bones, I've watched the series expand with each new adventure penned. In the end it is impossible to write something like this and not keep adding new characters. After all, if each story was only about our protagonist, no matter how special he may be, things would soon start getting very, very repetitive. Thus, to keep things fresh and new, we kept enlarging the supporting cast, both good and bad.

Ultimately a few of our colleagues and readers pointed out many of these figures were solid enough to warrant their own solo outings. We liked that idea and reached out to three writers we admire greatly; Fred Adams Jr., Andy Fix and Drew Meyer. We invited each of them to join us in this newest collection by giving us tales that would focus on one particular character in the Cape Noire saga. And did they ever deliver. The first three stories in this book are great and I had so much fun reading each of them. But they also ended up giving me one hell of a challenge. You see, while playing with Harry Beest, Sister Blood and Lt. Dan Rains, the guys went ahead and created even more characters to populate the streets of this fictional metropolis.

The plan had always been for them to deliver their stories and then for me to bring the various elements together tieing them up in a final bow with my own new Brother Bones outing. That was my goal at the start and I hope I've succeeded to some small degree. Another element I discovered about this particular collection is that continuity is a bitch and after having written lots of Brother Bones stories and comics, it was a chore to be sure I wasn't altering things that had happened before.

Gratefully I had Scaldcrow Games' amazing RPG game module, "Ron Fortier's Cape Noire" to use refer to whenever this old gray matter became less than clear on the names of certain people or the actual locales. The book, produced and assembled by T. Gleen Bane, his wife Theresa and the aforementioned Drew Meyer became a valuable resource and I thank them from the bottom of my heart for it every day.

There you go. Our fifth Brother Bones title. What's in store for the Undead Avenger going forward? Honestly, I wish I knew myself. At times the muse is maddeningly quiet and then, out of the blue it strikes, inspiring me to once again revisit those dark streets of Cape Noire and uncover what new horrors it contains. Here's hoping you'll join me.

RON FORTIER—Comics and pulps writer/editor is best known for his work on the Green Hornet comic series and Terminator – Burning Earth with Alex Ross. He won the Pulp Factory Award for Best Pulp Short Story of 2011 for "Vengeance Is Mine," which appeared in Moonstone's The Avenger – Justice Inc. and in 2012 for "The Ghoul," from the anthology Monster Aces. He is the Managing Editor of Airship 27 Productions, a leading New Pulp Fiction publisher and writes the continuing adventures of both his own character, Brother Bones – the Undead Avenger and the classic pulp hero, Captain Hazzard – Champion of Justice. In 2017, he was awarded the first, Pulp Grand Master by the Pulp Factory. Fortier also writes the highly popular Pulp Fiction Reviews blog.

You can find him at (www.Airship27.com)

ROB DAVIS—Comics and pulps artist and designer. Probably best known as the illustrator of Star Trek comics for DC and Malibu comics in the 1990s. He won the Pulp Factory Award for Best Pulp Interior Illustrations in 2009 and 2016 for illustrations in Sherlock Holmes Consulting Detective. He is the Art Director of Airship 27 Productions, a leading New Pulp Fiction publisher doing design work for all the books and illustrating many of them each year.

Can special bullets made of sacred jade finally end the un-life of Brother Bones?!

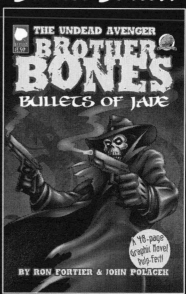

In his first comic book outing the Undead Avenger takes on CAPE NOIR's oriental underworld in a rambunctious 48 page tale of intrigue, suspense and excitement as only Airship 27 and Redbud Studio Comics can present.